2d

P9-BBP-985

Other St. Anselm's Mysteries
by Isabelle Holland

A DEATH AT ST. ANSELM'S

At an exclusive New York church known for its programs for the homeless, someone kills the wheelchair-bound church treasurer, whose tight control of the holy purse strings has made him less than popular. The evidence points repeatedly toward the Reverend Claire Aldington, a beautiful widow struggling to keep her family together. To clear her name, Claire is forced to unearth a series of dark, damning, and painful secrets, both clerical and personal.

"A murder mystery and a good one."
Newgate Callendar,
The New York Times Book Review

FLIGHT OF THE ARCHANGEL

Free-lance journalist Kit Maitland has been assigned to write an article about the Van Reider mansion, a property of St. Anselm's Church. Looking around the library of the old house, she discovers the body of a very recently murdered man, and to Kit's horror she is the prime suspect. So the investigative reporter must investigate a brutal murder, and in the process, she must face the truth about her own past.

"A beguiling mystery . . . the characters are sterling, admirable, and marvelous to find out about."

Los Angeles Times

Fawcett Books
by Isabelle Holland:

A LOVER SCORNED

Isabelle Holland

FAWCETT CREST   •   NEW YORK

A Fawcett Crest Book
Published by Ballantine Books
Copyright © 1986 by Isabelle Holland

Library of Congress Catalog Card Number: 86-8979

ISBN 0-449-21369-2

This edition published by arrangement with Doubleday & Company, Inc.

Manufactured in the United States of America

First Ballantine Books Edition: November 1987

I

THE FIRST BODY WAS FOUND EARLY SATURDAY MORNING BY A runner in Central Park. She was stripped to the waist and her shoes were missing. There was no handbag anywhere near. So the body lay in the morgue for two days while the police tried to find out who she had been. She was approximately thirty-five and in good health, the coroner said. The fact that her face had been beaten almost to jelly made any identification harder. Under the blood, her hair had been a dark honey blond, but there was no telling what color her eyes had been or what her features were like. She could have been said to have a good figure except that her breasts had each been mutilated with two savage gashes in the shape of an X, the lines meeting at the torn nipples.

"My God!" Lieutenant O'Neill said. "I've seen a lot of messy deaths. But this—"

"Yes, it's gruesome." The coroner pulled the sheet back

1

over the dead woman. "I suppose you're working on the fingerprints."

O'Neill shook his head. "So far, nothing there. Which means that she was never in trouble with the police, she was never on a Grand Jury, nor was she in any other occupation that required fingerprinting."

"Lotsa luck!" The coroner led the way out of the morgue.

FOUR DAYS LATER THE BODY WAS IDENTIFIED AS THAT OF the Reverend Ida Blake, an assistant rector at St. Timothy's Episcopal Church on East Thirty-Third Street. A widowed mother, living in California, came to claim the body, and Ms. Blake's brother, also a priest, flew in from England where he had been doing some research at Oxford.

Lieutenant O'Neill picked up his phone and dialed St. Anselm's number. "Mrs. Aldington," he said, when the church receptionist came on.

A young woman on the second floor of the parish house picked up the phone. "Claire Aldington," she said.

"This Reverend Blake—" O'Neill spoke without preamble. "Did you know her?"

"Hello, lieutenant," Claire said. She and the lietenant had been involved in a couple of cases together. "What a horrible thing to have happened! Yes, I did know her. Not well, but we met several times on committees."

"What kind of person was she?"

"What do you mean by that?" Claire asked quickly. Then added, "Sorry. I didn't mean to jump like that. But when police ask that question about a young woman I always feel they're implying she was promiscuous or something."

"You've never struck me as a militant feminist before." O'Neill knew that comment would add fuel to her paranoia, but he couldn't resist saying it.

She took a deep breath.

"All right, all right," he said hastily. "Don't get your hackles up! If it had been the Reverend Isaac or the Reverend Ian Blake I would have asked the same question.

After all, you're the only Episcopal priest I know—male or female."

Claire expelled her breath. "I should have known you were needling me. As I just said, I didn't know her that well. But since you brought up the phrase, she was a lot more of a militant feminist than I am. That is, she belonged to various women's rights groups, marched a lot and was fairly visible as a feminist. But then, so are thousands of other women in the city—in and out of the church."

"Umm," O'Neill said. "That raises certain . . . certain possibilities."

"Such as a rampant male chauvinist as murderer . . ." Claire paused. "I didn't mean that exactly."

"Why not? It's logical enough."

"Yes. But it somehow makes light of it—a cheap crack at an inappropriate time. How did she die? The paper didn't say."

O'Neill hesitated. "The details have been deliberately kept away from the press—and don't start giving me a hard time about the First Amendment! There are times when catching the criminal comes first—particularly if he has anybody else in mind."

"I couldn't agree more. So I'll withdraw the question."

"I'll tell you, Claire—" The Christian name slipped out before O'Neill realized it. "If you don't mind me calling you that." He was embarrassed and therefore brusque.

"I don't mind at all—" Claire was a little amused and also touched. "And I won't repeat what you tell me. You know I won't if I promise."

"No. I know you won't." He told her the grisly details.

Claire was silent for a moment. "That sounds like somebody who is truly insane. Or truly evil."

"Maybe they're the same thing."

But Claire was not to be diverted by what could become an interesting theological point. "My God! I hope—I devoutly hope—that she was unconscious when that happened."

"We have no way of knowing that, but I hope so, too."

He paused. "Beyond her being a feminist, was there anything else about her that you think would be helpful? We know she wasn't married. We're not sure whether or not she had a boyfriend. The rector of her church, the Reverend—er—"

Claire could hear him shuffling the papers on his desk. "The Reverend Dennis Burton," she supplied.

"Thank you. He said he didn't know. Another cleric there, the Reverend George Bruce, said he thought she did, but didn't know who it was. Her mother and brother don't know. We haven't found anybody else who does. Any ideas?"

"No," Claire said. She was silent for a moment, trying to remember if she had seen Ida arrive at various meetings or social occasions with a friend of either sex. "I don't have any ideas, not at the moment. Do you want me to see if I can find anybody who was a close friend? Or isn't that something you would do?"

"We'd try. But I think you'd have a better chance of coming up with an answer."

"All right." Claire's assent was less than enthusiastic.

"You don't sound too convinced."

"I'm not. I can't imagine why finding a good friend would—would be a problem. But if, by some stretch, it is, then you'll have to leave to my judgment what I can tell you."

"I tell you what no one else outside a few cops at headquarters know, showing a lot of trust, and you go into muttering and backing and filling about conditions if you find somebody."

"Yes, it's an unfair world. But speaking in my professional capacity, I can imagine circumstances where I'd find it some kind of betrayal to tell you what I've learned."

"Okay. But while you're being such a finely tuned person of honor, just remember that whoever did it is planning on his next victim. People with minds like that don't stop."

"I'll remember it," Claire said grimly.

* * *

THAT WAS THE FIRST WEEK IN APRIL. FOR THE NEXT MORNING OR two Claire opened up the New York *Times* with both hope and dread—hope that Ida's killer had been located, although she was moderately sure that O'Neill would have called her if that had been the case, and dread that yet another body had turned up.

Her paper was delivered to her apartment each morning. Usually, she simply folded it into her tote bag and took it with her to the office so as not to take away from her breakfast time with Martha, her stepdaughter, and Jamie, her son. But she now found herself eyeing the headlines and glancing quickly at the index on the front page of the second section before consigning it to her bag.

The fact that the victim was a woman priest was enough to assure any new development a prominent place. The papers and television news broadcasts had been filled with the murder, and Claire herself had been called on by two newspapers and three television reporters for comment. Other than expressing her regret, Claire had refused to comply. This was partly because she liked the media least when it was in its And-what-were-your-thoughts-Mrs.-Smith-when-you-saw-the-dismembered-body-of-your-daughter? mood, and partly because if there was a woman-priest-hating maniac going around, common sense dictated that she mantain as low a profile as possible.

She was slipping the paper into her bag when twelve-year-old Jamie said, a certain note of grievance in his voice, "You can look at your paper if you want to."

"Don't be a martyr," his eighteen-year-old half sister reprimanded him. "What with women clergy being knocked off, you can hardly fault her for being concerned."

Jamie helped himself to another muffin. "The kids at school think she maybe had another secret life. Like she was a priest during the day and a sex fiend at night."

"That's not funny," Claire said angrily. Children, she thought, changed places with bewildering speed. Two years before, Martha, with her anger and her anorexia, had been almost more of a problem than Claire could handle. Jamie, by contrast, had been a delight. And now, she thought, he was busy turning himself into that least attractive member of his sex, a thorough chauvinist.

"I was just telling you what the guys said."

"Not perhaps the most sensitive reaction to a truly horrible death," Claire said. But then, she thought, sensitivity was not where it was at with boys that age—or at least not where it showed. "Have you taken Motley out?" Motley was Jamie's dog, a mutt of many ancestors, who looked mostly like a shepherd-retriever cross.

"Yes," Jamie said, and sounded more like his old self. "He chased a squirrel—or at least tried to."

"Did the squirrel get away?" Martha asked.

"Didn't you have him on a leash?" Claire was both surprised and concerned. Jamie loved Motley more than anyone else, including, Claire sometimes suspected, his family. "You know he's supposed to be."

"Oh Ma! It's so boring like that. He gets more exercise if I let him free."

"It would be even more boring if he were hit by a car," Claire said. And then, "I'm surprised at you, Jamie!"

"Did the squirrel get away?" Martha persisted.

"Yes, the squirrel got away. And, if you must know, I couldn't find the leash."

Claire felt an odd sense of relief. If Jamie had really grown indifferent to his adored dog's safety then the change in him was much more serious than she had counted on. She was further reassured when he burst out, "You know I wouldn't let anything happen to him. I made him come to me before we got to every corner, then I took him across holding onto his collar."

"I wonder what happened to the leash?" Claire said. "You always hang it up on that hook in the hall closet, don't you?"

"Sure. And when it wasn't there I looked for it on the floor."

"As a matter of fact," Martha said, "it's in my room. I forgot. Sorry."

"What's it doing there?"

"I took it to try the effect of a thin leather belt on a skirt and I didn't have anything else that would do."

"You could have had Motley killed!" Jamie's face flushed.

"Come on, now, Jamie," Claire said pacifically. "You could have used some string. There's a whole ball of it in the kitchen. And Martha," she went on as Jamie mumbled something under his breath, "please always return that leash to its hook."

"Sorry—again."

Later, on the bus, instead of reading her paper or pondering Ida Blake and her terrible death, Claire found herself sitting with folded hands, gazing out the window and thinking about her two children: Martha, her late husband's daughter by his first wife, and Jamie, her own son.

Previously Martha, who had just returned home after three months in the hospital for anorexia, had complicated an already tense situation by succumbing to another attack. It was a time when Claire was involved in the scandal that shook St. Anselm's Church, of which she was an assistant rector. Since then Martha had done a right about-face and now, at eighteen, was getting excellent grades at school, had been accepted by the Ivy League college of her choice and was deeply involved in the school drama club. Having something to do with her energies besides starve herself, she had become more even-tempered and much easier to deal with.

Twelve-year-old Jamie was another matter. He and Claire had always been good friends, sharing not only the same red hair and gray eyes but the same humor and, for the most part, the same mind-set. In any situation, she could be reasonably sure as to how he would react. No more. There were still moments when he seemed the same good natured, not too meticulous, semislob of a boy that she had known

and delighted in. But they were few. The rest of the time he
talked and sounded like the ultimate hard hat. Claire, in one
furious moment, had dubbed him Much Macho, and was
even more enraged to see him react with satisfaction.

"After all," he pointed out, "a guy is suppose to be like a
man."

"But not necessarily like a klutz," she had replied
sharply.

Staring out the window watching Fifth Avenue pass,
Claire thought now, I shouldn't have let Brett talk me into
sending him to St. Stephen's. Brett Cunningham, Claire's
fiancé, had suggested taking Jamie out of the coeducational
school where he and Martha had gone and where he trailed
his older half sister. When she wasn't being anorexic and
neurotic Martha seemed to be unable to get anything but
A's.

"He lives with two women," Brett had said. "He ought
to go to a boys' school." And Claire had agreed. Now she
reminded herself that her beloved, Brett Cunningham, was
a conservative and a banker, and, in her surprisingly strong
attraction to him, she was inclined to forget that most of his
social ideas were supposed to have gone out in the fifties.
"Damn Brett," she muttered under her breath.

Still, she reminded herself as she got up to leave the bus,
Jamie had gone from being an indifferent student to a good
one. "And you can't have everything," she piously told
herself as she approached St. Anselm's door. And then
grinned when a small voice inside her asked, "Why not?"

THE AUTOPSY REPORT WAS MADE PUBLIC THE NEXT DAY, BUT IT
did not add much information to what was already known:
Ida Blake had been stunned by a blow on the head, but she
had died from a stab wound to the heart.

"I hope that means she wasn't conscious when the
madman cut her up," Claire said to her boss, the Reverend
Douglas Barnet, the new rector of St. Anselm's. He had
been away at the time of the murder, doing a stint as guest
lecturer at the cathedral in New Orleans.

"I asked that," he replied. "Your friend Lieutenant O'Neill said maybe, maybe not. She could have been stunned briefly, then come to when she was having her hands tied and been aware of what was happening."

"When I said to O'Neill I hoped that she didn't remain conscious, he said he did too. I wonder what made him express his doubts about it to you."

"I don't know. Why don't you ask him."

Claire liked the new rector, although he had not been at the church long enough for her to feel that she knew him, in addition to which he seemed, unlike the two previous rectors, to be reserved and somewhat withdrawn.

Feeling a little set back, Claire said, "I will."

There ensued one of those silences that sometimes occurred in conversations with the rector. Finally Claire asked, "Are you going to the funeral service tomorrow?"

"No. I have an appointment that I have to keep. You'll be going, of course. Will any of the others?"

"Larry will," Claire said, referring to the Reverend Lawrence Swade. "And I think Jim and Ann will." Jim Butler was another assistant rector, and Ann Morosky was a seminarian.

"Good!" said the rector, sounding indifferent. After another silent moment, Claire left.

On the way to her office she bumped into her colleague, Larry Swade.

"Why is it that whenever I have a conversation with the rector I always emerge feeling as though he wished I were someone or somewhere else?" she grumbled. Larry was a particular friend and she felt free to say whatever was on her mind.

He leaned his rotund form against the wall. "Because being a female cleric in a male bastion, you're feeling insecure. Or because being a therapist, it is second nature to you to look for the reason behind the reason. Or because it may be true." He paused. "Any of the above," he added helpfully.

"I should have known better than to ask you. None of the

above gives me any comfort. Are you serious or just being funny, as usual.''

He smiled. "Let me say that I don't think it's because you're feeling insecure. You seem blessedly free from any of the . . ." He stopped. A dull red slowly crept into his round cheeks. "Dear me," he murmured.

"Go on, say it!" Claire spoke in exasperation. "Any of the insecurities and defenses afflicting women clergy."

"I didn't say that," Larry protested.

"Wasn't it what you were going to say?"

Incurably truthful, Larry sighed and then nodded. "I don't usually put my foot into my mouth that far," he said. "For one thing, I'm too fat."

"Being fat is no guarantee against being prejudiced."

"True. What can I do to restore your good will?"

Claire thought for a moment. "You can take me out to the greasy spoon across the street and buy me some coffee."

"Done!"

Feeling a little guilty, they emerged from the big double doors of St. Anselm's parish on Lexington Avenue. The church occupied half the block between Park and Lexington avenues, with the church itself facing Park, and its parish house fronting on Lexington. Built half a century before, when the East Sixties were completely residential and "uptown" meant the East Sixties and Seventies, the church became known for its congregation of rich and near-rich WASPS, whose town houses surrounded the church. Now shops and boutiques lined Lexington Avenue, interspersed with delicatessens and coffee shops. There were, as usual, an assortment of street people on both sides of the avenue, some lining up for St. Anselm's daily meal for the poor, others groping through the litter baskets at the corners, and one, a woman, sitting with her back to a wall on one of the corners, her possessions in shopping bags around her, and a cat, with a collar and leash attached to the woman in some way, asleep next to her.

Taking advantage of a slight pause in the stream of traffic,

Claire and Larry unrepentantly jaywalked and went into the coffee shop.

"I have no reason in the world to feel guilty about Althea," Claire said, as they sat down at a small table near the window. "I've done everything I can to make her go into a hospital, but she refuses absolutely and the law is on her side."

"But you still feel guilty," Larry said.

"Yes. Don't you?"

"Compassion, yes. Guilt, no. It may be a comment on the state of my conscience or my laziness, but no, I don't. If no one had tried, I would. But I know you have, not once but many times. It's her choice. Therefore God bless her and let her be."

"And what about her cat?"

"It seems perfectly happy to me."

"I don't see how it can be. It isn't free to roam and it doesn't get any exercise."

"How well do you know cats?"

"Not very," Claire admitted. "We're a dog household."

"Well we have three cats. During the day they sleep, especially the older ones. And Althea's Dalrymple is nearly sixteen. Apparently the two of them walk a lot at night."

"Dalrymple? You mean that's the cat's name? I don't believe it!"

"Named after a psychic who found him when he was lost," Larry told her, launching into his English muffin with enthusiasm.

"You've been talking to her," Claire said accusingly.

"I always talk to her," Larry said. "She can be quite interesting when she isn't caught up in one of her hallucinations. Did you know she has her master's in mediaeval history?" He stared at Claire's stunned face. "Gotcha that time!"

"All right, Larry. We must have a chat about her soon. I take it you, too, have tried to persuade her to go into a psychiatric institution."

"Of course. But she feels they're full of Viking hordes

trying to overcome Arthur's Britain, and only by sitting, as she does each day, on the cliffs above the English Channel can she warn Britain in time. She's the only one who can do it, and she says that God Himself has appointed her this task."

Claire thought for a moment. "As delusions go, it's quite a nice one. I wonder what the delusion is of the madman who attacked Ida Blake."

"You're the therapist. What do you think?"

"That he was killing his mother, punishing women in general, women priests in particular—" She stopped abruptly, aware that she was about to violate her promise to Lieutenant O'Neill by mentioning the disfigured breasts. "Something like that," she finished. "By the way," she rushed ahead before Larry, who could be exceedingly intuitive, queried her about her unfinished sentence. "Lieutenant O'Neill asked me if I would talk to some close friend of Ida's to see if I could find out anything that might explain this . . . explain what happened. There's Sarah Buchanan, who was at the seminary with her and who's over at St. Andrew's. I can talk to her, but do you know anybody else?"

Larry chewed for a moment. "You might talk to Brett," he said, and then, "Don't you two ever communicate? What a silent marriage you're going to have!"

"Don't be an idiot. Of course we communicate. But he's been away on a business trip. I haven't seen him since Ida— since it happened. Why? Did he know her?"

"I believe so."

A small worm of jealousy threatened to slither through Claire's Eden. Ida had been quite pretty. Fiercely she crushed it. "How strange! He never mentioned it to me."

"When's he coming back?"

"End of the week, I think. The last time we spoke he said he had called a couple of times, but either I wasn't there, or whoever was home forgot to tell me."

"I wonder if he knows about it."

"He's bound to, unless he's been cut off on some desert

island remote from any newspaper, radio or television—if there is such a place nowadays."

"Or been captured by some capitalist-hating terrorist."

"Don't say that—even jokingly!"

Larry put out a pudgy hand and grasped her arm. "Sorry—of course it was a joke! But you have to admit he is the very model of a modern major capitalist."

"I'll have you know he's a very kind man!"

"I do know it, Claire. The two terms are not necessarily irreconcilable. And I am truly impressed with your defense of him. You are in love."

"Why else would I be planning to marry him?"

"Knowing you, no other reason at all. By the way, why are we out here having coffee when I, for one, have work to do inside? I had the feeling there was something, something about the rector, that you wanted to discuss away from the sacred walls."

Claire paused. Finally she said, "Now that I've lured you out here, I feel foolish saying this, but—here goes! Does it ever strike you that he . . . well, that he isn't quite . . . quite present? That he operates with part of his mind, but the larger part is somewhere else? It's hard to say what I mean, exactly. He's a good administrator. His sermons are quite respectable, if less than stirring, and he reads the liturgy well. But—"

"But you think he's doing it all on automatic pilot."

"Exactly! So you have noticed!"

"How could one not?"

"But he was the choice of both the search committee and the vestry. I can't believe they were all half asleep."

"I suspect that after the *Sturm und Drang* of the past few years the ordinary seemed powerfully attractive."

"I don't think he's ordinary," Claire said. "If he were ordinary he'd make polite noises. Barnet doesn't do that."

"You should be asking Brett these questions," Larry said, looking at the check the waitress had handed him. "He's on the vestry."

"When he comes back, I will." She paused. "Don't tell

anyone this, but I think Brett was one of those who didn't vote for him."

"I've always thought Brett a very sound man."

THE FUNERAL SERVICE TOOK PLACE THE FOLLOWING MORNING AT St. Timothy's. As she listened to the old, beautiful words Claire was struck again by the horror of the tragedy, but this time not so much with sorrow at what happened and her prayerful hope that Ida had not known what was being done to her, but at the very bizarreness of the crime itself.

Against her will, past the flow of words of the scriptures and the gospel containing the promises of hope and resurrection, Claire's mind picked and chose among the facts given in the newspapers and broadcasts and worried at them. Whether or not Ida herself was a runner Claire didn't know, but she was not in running attire when she was killed. That being the case, what was she doing in Central Park? If there had been any reason suggested in the paper, Claire had missed it.

". . . for we are more than conquerors" read the young man at the lectern. He was slight and fair-haired and reminded Claire of Ida. She glanced at the printed program. "Epistle—The Reverend Hector Blake." So that was Ida's brother.

What was Ida doing in Central Park dressed in—but what she was wearing above the waist was mere conjecture. As though Claire had seen the body, she saw, in her mind, the indignity of the gashes and could feel herself shrink. She looked down and felt Larry's hand on her arm. Her own hands, she noticed, were clenched. Firmly she fixed her eyes on the magnificent stone reredos behind the altar and tried to keep her mind on the gospel.

It was during the short homily that Claire's eyes, glancing around the church, saw Brett Cunningham. He was in the first pew on the other side, sitting with an elderly woman. He didn't call and tell me he was back, Claire found herself thinking, and once again pushed back the unworthy senti-ment that the thought produced. What's the matter with me, she wondered? It wasn't as though Brett had not, in fairly conventional fashion, done the pursuing in their relationship. Starting out with dislike and suspicion when they had first been thrown together, she had come grudgingly to admit that this banker and vestryman, who represented what she considered all that was tradition-bound and reactionary in the Church, was not only considerate but also kind, not only highly intelligent but perceptive. Once he had said to her, "As far as the social mission of the Church is concerned, we disagree about means, not ends. I refuse to allow that you and your cothinkers have a corner on all the virtue, much as you yourself think it!"

"I do not!" She had protested.

"Yes you do. You can't help it. You were brainwashed by Patrick." Patrick, her late husband and also an Episcopal priest, had been a marching, protesting child of the sixties.

"True, but there are worse things to be."

"Agreed. Shall we go on with our political fight or shall we go out to dinner?"

That was how he won battles, she thought irritatedly. He smiled, conceded, and changed the subject. "You don't fight," she once said.

"What's the point? Are you going to change your mind?"

"No."

"I didn't think so. Neither am I. Are you hungry?"

And so the courtship had gone. And then she had discovered how profoundly this forty-seven-year-old banker, urbane and rather austere, could light fires within her.

The first time this had happened she said, stumbling and happy, "I didn't know . . . it's never been like this."

His thin, strong hand outlined her face and mouth. "Not for me, either."

Looking now across the church, what she saw mostly was his back in its dark blue pinstriped suit and above that, his dark hair, flecked here and there with gray. He must have become aware of her, because he half turned and she saw in profile his angular, thrusting nose. Then he turned a little more and their eyes met, his blue, hers a greenish hazel. He

gave a slight smile. Her heart gave two beats. She could feel
the blood rush into her face, as though the whole congregation must see what was in her mind. Quickly she tugged it
back. This was Ida's funeral. Ida, who had died a violent,
loathsome death. How could she have forgotten? And why
was Brett up there with the woman who was undoubtedly
Ida's mother?

When the service was over, Brett led the elderly woman
in the procession following the coffin. She looked, Claire
thought, like a small, frightened, and very angry bird. The
anger, which was marked, was natural, Claire told herself.
Natural or not, it held and dominated the pinched features.
Quickly Claire looked up at Brett. He eyed her steadily but
then glanced down as the woman beside him said something.

Outside St. Timothy's Claire was standing with Larry,
waiting for Ida's mother and brother to appear so she could
express her sympathies and then be free to leave.

"I didn't know Brett knew them that well," she said to
Larry.

Before he could reply Brett came up, still with Mrs.
Blake on his arm. Claire spoke her regrets.

The angry, birdlike eyes looked at her. Amazingly, the
woman said, "You didn't like my Ida, did you?"

Claire immediately became away of Lieutenant O'Neill,
looking as much as possible like a member of the congregation, standing within earshot.

"I didn't dislike her, Mrs. Blake. We just didn't see eye
to eye on a couple of things."

"It's people like you bring sadness into the world," she
snapped.

"Mrs. Aldington may have disagreed with Ida, Cousin
Helen," Brett said. "But she would never bring sadness,
only good will and joy."

Tears pricked Claire's eyes. "I didn't realize you were
related," she said.

"Second cousin." He smiled a little.

"You're not even sorry," Cousin Helen went on as

though neither Claire nor Brett had spoken. She was like an obsessed child, Claire thought.

Brett spoke. "I'm sorry Ida is dead, most especially about the way she died. And so is Claire. And if you don't apologize to her now, Cousin Helen, I don't care how great your loss is, I'm not taking you home."

It was both sad and funny, Claire thought.

"It's all right, Brett." Claire tried not to feel unbecomingly happy at his defense of her. "I understand."

Mrs. Blake brought her cane down onto the ground, missing Claire's rather fragile sandals by less than half an inch. "It's your fault. I know all about what you did to Ida. She told me. Well, I have means of doing something about that. You'll be sorry. Brett was meant for Ida, and you took him."

She's nuts, Claire thought to herself, and then jumped as the old woman smiled grimly and said, "No, I'm not nuts! You'll see! Come, Brett!"

II

CLAIRE WAS SITTING IN HER OFFICE THAT AFTERNOON WHEN Brett called her. To her horror, Claire heard her voice say accusingly, "I didn't know you were back."

"Sorry about that, darling," Brett replied, and Claire felt her heart skip at the endearment. It had all the more impact because Brett was not given to using it. "I wasn't planning to come back this soon. But Helen tracked me down and asked me to accompany her to the funeral. Apparently, with Hector up in the chancel with the other priests she felt, as she put it, alone and abandoned. As you may have noticed, she's given to dramatic phrases."

"Yes indeed—especially since I seemed to be the target of one or two. Where on earth did she get that business about my not liking Ida?"

"Probably from Ida, who told her that the two of you didn't always agree. You have to realize that with anyone like Helen, to disagree about anything means to be the

18

enemy. With her, disagreement and dislike are the same thing."

"Why didn't you tell me you were related? I couldn't have been more surprised."

"I suppose it never came up. I certainly wasn't deliberately withholding the information. How about dinner?"

Claire paused. Even though Martha was almost an adult and very responsible, Claire didn't like to leave her and Jamie alone more than one night in the week, and she had already been to dinner and the theater with one of the parish families. But Brett was Brett. "I'd love to. I've missed you. When and where?"

"How about my club at seven?"

Claire was amused. Elite all-male clubs were among Ida Blake's pet dislikes. "When you think of the amount of business networking that goes on there!" she would fume. And then Claire remembered how Ida died, and her amusement stopped.

"You're on!" she said.

"What was all that hesitation about? I thought for a minute you'd hung up."

"No, I was remembering how your Cousin Ida felt about male bastions like your club, and then it stopped being so amusing when I remembered how she was killed. Do you think some demented male chauvinist murdered her?"

"I doubt it. Ida had her share of contemporary opinions but she wasn't the most militant around. If some antifeminist had gone nuts with fury and wanted to kill a women's rights representative, he could have found a far more telling symbol."

Suddenly Claire remembered Lieutenant O'Neill's questions.

"Brett—do you know if Ida had a boyfriend? Lieutenant O'Neill called and asked me to find out anything I could about her friends and associates. I was thinking of telephoning Sarah Buchanan, but you'd probably know more about her than Sarah. Particularly," Claire went on, unable to suppress her lively sense of mischief, "since your cousin obviously had you in mind for her daughter."

"I'd give much if Cousin Helen weren't as batty as she is and would keep her mouth shut. I knew that statement of hers was going to cause me a lot of trouble. To answer your question about a possible boyfriend, I don't know. Strange as it may seem to you, what with all this maternal shoving going on, I didn't know Ida that well."

Claire felt a surge of reassurance, and was able to say sincerely, "She was very pretty."

"Do I get the feeling that you're trying to provoke me?" Brett asked. "Now, that's very flattering."

Claire laughed. "No, I am not trying to provoke you, and conceit will get you nowhere."

"See you then at seven," Brett said cheerfully.

DINNER WAS AS DELIGHTFUL AS SHE KNEW IT WOULD BE. Afterwards she couldn't have said what she and Brett talked about except that his wry comments kept her amused. Yet by the time dessert arrived, she had the strong impression that underneath the humor there was strain.

"Are you worried about something?" she asked abruptly, as he refilled her glass with white wine.

He didn't reply for a moment, then said drily, "No wonder you're good at your job!"

There was another pause.

"Well?" Claire said, then added more gently, "I don't mean to pry. Maybe you'd rather not talk about it."

"Let's get this out of the way," Brett said, watching the waiter pour their coffees. Pulling the check over he signed it. "That's all, thanks," he said, and the waiter left.

"It's not so much that I don't want to talk about it. And I'd certainly rather talk to you than anybody else. It's just the ostrich part of me that would like the whole mess to go away."

"Ida?"

"No. Not Ida." He paused. "Adam." Adam was Brett's

son. "A . . . a colleague of mine in San Francisco called the other night and told me I'd better get out there. The police had tried to reach me in our West Coast office. I took the next flight and got in touch with the police as soon as I hit the airport. It seems that Adam has been living on the streets for about three months and had been taken to the hospital after an overdose of drugs." Brett was staring down at his plate as he said this.

"Is he all right now?" Claire asked quickly.

"I don't know about all right. He's alive."

"Did you know about . . . about his being on the street? Or about the drugs?"

"No, but I should have. He'd call me from time to time. I assumed it was from his apartment. But it must have been from a pay phone with a credit card—probably stolen—because I never heard any operator or dropping coins, so I took it he was all right as he ever was. But according to the police he got evicted from his room in February and has been roaming ever since."

"He didn't let you know?"

"He's a leftover from the sixties. I'm the Enemy."

"But still he called you."

"Only when he wanted money."

"How could you send it if he didn't have an address?"

"It turns out I sent it to the apartment of a friend of his. The friend would give him the cash representing the amount of the check I'd sent, then Adam would endorse it to his friend."

"It didn't strike you as odd when the check came back."

"The cancelled checks are held by my secretary, who then reconciles them with my checkbook."

"Umm." Claire remembered that when she first knew Brett she had asked him what his grown son was doing. His reply had been, "Playing the guitar and finding himself." "I guess he didn't find himself," she said now.

"No, it seems not."

"Where is he at the moment?"

"In a rehab—one suggested by Ida, by the way. She'd known Adam well when she was young, so she seemed the logical person to ask."

Except, Claire thought, that it was just as logical to ask her, his fiancée and a therapist to boot. But to point that out seemed churlish. "Which one did she suggest?"

"St. Jude's in Colorado. I took him there before I had to come back for Ida's funeral."

A silence fell. The ease during dinner had gone.

Claire asked, "Would you like to talk about it? About Adam?"

He smiled. "Not now. Another time." The strain was still there. Claire glanced at her watch. "I guess I'd better be getting back. I don't know how successful Martha is at cracking the whip. If she isn't, I could get home to find Jamie watching the Late Late Show."

"I was hoping you'd stop by my place for a—er—brandy before going home."

Claire had been planning to, but now she knew she was going to refuse. It seemed incredibly petty that she should want so much for Brett to tell her the real reason he had confided in his cousin Ida, whom he claimed not to know well. But Claire was aware that he was not going to tell anything more.

"Another time," she said.

Their kiss, when he handed her over to the doorman of her building, was as decorous as any maiden aunt could wish. Illogically, it made her furious. "Good night," she said coldly.

SHE CALLED SARAH BUCHANAN BEFORE SHE LEFT THE HOUSE and made a lunch date with her. Sarah, who was an ordained priest, helped out on Sunday mornings at St. Paul's, a small church on the Lower East Side. But her main job was editing one of the magazines put out by the Church.

"How's your area for restaurants?" she said. "We have nothing except one second-rate Chinese place, a pizza

parlor and a deli, and about three hideously expensive
gourmet eateries, each sporting about four stars.''

"Let's go to the International," Claire said, naming her
club. She felt slightly guilty as she always did, because she
couldn't possibly have afforded her membership on her
salary, but with the money from her late husband, Patrick, it
was one of the amenities she could enjoy.

"That means you pay," Sarah said. "Since I'm broke,
I'm going to accept with pleasure."

"That's the girl!"

The Women's International Club was in the East Seventies. About half the membership was professional and half
what was politely called general—which meant wives and
mothers engrossed in home, family and volunteer work.
Club members were happy to talk about other members who
were lawyers, doctors, corporate officers, college presidents, and leaders in the arts, but, when pushed, had to
admit that the "general" were the ones who, perforce, did
the work of the club.

Claire and Sarah chatted over a glass of wine and the first
course. Then Sarah said, "You want to talk about Ida, don't
you?"

"Yes. The lieutenant in charge of the case asked me a
couple of questions about Ida that I couldn't answer, and
you're the only one I know who knew her well." Except
Brett, she thought and then reproached herself. Why
couldn't she accept as true his statement that he didn't know
her that well.

"Well?" Sarah said. There was a slightly puzzled note in
her voice.

"Sorry. I was woolgathering. What did you say?"

"I asked, What did you want to know?"

"I guess, first, did she have a boyfriend? At least, that
was the question the lieutenant asked me. And let me also
reassure you that anything that is not for his ears will be
kept in confidence."

Sarah was staring at her in an oddly quizzical way. "Okay." She paused. "Did she have a boyfriend? Yes and no. As a matter of fact, she went out with several guys. But there was one who was special. I know, because she told me."

"Who was it?"

"I don't know. She never identified him. I used to tease her about that, but she'd just laugh and say that discretion was the better part of candor."

"And you had no idea at all?"

She shook her head. "Sorry."

Claire paused. "Did you hear the details of how she died?"

"There's a scuttlebutt going around that she was mutilated in some way. Is it true?"

So much for Lieutenant O'Neill's attempt to keep all the details secret, she thought. However, Sarah hadn't mentioned the exact nature of the slashes, and Claire didn't think she should go into further detail. "Yes, Lieutenant O'Neill was determined to keep that out of the press. But I guess it's more than can be expected that he can sit on it entirely."

Sarah winced. "How horrible! Some woman hater, I suppose."

"Or woman-priest hater."

Sarah stared at Claire. "What a cheerful thought!"

"Comforting, too."

"Do the police have any clue, or even the beginnings of a clue?"

"If they do, they haven't told me. I hardly knew her. What kind of person was she, Sarah?"

As Sarah hesitated, Claire silently cursed herself for such an open-ended question—the kind of question that frequently produced frozen silence. Ordinary perception, let alone her training as a therapist, should have made her go about it a different way.

While she was trying to phrase another query Sarah said,

"Sorry. Maybe because there's now such wild speculation in the Church and generally, I suppose, as to what kind of person Ida was, I buttoned up."

"I, of all people, should understand that. It's exactly the way I reacted when O'Neill asked me."

"The truth of the matter is that Ida was so ordinary—your nice, bright, wholesome girl, who came along at a time when it was possible for a woman to be ordained and who decided to devote her life to serving God and her fellow humans."

"Yes, that was my impression. But having encountered her mother, I wonder how on earth she could have grown up to be wholesome and ordinary. Have you met the dragon lady?"

"No. She lived in California and whenever Ida wanted to see her, she went there rather than Mrs. Blake coming here. But I know what you mean. I saw her at the funeral."

"She put the hex on me, you know. She said I had never liked Ida—which is not true—and that I had prevented Ida from winning Brett, which Brett swears is also not true."

Claire smiled when she said that, and expected an answering smile. Everyone knew about her and Brett's engagement. They were only waiting till the end of the school year to get married, when Jamie would be off at camp and Martha would be involved in Provincetown in a theater project.

But Sarah wore a look of acute discomfort on her face before she finally produced a weak and unconvincing smile.

"That was supposed to be funny," Claire said.

"Yes," Sarah echoed, and glanced at her watch. "I really have to get back pretty soon. We're on the point of going to press, and you'd think we were the New York *Times* for all the fuss it generates."

"Whoa! Sarah, why are you looking uncomfortable when I mention Brett? Did that evil woman Mrs. Blake spread her poison around the place? Is what she said to me not news to you?"

As Sarah continued to look uncomfortable Claire said, "Come on, Sarah. If it's true, the least somebody can do is tell me."

She sighed and sat back a minute. In the brief silence that followed, Claire heard, as though from another planet, the babble of women's voices at the various luncheon tables, punctuated here and there by tenor and baritone sounds coming from male luncheon guests.

"All right," Sarah said. "Ida once said that you had come along and driven a big hole in her and Brett's relationship." As Claire stared she went on. "According to her, they were on their way to being engaged when he met you and—er—fell hard for you."

"You mean I seduced him with my wicked wiles."

"Something like that."

"The ironic part is that I didn't, unless you call having one battle after another a new form of seduction."

"What kind of battle?"

"Anything, but mostly political as it applied to the church—St. Anselm's—and what was going on there at the time. I never before looked on myself as a flaming liberal, but against Brett's solid reactionary impulses I sounded like Che Guevara!"

"I never knew Brett was such a conservative. Ida always said he did a lot of pro bono work and was very generous with his money to people who needed it—her mother for one."

Claire saw then that she had put herself in the unlovely position of attacking her own fiancé and having her rival's representative stick up for him. Only her rival was now dead.

"He is generous," Claire said. "I guess I was reacting to Ida's accusation."

"Well, I didn't want to tell you, and I had come here with the firm determination not to tell you, but it somehow came out."

"In that case, why did you agree to meet me and talk to me? You knew I was going to ask questions about Ida."

"Because I'm as anxious to help the police find her killer as you are, and I didn't think her relationship—if that was what it was—with Brett and therefore with you, particularly relevant. I'm assuming that some evil nut has done the killing, and if he did it because he didn't like women priests, then I have a vested interest in his being caught."

"Yes. We all do." Claire dragged her mind away from Brett and his connection with Ida. There was something he and she would have to thrash out. "Let me get this straight. The boyfriend that you say Ida was so mysterious about— that wasn't Brett, was it?"

"Oh no. Brett and she were past history. This was somebody else—at least I think so."

Claire tried to collect her fragmented attention. "My own impression of Ida was that she was a fairly militant feminist. She belonged to the obvious organizations and I've even seen her on local television news picketing some place along with the other feminists. Is that impression right?"

"More or less. I belong to some of those same organizations and would see her at meetings. But I was never sure how committed she was—I can't tell you why. I sometimes had the impression that she was going through the motions and that was all."

Claire sipped some coffee and signed the check, which made her think again of Brett and their dinner the previous evening. Since a complex rush of emotion seemed to follow that thought, she wrenched her mind away. "How long had you known Ida? Just since you were clergy together in New York?"

"No, we went to school together—not college or even high school," she said as Claire looked up. "But when we were around seven to ten we attended the same polite little girls' school here in the city. Then her mother moved to California, and though we wrote occasionally, I didn't see her again until she became a seminarian here."

"Did you see a lot of her?"

"Well, we had dinner every week or so, and then we'd meet at functions. One way or another, I saw a fair amount of her. And now I really do have to split. My boss is one of those who feels the Church made a grave mistake in letting women be ordained, and I don't want to feed his paranoia by being late around production time. Thanks for the lunch!"

CLAIRE WALKED BACK TO THE CHURCH, HER MIND A JUMBLE. As she passed the reception desk, she automatically took the messages handed out to her by Darlene, the receptionist. "Thanks," she said automatically.

"You okay?" Darlene asked.

That brought Claire around. "Yes. Why? Do I look unokay?"

"Sort of like if somebody ran over you you mightn't know it."

Claire grinned. "That bad, huh?" There was, within her, a pain waiting to be recognized and acknowledged, but she was determined to keep it at bay as long as possible. She glanced down at her messages. Her three o'clock client, a somewhat flaky young woman, had cancelled and would call later to make a new date. Her five o'clock client had called because she was in the middle of an anxiety attack and wanted to be called back immediately. Claire glanced at the time of the message: twelve-fifteen. Either the attack had receded or the client had done something constructive or destructive to alleviate the anxiety.

At that point the switchboard buzzed again. Darlene answered, murmured, "I'll see if she's in," and pushed the hold button. "It's that Barbara Davis," she said. "She called you earlier. It's one of—"

"Yes, I know," Claire said. "Tell her I'll call her right back as soon as I've reached my office."

Darlene murmured this into the phone, then listened for a minute and said, "But she'll call you right back. She bsaid so. Oh all right." Darlene pushed the hold button again. "She says she's on the point of suicide."

An unprofessional impatience seized Claire. She was visited by an intense desire to shout into the phone, "Knock it off." Although there was a ninety-nine percent chance that Barbara was simply bluffing to get Claire's attention, Claire knew she couldn't ignore that one percent possibility that she just might try it. She reached for the phone. "What's the matter, Barbara?"

Five minutes of listening later she said, "All right, we'll talk about it when you get here at five." She handed the phone back to Darlene.

"And Mr. Barnet wants to see you ASAP," Darlene said.

"Why didn't you tell me that right away?" Claire asked indignantly. "I could have missed Barbara's call then."

"She might have committed suicide."

"In a pig's eye," Claire said angrily. "You know better than that."

Darlene grinned. "But I can't make those judgements. You know I can't."

"No, that's true. You can't. But you don't have to gloat."

Claire went into the downstairs ladies' room to straighten herself before seeing the rector. If it had been Larry Swade who wanted to see her, she would have gone as she was. With Douglas Barnet, her boss, she wanted the security of looking her best.

After washing her hands, she brushed back her heavy, waving dark red hair, powdered her nose and smeared lipstick on her oversized mouth. Above it, greenish gray eyes between rows of black lashes stared back at her. Then she looked at herself in the anteroom's full-length mirror. Always slender, she had recently lost weight for no good reason that she could think of. "It's not as though I don't eat," she grumbled to herself, patting and pulling into place her well-cut gray flannel coat and skirt. Patrick, her late husband, had once said in an unusually frivolous flight for him, that she had the legs of a chorus girl. The thought seemed to give him much satisfaction. Her legs were still good, Claire thought, trying not to feel too pleased. Far below the austerity of her clerical collar and black rabat, her black sandals lent an almost wanton touch.

"COME IN," DOUGLAS BARNET SAID.

Claire walked into the large corner office on the first floor. Books rose to the ceiling on two walls. Windows looking out onto Sixty-second Street occupied a third, and portraits of previous rectors covered the fourth. It was the richly furnished room of a once wealthy parish, and of all the parish rooms, including the church itself, showed least the diminishing wealth of an increasingly mixed congregation.

"Ah, Claire!" Douglas turned. "Thank you for coming by. I'd like you to meet my sister, Penelope Morgan. I'm delighted to say she'll be living with me, her old bachelor brother."

Claire turned. A tall woman who had been examining one of the portraits turned and held out her hand.

"Claire Aldington, isn't it? How nice to meet you! Douglas has spoken of you often."

Claire found herself looking up into a pair of slate blue eyes in an angular, handsome face not unlike the rector's. She must be nearly six feet, Claire found herself thinking. "How do you do?" she murmured. "Is it Mrs. Morgan?"

The woman smiled. "Miss, actually. Douglas and I are only half siblings. Our fathers were different. Mummy came to England after Douglas's father died and married Daddy, who was English."

"It will be very nice for Douglas to have you here. The rector's apartment is really too large to rattle around in alone."

"And he doesn't eat properly," Miss Morgan said severely. "I think he lives off cottage cheese and ice cream."

A passion for America's favorite dessert seemed such an

innocent addiction, so out of character. "You're like my son, Jamie," she said to him. "He doesn't eat ice cream. He inhales it."

"You must come and have a bite with us soon. And bring Jamie—he and Douglas can gorge together."

It was such a unlikely picture that Claire found herself unable to imagine it. "I take it you've just arrived from England," she said, to avoid the embarrassed silence that so often occurred when she was with the rector.

"Actually, I've been over here for a bit, staying with Douglas off and on, but only just now decided that he really wasn't fit to be alone." She smiled gaily at her brother, and he gave her a rueful, twisted smile back.

"We bachelors cherish our independence, you know."

Claire's memory suddenly produced the biography of Douglas Barnet that, along with biographies of the other candidates for the rectorship, had passed around the church. "But you were married, weren't you, Douglas?"

"Briefly. My wife died. Now I've got to get some work done before I go back to the apartment, my dear. So I know you will both excuse me."

"We know when we're being given the push, don't we Mrs. Aldington?"

"Please, it's Claire. We're not very formal around here."

"Of course. And I'm Penelope—Pen for short."

"Is there anything I can do to aid the settling in?" Claire asked quite sincerely, though devoutly hoping there wasn't. Then she berated herself for lack of common charity. She was quite sure that if the roles had been reversed, Miss Morgan—Penelope—would have outdone herself to make Claire feel at home.

"How kind of you to ask! I don't think so. I've been stocking up ever since I first arrived. Talk about the cupboard being bare. I opened the fridge and found in isolated splendor a carton of milk and a box of cigars."

Claire burst out laughing. "Why the cigars?"

"According to Douglas, it keeps them fresh."

"I've never seen him smoke one—or a cigarette for that matter."

"Oh no! It's a secret vice. A man like him has to have one, you know, or he'd be unbearable!"

Claire gave Penelope a swift look and caught the ironic glint in her eye. "I adore my brother," Pen said. "He is much older than me and when we were children he was almost like a very young and rather indulgent father. But I soon realized that with his strong spiritual bent he could easily become sort of a fanatic church guru if he didn't have some human failing to hold him down."

"And cigars were it."

"Yes. I loathe the smell, but find it all rather endearing."

By this time they were at the reception desk. "Have you met Darlene?" Claire asked.

"Actually, you're the only person on the staff I've met. So I should love to meet her."

Claire performed the introduction and watched while Penelope charmed Darlene. She was, Claire decided, going to be an enormous asset for the rector. If she came on a bit strong, then all the more to the good with her brother frequently radiating some kind of repression.

By this time, attracted by the noise, Larry Swade's ample form came ambling down the hall. Claire smiled and performed the introductions.

"You must both come to dinner," Penelope said, "as soon as I can get some order into the place."

"Love to," Larry said.

"Me, too," Claire chimed in. "And don't forget, if you need any help, give a shout!"

"I certainly will. Well, see you anon." And Penelope went down the shallow steps to the front door.

"That should go a far way towards making Doug more cheerful," Claire said, as they both walked to the stairs and Larry's office.

"I should certainly think so. Of course, a wife would be even better."

"That's just because you and Wendy seem to have found the perfect formula. And she spoils you rotten."

"That she does," Larry responded happily.

"Doug said that his wife died after brief marriage. It's odd. I have a hard time imagining him married. I wonder why."

"Because he seems so much the perfect celibate. Almost like a Catholic priest."

"No," Claire said slowly. "Not so much like your run-of-the-mill parish priest. More like a monk."

"You're right." Larry paused and then went on. "I wonder if all the implications of that are true. If they are, then the likelihood of his marrying again are small."

"I assume you're talking about what seems to be his natural bent for celibacy."

"Yes, of course, I'm not implying anything else. The trouble with even speaking the word celibacy in today's world is that people promptly assume that either you mean something else or the poor man is in a disordered state. I mean exactly what I said: that he seems the perfect celibate. There are such beings. My uncle was one. I doubt if he had a sexual encounter of any kind in his entire life, which he spent, by the way, sitting in one of Boston's better men's clubs, reading and—very occasionally—playing whist."

"You mean bridge."

"No I do not mean bridge. I mean whist. Uncle Jeremy considered bridge a vulgar game."

Claire had this sudden vision of an older Swade, stout and cheerful—in fact, remarkably like Larry—sitting behind a newspaper in his club, or playing at a table for four. "I bet he looked like you," she said.

"I look like him, as a matter of fact. He and my father were twins. And I am certainly like my father. But I am not a celibate."

"Viewing your large and growing family, I would certainly say not." Reaching the stairs, Claire turned to go up.

"By the way," Larry said. "How's Brett?"

"Fine," Claire replied shortly.

"That's good," Larry said. "Because the last time I saw him—that is, the last time before Ida's funeral—he didn't look fine."

Claire turned back from the first step. "When was that?"

"As a matter of fact, it was last Thursday, at his club—speaking of clubs. He was there having dinner with Ida."

III

CLAIRE STARED DOWN AT LARRY. SHE HAD AN ODD FEELING THAT she was watching herself from a great distance and was noticing her sense of shock, then her anger and hurt.

"You're sure you mean Thursday," she said.

"Yes. Why?"

To no one else would Claire have said what she then did. "Because according to my beloved, he was in Colorado putting his son into a clinic last Thursday."

"Come back to my office," Larry said. "Judging by the look on your face, this needs talking about."

"What's to talk about? For reasons of his own he lied to me."

"Claire, I have known Brett Cunningham a lot longer than you have. He's one of the most honorable men I know."

"I didn't say he wasn't. I just said that on that occasion he lied."

"Why on earth would he do that? Come on, Claire. Be reasonable and be fair."

"He probably did it because by that time I had additional reasons to feel that he had more than a cousinly interest in Ida Blake. And incidentally, only after she died did he happen to mention that they were cousins."

"So? I'm quite sure that Wendy has dozens of relatives she's never told me about."

"Even the young, handsome ones?" Claire asked wryly.

"Claire, you're being absurd."

"Am I? Yes, I suppose you're right. Forget the whole thing!" She smiled and went quickly upstairs. She could hear Larry's heavy tread beginning to come after her and was relieved when Darlene's voice said from below, "There's a phone call for you from the bishop's office, Mr. Swade."

Not that that would keep him long, Claire thought, and found herself wishing intensely that she had not opened her Pandora's box in Larry's presence, nice as he was. Fortunately, her first client of the afternoon was due in less than five minutes. Claire paused as she heard lighter footsteps coming up the stairs. In fact, the client was now near the door. Larry would not think of interrupting her in the middle of a session, and by the time her appointments were over, she was determined that she would have thought of a way of getting out without anyone hearing.

When her last client left, Claire packed books and papers in her tote bag and left her office just as her phone rang. Convinced it would be Larry, Claire ran to the end of the upstairs hall in the opposite direction from the stairs, then went through the musty library, containing mostly scholarly tomes on theology, through an empty office on the other side, and down some narrow stairs. In front was a door that led into the church itself. Claire glanced at her watch. Evening prayer would not have begun yet. It was celebrated twice a week and Claire loved to attend, but this time she passed quickly down the side aisle and out. She was halfway home before it occurred to her that if Brett had had dinner with Ida the night before she was killed, then he would be—if he were not already—of great interest to the police. Serve him right, she thought angrily and was embarrassed to note that she was talking aloud to herself and people were turning around as she passed. If it weren't so awful it would be funny, she finished in her internal conversation.

JAMIE WAS WATCHING THE NEWS WHEN SHE ENTERED THE apartment.

"Homework done?" she asked.

"You know, Ma, you're getting to be authoritarian," Jamie said. "You don't even say hello when you come in."

Claire walked over, raised his head by his red hair, kissed his cheek and said, "Hello, darling, is your homework done?"

"Almost."

"Previous experience tells me that that means no. Go and do it."

"That's not fair. I've done some, I tell you."

"Like what?"

Silence.

"Well?"

"I copied the assignment into my book."

"But you haven't actually worked it."

"I'm going to, later."

Claire turned off the television. "Now."

As Jamie grudgingly pulled himself off the floor, Motley, who had been lying beside him, also stood up.

"Has Motley been walked?"

"I'm just going to walk him now."

"And not only round the corner, Jamie. He's a big dog and he needs plenty of exercise."

"I know that." Jamie tugged the leash off the hook near the door. Then he put on his jacket. Without saying anything further he left, Motley loping happily beside him.

Claire sighed, moved to turn on the news again, but then

went down the hall to her stepdaughter's room. "Martha!" she called, knocking on the door.

"Come in, but come in quickly."

Claire, wondering what that command portended, turned the knob, opened the door and then jumped as something streaked past her.

"She's out!" Martha yelled, tearing past Claire in pursuit.

"What the—" Claire said, and returned to the living room as Martha pounced on a small strip of fur and picked it up.

"Bad Patsy!" she said lovingly, stroking the kitten.

"That's a kitten," Claire said, stating the obvious. "I wonder how Motley will react."

"Motley would swallow her in one large bite."

"Not necessarily," Claire said. "When I was growing up we mixed cats and dogs. He probably wouldn't attack a kitten. But where did she come from?"

"Ellen called me up and said she had two kittens, one for the taking." Ellen was Martha's best friend.

"Did she know by Divine Revelation that you wanted a kitten?" Claire asked, going over and taking the small gray and white kitten from Martha's hands, "or did you happen to mention that you were interested in having one? I must say, she's adorable. What's her name?"

"Well, the first time I went over and picked her up, she growled at me and then spat, so I called her Feisty von Spatsburg, in honor of her white spats and white military mustache. But I think she must have been upset then, because she's really sweet and affectionate, so I've brought her name down to Patsy. Do you think it suits her?"

"Definitely." Claire, grinning, had put Patsy down and was dangling her key chain above the kitten's head. Patsy on her hind legs was displaying her gray and white stomach and her white mustache. Claire bent, picked her up again, cradled her and stroked her back. An astonishingly large purr started.

"Can I keep her?" Martha asked anxiously. "I really was

going to tell you tonight, because I knew how much I
wanted to have her, but as long as there was a chance I
couldn't, I didn't see any point in, in—"

"—getting into a row with Jamie?"

"You do understand. I knew you would."

"Of course. I'm sorry you didn't know that automatically. What you want is just as important as what Jamie wants.
And if you don't know that it must be my fault."

Martha came over and hugged Claire, kitten and all. "It's
not your fault. You've been wonderful!"

To her astonishment, Claire felt tears spring to her eyes. I
must be coming unhinged, she thought. "Thanks for the
vote of confidence," she said as casually as she could.

Martha put her head on one side. "Are you upset about
something?"

"Just because I become slightly tearful at a compliment?"

"Yes. You don't usually. And I've thought lately that
there was something bothering you."

The distance Martha had come from the self-absorbed
anorexic girl was remarkable, Claire thought, wishing
nevertheless that her stepdaughter had not become quite so
perceptive. "Yes," she finally said. "There is. But I'd
rather not talk about it at the moment."

"All right. But, as you'd be the first to tell somebody,
don't lock it away inside."

Claire smiled and handed over the kitten, who was now
asleep. "Yes, Madame Therapist."

"By the way, Brett called." As Claire's head snapped up,
Martha said, "In case you didn't know."

"I didn't. Who was going to tell me? Jamie?"

"I guess he forgot."

"I guess he did," Claire said grimly. "When did he
call?"

"Just before you got home, I think." She paused. "He
wanted you to call him back right away. At least, I think
that's what he said."

Fighting a strong desire to annihilate her son when he got

home, Claire went to the phone in the hall and dialed Brett's home number. After five rings she hung up. There was a telephone in his study and one in his bedroom. If he were there—and answering the phone—he'd have had more than enough time to pick up the receiver. On the off chance that he was still in his office at a quarter to six, she dialed his bank. This time the phone was picked up immediately by one of the young male assistants, who told her cheerfully that Mr. Cunningham had just left.

"Thank you," Claire said, and hung up. Well, she thought, she'd tried.

Going into the kitchen, she put on a huge apron, got the makings for dinner out of the refrigerator and started preparing chicken legs for baking. These were in the oven and Claire was putting some defrosted peas into a pan of boiling water when the front door opened and Motley bounded into the kitchen followed closely by Jamie. Patsy, the kitten, hovered over by Martha, was eating ravenously from a small dish in the corner beside the stove. Several things happened at once. Martha gave a squeak of fright. The kitten looked up, saw the canine monster bearing down on it, arched its back and spat.

"Who the hell brought that cat in here?" Jamie demanded angrily.

"It's mine," Martha said, bending down to snatch the kitten to safety.

"Just everybody stop and be quiet," Claire said, and then as Jamie continued to mutter, "I mean everybody and NOW!"

It had the desired effect. Everyone, including the kitten, froze.

"Now," Claire said. "Martha, back off. Let's see what happens between the kitten and Motley."

"I don't see why—" Jamie started.

"Be quiet, Jamie, for the Lord's sake. Now just shut up!"

Motley stared at the kitten a few feet away, and the kitten, barricaded behind its dish, stared back. Claire felt, rather than saw, Martha tense, ready to act. Quietly she put out a hand. Finally Motley and the kitten were nose to nose. Then, astonishingly, Motley tentatively licked the kitten's head. She put her ears back and bore it heroically. Then, after a while, her tongue went out and she licked Motley's head in return. There was a collective sigh. Immediately after that, Patsy spat. Motley moved back.

"All right," Claire said. "As you can see, this doesn't mean that the lion is about to lie down with the lamb immediately. But I think when the two of you are here they should spend some time together. When they're really friends, they'll be nice company for one another when they're alone."

"I don't think a dog—" Jamie started.

Claire turned. "Jamie, you're my son and I love you, but if you make one remark like I think you're about to, I'm going to hit you on the head with this pan. So be warned."

Jamie gave her a disgusted look. "Come on, Motley. Let's go."

But for once the magic words did not have their usual effect. Motley stayed right where he was, sitting on his haunches on the floor, staring at his new friend, who continued to eat her dinner. Jamie stamped out. Martha giggled. Patsy, with nerves of steel and an untroubled sense of her own importance, polished off her food.

"Motley!" Jamie called from the direction of his room. Motley stood up.

"Come here!"

Motley accepted the inevitable and hurled himself from the room. At that moment the phone rang.

"Get that, will you, Martha," Claire asked, trying to ignore the beating of her heart.

Martha went down the hall and picked up the phone. "Hello," she said. And then, "Oh, hi! Just a minute. It's Brett for you."

At the phone's first ring Claire, suspecting that—afraid that—it might be Brett, had made an iron pact with herself that she wouldn't answer the phone. A civil "Tell Brett that

I'll call him back" would be appropriate. Nevertheless, she found herself going down the hall and picking up the phone.

"Hello Brett."

"I tried you before, at work and at home. Didn't Jamie give you the message?"

"Afraid not." She could hear the icicles in her own voice.

There was a slight pause. Then Brett said, "Do you think you could put aside your anger with me for a while and help me entertain Doug Barnet and his sister? This wasn't a planned thing—it just came about, and I think it would be a lot more amusing for them if you were there."

Claire knew he was right. As one of the assistant rectors she ought to accept. It would be the least she could do to welcome the rector's sister. But she said, "I've already started dinner here."

"Come on, Claire. It's not as though you lived alone, eking out groceries from week to week. You have two young people there who can easily eat up anything you prepare."

"All right. Where and at what time?"

"My club as soon as you can get there. The Barnets are due in half an hour."

BRETT'S CLUB, THE OLDEST AND MOST DISTINGUISHED OF THE male clubs in New York, was on Fifth Avenue in the upper sixties, and its entrance hall was, to Claire's mind, a cross between an English manor and a pagan temple, the pagan aspect springing from the domelike ceiling with a frieze of nymphs and fauns running around immediately beneath. On the other hand, the wood panelling, to say nothing of the elderly male servitors, gave it an English air.

In deference to the semiformality of the occasion, Claire had put on an emerald green silk dress that made her eyes almost as green by reflection and brought out the red in her hair. The Barnets were already in the big lounge, sitting with Brett in an alcove around a table bearing drinks and hors d'oeuvres.

Brett and Douglas Barnet rose as she approached. Claire was aware of the strained look on Brett's face, and the intense blue of Penelope Morgan's eyes.

"Sorry to be late," she said. "I had to make sure there would be peace in my household before I left. My daughter acquired a kitten, and I wanted to be certain that my son's large dog wouldn't swallow it whole."

"If the kitten is young enough," Pen said as Claire sat down, "that should be no problem. We had lots of dogs and cats at home."

Brett summoned the waiter. "What'll you have?" he asked.

Claire glanced swiftly around. Brett was obviously having his usual scotch and soda. So it seemed was Douglas. Pen's drink could have been either a club soda with lime or a gin and tonic with lime. "Gin and tonic, please."

She turned to Penelope. "Has the moving in and unpacking improved any since this morning?"

Pen laughed. "Hardly. I put three things away and four more seem to appear in the middle of the floor."

The conversation revolved for a while around the problems of moving from one location to another, from one country to another. After they went into the dining room it seemed to center around different practices in the Anglican communion between Britain and the United States and low church and high church. "Of course," Pen said, "Daddy was quite high in his parish and stuck to it when the congregation and even the vestry seemed to get sloppier and sloppier."

Claire, listening with half an ear, wondered how much age difference there was between the half siblings. Their common tie was their mother, whom they must both resemble with their angular good looks—looks which Claire admitted to herself were more suited to Douglas's male appearance than to Pen's female. Yet she had both power and attractiveness. Douglas Barnet, Claire decided, looked as though he was in his early fifties; Pen, probably fifteen years younger than that.

"You can't yank people up too fast," Douglas was saying. "It's not fair to them and they'd probably leave and go to some other parish. I think, at St. Anselm's, there could be a stronger emphasis on the Catholic tradition and I intend to support that as much as I can, but it has to be done gradually."

"How do you feel about women's ordination?" Claire asked, diving off a high cliff. If he were among those who didn't care for women priests, he could make life difficult for her.

"If they are all as competent and devoted as you, Claire," Douglas said with a smile, "then the more the merrier."

Claire caught Brett's somewhat sardonic glint and smiled wryly. "I really wasn't looking for a compliment. It was a serious question."

"And although it contained a well-earned compliment, I meant every word of it."

"Of course in England we haven't come that far," Pen said. "I'm afraid we rather lag behind in such matters."

"Well, someone doesn't like them," Claire said slowly. "I'm thinking of Ida Blake."

"It's horrible and shocking," Pen said. "Doug and I met her once or twice. Such a lovely girl. Such a horrible crime."

"And we don't know that it was her being a priest that—er—motivated the killer," Brett put in.

Oh don't we, Claire thought, remembering the savage cuts on Ida's body. What else could those cuts mean? Looking up, she encountered Brett's eyes looking gravely at her and decided to change the subject.

"How long did you actually live in England?" she asked Douglas. "I mean, when your mother married Pen's father, did you go over there with her?"

Douglas smiled at his sister. "Only for vacations. I was in prep school here, and my uncle, who, with my mother was appointed guardian, felt that as an American I should remain here for schooling and I think he was right. But I was there for holidays, and, of course, after getting my first degree here, I did go to Oxford, so I saw far more of my family then."

"Was your father a clergyman too?" Claire knew she ought to remember this from the information the search committee had supplied, but she couldn't recall what his father had done.

"No. Father was a businessman. My uncle, the one I stayed with after father's death, was a priest."

"And was he very high church?" Brett asked, absently eating his dessert.

"No. He was somewhat more like a rector St. Anselm's had once, the Reverend Norbert Shearer—a complete activist. As far as he was concerned, the Church existed only to push the social gospel."

Brett smiled. "So in a sense you're a rebel yourself."

"Yes. You could say that. Of course, I think I was much influenced by my stepfather, Pen's father."

"Didn't going from one to the other, from your uncle the activist to your stepfather, the Anglo Catholic, give you a slight case of theological or at least ecclesiastical schizophrenia?" Claire asked.

"Nonsense!" Pen said bracingly. "It gave him a wonderful place from which to judge for himself. Now tell me, Brett and Claire, what do I do about some of the social activities of the parish. I'd know what to do in England, and Douglas has given me his ideas, but I'd like to have yours."

The conversation meandered around the subjects of the Altar Guild, the women's groups, the outreach programs, and various other activities. Listening to Brett's answers, Claire found herself once again admiring his detachment. From his comments you couldn't tell what he liked or didn't like. The one exception was the feeding and overnight sheltering of about thirty homeless men and women.

"I'd like to see us increase our commitment to that," Brett said.

"Well, what's to prevent our taking in fifty?" Pen asked. "Heaven knows the parish hall is big enough."

"It's a matter of city law. You can't house more than so many people with only so many bathrooms available to them."

"How silly!"

"Yes, well," Douglas pointed out, "it's a necessary law in the sense that it was passed to protect people from landlords who'd cram them in without the proper amenities and charge them as much rent as they could get. In this particular case it's a block to helping more of the street people. All of us are trying to get around it some way."

Douglas paused for a moment then turned to Claire. "Any news from your friend, Lieutenant—er—O'Neill, as to how the investigation is going?"

"Investigation?" Pen asked before Claire could answer.

"Yes, the police investigation about Ida Blake's death."

"Oh yes, of course, poor girl! Haven't they come up with anything at all?"

"Not that I know of," Claire said. "As a matter of fact, I haven't talked to him since before Ida's funeral." She looked straight across at Brett. "I believe you saw her after I did. Didn't you have dinner with her the Thursday before she died?"

There was a bare hesitation. Then Brett said, "Yes, I did. I had to come back from Colorado for a day and a night, and I had dinner with her the night I was here before going back the next day."

"My goodness," Pen said. "That sounds terribly rich and important. Like a film star. What did I hear some American actor say over the telly in London once? Something about being bicoastal?"

"I don't aspire to such glamor. When I called my office I was told about a directors' meeting I knew I couldn't miss. When I came back I called Ida—my cousin—and we had dinner together."

"I didn't realize you were related," Douglas said.

"It must have been horrible for you—the way she was killed," Pen put in.

"It wasn't pleasant for any of us," Brett said.

Douglas and Pen excused themselves not long after dinner. When they were collecting their coats Brett said abruptly to Claire, "I think we have to talk in peace and quiet." After the others had left he pushed her into a taxi and gave his own address.

Brett lived in a small apartment house in the East Seventies. There was no doorman. He let himself and Claire into the locked front door, then, on the fifth floor, into his apartment. It was surprisingly large, with two bedrooms, two baths, a living room and a study. It was the latter room they went into. Claire sat down on the sofa as Brett went over and turned on the answering tape of his machine. There were half a dozen messages, five of them obviously business related, but one from Lieutenant O'Neill requesting Brett to call him at his earliest convenience.

"Everybody wants to talk to me about Ida," Brett said, as he rewound the tape. "I'll call him later."

He poured them each a small scotch and water from a tray on a table, sat down in a chair near Claire and said, "I wish you had the confidence in me that I have in you. If I heard you were having dinner with some attractive guy younger than I, I suppose I could see where I might be upset, but I still don't think I would be, not if you had assured me, as I have assured you, that there was no reason."

"I guess that makes you more confident than I am. But I also feel that if you had told me from the beginning that you were related to Ida, then I'd be much less suspicious and prickly now. But you didn't. And you lied to me. You told me you were out in Colorado with Adam when you were in town having dinner with Ida. I should think that would make anyone suspicious."

"As I am sure you realize, I didn't lie to you. But I will admit I didn't tell you the whole truth. As I said this evening, I had to come back anyway. There was an urgent message from Ida to call me. I did. There was something— something confidential—she wanted to talk to me about. So we had dinner. I should have told you that much. But there was a reason I couldn't go into it further. A reason which I'll explain to you someday. I can't now. All I can do is ask for your trust."

"'Trust me,'" Claire said drily. "Girls learn that it's the kind of thing men say when they are ready to pull a fast one."

"I'm sorry you feel that way," Brett said. He rose. "I'll take you home."

There was something about the way he was looking at her that made her heart turn over. Her anger receded. She got up and walked over to him. "No, don't. I'm sorry." She put her arms around Brett and kissed him. He responded with a vigor that almost literally took her breath away. "I don't know why I was such a fool," Claire said, when she could. "Larry said you were one of the most honorable men he'd ever known, and he's right."

Half an hour later Claire had forgotten all about Ida, her relationship to Brett, and even her murder. But she was reminded unexpectedly. Brett's phone rang. They both listened to the tape. When Lieutenant O'Neill's voice came on Brett said, "I suppose I'd better pick it up." He lifted the receiver from the phone on the end table beside the sofa and pushed the button to stop the tape.

"Hello, Lieutenant," he said. "What can I do for you?" After a moment of listening he said, "Yes, it's true. I came back from Colorado and had dinner with Ida and then flew West again." There was another pause, then, "You'll be interested to know that Claire, who is sitting here, just asked me that question half an hour ago. No, I didn't answer her either. Where does that leave us? All right. I'll see you tomorrow morning at nine." He put down the phone.

"Do you think he'll respond as lovingly as I did to your request to trust him?" Claire said amiably. She was feeling relaxed and happy.

Brett made a face. "If you're speaking literally, I should hope not. But I also hope I can stall for a little time." He came back to the sofa. "Where were we?"

"At the point, unfortunately, where I have to go home."

"Couldn't you stay a little longer?"

"Brett darling, I would if I didn't have a sneaking fear that Jamie will have spent the entire evening watching television."

"You told me he got good grades. How can he get good grades if he spends his time in front of the tube?"

"Because he has grown into an extremely quick study. Quicker than I often wish he were. I preferred him when he was a plodder. At least he showed guilt when I pushed him off to study. Now he just says he's going to get an A or B anyway, so why am I giving him flak?"

"I thought this school might take him out from under Martha's shadow and encourage him."

"It has. It has also made him into a fourteen-carat male chauvinist."

"It's a phase. He'll grow out of it."

"I devoutly hope so."

WHEN CLAIRE GOT HOME SHE FOUND A NOTE BESIDE THE telephone in Jamie's handwriting. "Lieutenant O'Neill wants you to call him whenever you come home, no matter how late." The latter part was underlined and seemed somehow to carry a reproach. Staring at the square handwriting, Claire felt a sudden rush of affection for her occasionally tiresome son. Much Macho he might be in his worst moments, but he could also—at unexpected times— be sweet and surprisingly tender-hearted. She was beginning to wish that she had come home a little earlier, when she heard a sound from the other side of his bedroom door that seemed to indicate he had not bedded down for the night.

Going down the hall she knocked on his door. Silence. That could mean that he really was asleep, or that he had not done his homework and didn't want to talk about it. Edging the door open an inch, she said, "Jamie? Are you really asleep, or are you just pretending to be?"

There was silence, then a sigh. Then a light clicked on. "All right, Ma. I haven't done all my homework."

Jamie, clad in red pajamas, sat up in bed and punched the pillows behind his back. "If you want to blast me, go ahead."

Instead, she went over, sat down on the bed, put her arms around him and gave him a big squeeze. "That's terrible, if every time you see me you think I'm going to light into you!"

"Well, I got kind of—er—sidetracked."

"With what?"

Jamie lowered his gaze. "Nothing really." But his hand crept towards one area of his quilt. Beating him to the draw, Claire put out her hand and discovered what felt like a book. Pulling it from out of the covers, she looked at the title: *Dog Stories*.

"Is that what distracted you?"

"Yeah."

"What did it distract you from?"

"Algebra and American history."

"I think I'd rather read dog stories, too, than algebra and history. But they're not going to get you into college."

"Ma—d'you think I could be a vet?"

"If you want to be, of course. When did you think about this?"

"Oh—it's been in my mind for a while. And tonight, what with Martha's kitten, I got to thinking . . ."

"Your're going to have to do well in science. Veterinary medicine is not that different from human, and I've heard that vet schools are a lot harder to get into."

"Yeah, I talked to Brett about them when he was last here."

"You talked to Brett about going to veterinary college?"

"Yeah, he said he'd look up some stuff about them for me. I thought it was pretty neat of him."

"He didn't say a word to me about it."

"Well, it was between us. Why should he? Ma—when are you and he going to stop fooling around in his apartment and get married? Then you could see him and stay home."

Claire felt herself blushing violently. "You're making me blush."

"Just thought I'd mention it." Jamie slithered down under the covers. "Night."

Claire kissed him, turned out the light and went down the hall to the sitting room, picked up the phone and dialed Lieutenant O'Neill's number.

IV

"DID YOU TALK TO YOUR FRIEND ABOUT IDA BLAKE'S BOY-friend?" O'Neill asked when he came on the phone.

"Yes, I did. And it seems there was a boyfriend, but she doesn't know who."

"From what I've picked up, Brett Cunningham, your guy, was once her boyfriend."

"Yes. I hear the same," Claire said. "But I also hear that that was a thing of the past. And Brett says it was never a—er—romantic thing in the first place. They're cousins."

"So I understand. I also understand that he had dinner with Ms. Blake the night before she died."

"Yes. He did. As he told you on the phone earlier. I was there."

"So you have no idea who her current boyfriend might have been."

"None. Why is it so vital?"

"According to the medical examiner, she had a recent abortion."

"What?"

"Yeah. Something of a surprise, isn't it? I take it you didn't know."

"No, of course I didn't know. How—how did they know?"

"I don't know all the medical ins and outs. But it's something to do with the fact that the uterus was enlarged. So they took certain tests and verified a recent abortion."

"Good heavens!" Claire said.

"And of course you have no idea of who . . . who might be the father," O'Neill commented drily.

"I'm afraid I can't be of any help. I just don't know."

"Okay."

"Does anybody else know this?" Claire asked.

"Not yet. Not unless it's going to be leaked by somebody in the examiner's department."

"You mean like the slashes on Ida's breasts. That seems to have got around, although it hasn't been in the papers."

"It hasn't been in the *Times*. I think it was hinted at in one of the afternoon sheets."

"What are you going to do now?"

"Keep on digging."

WHEN CLAIRE GOT TO HER OFFICE THE NEXT MORNING SHE HAD a telephone message from Mrs. Blake waiting for her. "She says," Darlene had written on the pink form, " 'I want to see you at once.' By the way she sounded, I'd take a lawyer." There followed a telephone number that looked as if it belonged to a hotel.

Claire dialed the number and discovered that Mrs. Blake was staying in a quiet, very expensive hotel on the Upper East Side. When Mrs. Blake answered, Claire identified herself. There was an indrawn breath.

"I wish to see you, Mrs. Aldington. Please come to my hotel suite as soon as you can."

"I will be glad to come and see you, Mrs. Blake, but I don't respond well to orders. Brett tells me that there was no understanding of any kind between him and his cousin, and that our engagement had nothing to do with Ida whatsoever."

"That is not true. There was a long-standing arrangement between them. It was only a matter of time. But then he met you! I want to know in your own words what you did and what lies you must have told Brett Cunningham about my Ida."

"I told no lies. Ask Brett."

"What's the use of that? He's besotted. He'll say what you tell him to say. I brought up two children. Now one is dead and I don't know the other."

Responding to the grief in her voice, Claire was about to say something conciliating when Mrs. Blake burst out, "I have a good mind to call up one of my friends in the press and tell her the entire story."

Claire wanted to laugh. She also felt sorry for the foolish and ill-tempered old woman. "By all means do so. I have no idea what the quote entire story unquote is. And I can't imagine that the public at large would have the slightest interest in me or anything about me."

"Perhaps not. But Brett Cunningham is an internationally known investment banker. Tales about his undignified goings on could shake confidence in him."

Claire was now thoroughly irritated. "Mrs. Blake, you would not do any serious harm to either him or me, and all you'd do would be to make your daughter—your unfortunate daughter—look, well, pathetic and absurd. It's ridiculous! Brett hasn't done anything wrong—even if he had left Ida for me. He's a widower, free to choose whom he wants."

"Perhaps, but it would not make either you or him happy to see his son's story in public print—the drugs, the alcohol, the squalor of his street life, and the lurid events in which you were involved a few years ago, with your stepdaughter's anorexia, and the highly suspicious death of the rector of your church."

A shiver broke over Claire, not because she thought for a moment that any paper would have the smallest interest in what amounted to old news, but because of the venom and vindictiveness coming through the phone.

"All of that—about Norbert—has been in the papers, Mrs. Blake. I cannot imagine why you think this would be some kind of threat. And I don't know what it is you want."

The imperious command snapped out, "I want you to come here." Then the aging voice changed, almost faltered. "There is something I have to tell you."

But Claire herself was angry by now. "I'm not coming, Mrs. Blake. I would have been perfectly willing if you had asked me in the usual way. But after threats like this I wouldn't dream of it. If you want to see me, you can make an appointment and come down here to the parish house."

When Claire hung up she found she was shaking. For a moment, she stared at the phone. Then, abruptly, she got up, ran down the stairs and back to Larry's room. His door was open, but he wasn't there. Going back down the hall, Claire stopped at Darlene's desk. "Do you know where Larry is?"

"Taking communion to a couple of shut-ins. You know, Mrs. Lang and Mrs. Benson."

"Oh. I wonder when he'll be back."

"Well, he has that conference up at the cathedral to go to this afternoon."

"Damn!" Claire said. Slowly she mounted the steps.

Never had she felt less like doing her job, but training and discipline had given her the ability to block out everything except the client sitting across from her.

At twelve, when the last client of the morning had left and she had a break until three, Claire called Brett at his bank. But his assistant said that he'd been out all morning and was not expected in till later in the afternoon. "Will you ask him to call me when he comes in," she said, and left her name.

On a sudden impulse she put on her coat and left the parish house. Heading towards the subway, she passed Althea sitting on her corner and wished her a pleasant good morning.

"Dalrymple's not well. So it's not a good morning," the woman said.

Claire stopped. "That's your cat, isn't it?"

"Yes. Look at him! His fur's not right and he won't eat." She indicated, with a surprisingly clean hand, the black-and-white cat sitting huddled on top of a pile of clothes. It was true, Claire thought, that his fur looked scraggly, but her knowledge of cats was not up to her experience of dogs. Tentatively, she out out a finger. Dalrymple spat.

"You see?" Althea said. "He's not himself." And she began to cry.

"What about a vet?" Claire asked.

"I don't have any money and anyway I'm afraid they'll take him away from me because I don't have a home for him. And I couldn't bear that. But I can't stand for him to be ill, either. I've been waiting for Mr. Swade to come out, but I haven't seen him. Would you please take Dalrymple to a vet for me? Please!"

Claire paused. She was on her way down to St. Stephen's to see if she could elicit any information about Ida from George Bruce, who was the second assistant rector, Ida having been the first. Obviously, the police would have talked to him, but Claire thought that, as a colleague, she might ask different types of questions and thus get different answers. She wouldn't have time to take Althea's cat to the vet and see George, since her first afternoon client would be at St. Anselm's, ready and waiting, at three.

"When will Mr. Swade be back?" Althea asked despairingly. "I know he would do it for me."

Claire recognized manipulation when she saw it. And there was no question but that Larry would indeed drop everything and do it. He talked less demagoguery than many of his fellow clergymen. But on an individual, person to person, level, he probably did more than anyone else.

"What vet would Larry take him to?" she asked Althea. "Do you have one you see?"

"Dalrymple likes Dr. Rosenthal. He's on East Seventy-third. He's very simpatico."

"I—I guess you don't have a carrier."

For the first time since Claire had known her, Althea stood up. She was tall and stately, and in her full-length skirts reminded Claire of a picture she had seen as a child, entitled *The Gypsy Queen*. Then she bent, collected the cat in her arms, complete with leash and harness, and thrust him into Clair's arms. "Here! God go with you both!" she said dramatically. Then she sat down. "You'd better take a taxi," she added prosaically.

The first taxi driver said, "I don't take no animals out of boxes." But the second seemed undismayed. Dalrymple sat in Claire's lap unmoving, almost limp, his previous irritability gone. However, after a while, as Claire stroked him, she heard the beginning of a purr. How wonderful cats were, she thought. It was so easy to know when you pleased them. Would the world be a better place if humans showed an automatic and involuntary response to people who made them happy? Probably. And therapists would become redundant.

"Well," the driver said. "Here we are."

Dr. Rosenthal's practice was on the ground floor of a town house. Obviously he was popular with more than just Dalrymple. A collection of cats and dogs and their owners sat in the waiting room. About an hour later he got to Claire and her charge.

Dr. Rosenthal turned out to be a young man, thin, with dark curly hair, dark eyes, and gentle hands. "That's Dalrymple," he said before he even glanced at the card the receptionist had made out. "Where did you get him?"

"From Althea." Claire repressed an urge to explain she

hadn't stolen him. "She said he's sick and asked me to bring him."

"Umm." The vet stroked him, looked in his mouth and then put a thermometer up his rectum. "Did she say in what way he was sick?"

"No. Just that he wasn't himself."

While Dalrymple was having his fever checked, the vet looked down his throat, at his teeth, into his ears, and put his stethoscope against his side. Then, with strong, sensitive fingers, he felt the cat's abdomen and sides. After that he removed the thermometer, looked at it, shook it down and put it into a glass with liquid.

"Does he have any fever?" Claire asked.

"Yes. Some. And his bladder's full. It's often the case with altered males. I suppose Althea is enjoying her usual place of residence." He glanced at her. "The corner of Sixty-third and Lexington."

"Yes."

"I think he may have an infection. And, of course, he's an older cat."

"Larry—my colleague—said he's nearly sixteen."

"Yes, and considering everything, he's remarkable for his age. I'll keep him here for a couple of days. Tell Althea to call me."

"All right."

"Are you paying for this?"

"Yes."

The vet smiled then for the first time. It made him look much younger. "You can consider this your good deed for the week, although from your garb and round collar, I must suppose that good deeds are your stock in trade."

"Not as much as they should be. Here, this is my phone number. If you have to get in touch with me, you can call me at the church or at this number at home." Hastily she scribbled on the card.

He took the card and looked at it. "Episcopal?"

"Yes."

"Obviously I'm behind the times. I didn't realize they had women ministers."

"How could you not know? There's been a lot about it in the papers since the bishop ordained the first woman nearly ten years ago, and even before that."

"I was about to say that Mother would be pleased, but I'm not really sure. She was pretty traditional."

"Your mother? Aren't you Jewish?"

"On my father's side. But Mother isn't. She was an Episcopalian—furthermore, the daughter of an Episcopal bishop."

Claire groped in her mind for a moment. "Then your grandfather must have been Bishop Lethridge from Chicago. I think I knew your aunt, who married an Episcopal priest. She always said that her sister had married a doctor from New York named Rosenthal. I don't know why I didn't think of it sooner."

He grinned. "Small-world department."

"But you became a vet, not a doctor."

"I always tell Dad that my patients are nicer than his. And they are. Look at Dalrymple here!" He had been stroking Dalrymple's head and back and the same deep purr that Claire had noticed before was sounding again.

She said, "What kind of a life is it for Dalrymple?"

"If he were younger, not much. But he's old now and mostly sits and sleeps when he isn't eating. And he's with somebody who loves him and whom he loves. For an aging cat it sure beats a back alley or the gas chamber."

"I wonder how long Althea has had him?"

"Since he was a kitten. But she hasn't been sitting on a street corner all that time—only the last two or three years. Before that she had an apartment and a job. Then her illness hit again, or she stopped taking her medicine. Anyway, the day came when she was evicted. And she's been sitting there ever since, living her dreams."

"According to Larry Swade she believes she is guarding the British coast and Arthur's Britain from the Norse invaders."

"Yes, that's what she told me. Sometimes Dalrymple here doubles as her steed."

Claire picked up her coat from the chair. "I'll give Althea your message." She started out. "I must say it seems terrible to me that people like Althea—people whose only crime is that they're ill—should have to sit on street corners."

"In general, I agree with you. But Althea doesn't have to sit there and she isn't destitute. Her family is not rich, but they could afford some help. And to be fair to them they've tried and tried to get her into a hospital. But she won't go, and when she does go, she won't stay."

"But why?"

"For one thing, they wouldn't let her have Dalrymple."

"No, I suppose they wouldn't. Where does she sleep at night?"

"I don't know. I haven't asked. Are you going to come and pick Dalrymple up, in which case I will call you? Or shall I send you a bill?"

"If I don't pick him up, I suppose Althea will. But how will she know when?"

He smiled again. "Because you will tell her to call me. She would anyway. Are you going back there to see her?"

"Of course. What shall I tell her besides asking her to call you? Just that he has an infection?"

"Yes. I'll know more when I get some blood tests back. Give her my best."

"I will. By the way, if I pick Dalrymple up, I'll pay you then. If I don't, then send me the bill."

Claire glanced at her watch as she left. Two-fifteen. She had just enough time to snatch a sandwich in a coffee shop. First she went back to Althea. "Dr. Rosenthal says Dalrymple has an infection and his bladder is full, so he may have trouble there. But he'll know when he gets blood tests back. You're to call him." She hesitated. "Do you want me to pick him up for you?"

"It would be a great kindness," Althea said in her stately

way. She looked worried. Her dark eyes darted here and there. "I can't concentrate on what I'm supposed to do when he's not here," she said.

"What is that?"

"You know the answer to that perfectly well. But I will tell you anyway. It's keeping Britain safe."

"I see." Claire bit back a question as to whether Mrs. Thatcher was aware of Althea's helping hand.

"You think I'm crazy."

"Actually, I was thinking of Margaret Thatcher, the current English prime minister."

"Ah, she will be in the past. The great cycle begins soon again."

Claire bumped into Larry Swade as she came into the front hall. "How do you feel about the cyclical view of history?"

"You've been talking to Althea, I see."

"I've been taking Dalrymple to the vet in your place."

"That's good of you, Claire. I'm terribly afraid that some day some public-spirited person will force her to go into some institution or other. She almost certainly couldn't take Dalrymple there and without him I think she'd die."

"If she got her mind back, wouldn't it be a fair exchange?"

"For how long? They can't keep her for over two months. She could sue them for her release, and then when she came out there'd be no Dalrymple."

"So it's better for thousands like Althea to sit on the streets? I really can't accept that, Larry. There ought to be somewhere for them."

"In the first place," Larry replied, looking through his mail, "I wasn't speaking of thousands. I was talking about Althea. In the second place I agree with you, there ought to be places—halfway houses, semishelters, etc. But I'm not sure that they'd do Althea any good, and it's almost certain that they wouldn't take pets."

"They would if Dalrymple were a guide dog," Claire pointed out.

"I'd give much to see you defending Dalrymple's presence with the Housing Authority on the grounds that he stood in the role of a guide dog."

"I'll work on it. By the way, how come Althea didn't see you when you came in?"

"I came through the church."

"Avoiding her?"

"No, I was not avoiding her. I like Althea."

"So do I, somewhat. But Dalrymple certainly prevented me from going to see George Bruce."

"About Ida?"

"Yes."

"I heard—" He stopped. "I really hate gossip," he said.

"In this case, it might help clear up a murder."

"Yes. All right. I heard, but about thirdhand, that Ida had been seen out with Giles Fairmont."

Giles Fairmont was the new rector of a church down in the East Village, the one where Sarah Buchanan helped out on Sundays. Claire, who had seen him only once or twice and had never talked to him, recalled him as in his early forties, tall and craggily handsome. He favored slightly long hair and, according to rumor, was originally English.

"I wonder if Sarah knew that," Claire said.

"Why?"

"Because if she did, she was less than candid with me. I took her out to lunch and asked her about Ida. Specifically, whether she had a current boyfriend."

"I told you it was only a thirdhand rumor," Larry said, looking unhappy.

"Don't worry," Claire said placatingly. "I won't do anything terrible."

"Yes, but I don't have much confidence that you and I would agree on what is terrible."

"What are you afraid I might do, Larry? Sic the police onto her?"

"No. Just, Just—er—precipitate things."

"What things?"

"I don't exactly know."

"Are you having an ESP attack or something—My God!"

"My God what?"

"I suddenly remembered where I heard the name Dalrymple before—she's that friend of Kit Maitland's,* that loony lady who lives in the same building with her down in the Village. She's the one who's into ESP and tarot and the like. You said Dalrymple was a psychic, but I didn't make the connection. What on earth was her first name?"

"I haven't the faintest idea, but she sounds fascinating."

"She is," Claire said. She was silent for a moment.

"And?" Larry asked patiently.

"Nothing really, except that Kit told me she kept throwing out clues when Kit was trying to track down a murder. How weird! Not that Kit could understand precisely what she was saying."

"She'd make a nice change from Lieutenant O'Neill," Larry said. "Why don't you look her up?"

At that moment Darlene at the reception desk called across the square hallway, "There's a call for you, Claire, from Lieutenant O'Neill."

"Speak of the devil," Larry said. "Toodle-oo. I'll see you later."

"I'll take it in my office," Claire said, and headed for the stairs.

"This'll be on the news tonight and in tomorrow's papers," Lieutenant O'Neill said abruptly, "but I thought I'd let you know first. Investigation has indicated that Ida Blake was not killed in the park. She was killed somewhere else and taken there. And she was drugged before she was killed."

Claire drew in her breath sharply. "There's something . . . something awfully planned about that."

"Yes. I don't think it was an impulse thing. Have you been able to dig up anything at all about a boyfriend?"

---

* Flight of the Archangel.

"No," Claire said.

The lieutenant paused. "Somehow that doesn't sound like the whole truth and nothing but the truth."

"It isn't. But the only suggestion I did hear was a thirdhand rumor."

"Most police investigations—the successful ones—wouldn't get off the ground without those. Who is it?"

"Lieutenant, I want to do something myself before I tell you that. I don't want to be responsible for some entirely innocent person being strong-armed by the police on nothing but a piece of gossip."

"We don't strong-arm people, Mrs. Aldington. And I must remind you that this is an ongoing police investigation of a particularly nasty murder of one of your colleagues. Have you seen today's paper?"

"No."

"Well, take a look at it and then call me back."

But Claire could not open her paper until four-thirty when her last client left. Then she took her copy of the New York *Times* out of her tote bag and spread it on her desk.

The *Times,* in its dignified way, recapitulated what had appeared before and of course said nothing of what the lieutenant had just told her. There was only one sentence that leapt out at her. Tucked at the end of the last paragraph, which restated who Ida was and what church she was connected with, was a statement that the well-known investment banker Brett Cunningham was distantly related to the late Ms. Blake, and had been considered something of a close friend and escort.

For which read, Claire thought angrily, boyfriend. Surely the venomous Mrs. Blake had not been able to get through to a *Times* reporter! Yet this was the first instance that his name had been given in connection with the Blakes. Even the accounts of the funeral had not mentioned him. What would be in the other papers? Claire picked up the phone. "Darlene, do you have either the *News* or the *Post?*"

"I have the *Post,* and somebody left the *News* on the table out here. Why, do you want them?"

"Yes. I'll be right down."

Leaning over the hall table, Claire perused the two papers and felt her blood pressure rise. Neither used the term "boyfriend" when referring to Brett's relationship to Ida. But the implication in each was clear. Brett Cunningham, internationally known banker and financier, had been, in the words Hollywood had made immortal, "a great and good friend" of the late Ms. Blake. And the widowed lady's mother, Mrs. Blake, was quoted as stating that it would only have been a matter of time until the relationship was formalized.

At this point Claire regretted bitterly her refusal to let Brett announce their engagement. Claire's argument had been that formal engagements appearing in the press were for the very young and, for the most part, for the previously unmarried.

She left the papers, went upstairs and dialed Brett's direct office number. "Have you seen the newspapers?" she asked, almost accusingly.

"I have. I don't think I would necessarily have described myself as an international financier—I think that's a bit grand."

"And how about your role as quote great and good friend close quote of the late Ms. Blake?"

"I think I see Cousin Helen's clumsy hand in that."

"But why is she doing it? She threatened me this morning, you know, because I wouldn't drop everything and go and see her."

"Yes. She told me about it at great and boring length."

"But what's her motive?"

"Partly frustrated rage and partly something else. But I'm not quite sure what it is."

"She also threatened to call up her quote friends close quote in the press and give them Adam's drug story, and the gorier details of my involvement with the murder at St. Anselm's."

"I did tell her that if she did any such thing I'd be happy

to hand back her portfolio for her to find another manager and if she embarrassed you in any way she would be very, very sorry."

"What would you do to her?"

"Since I wasn't quite sure what I could hold over her head, I made the threat as vaguely ominous as I could. She has the manners of a bad-tempered child, but she's not stupid."

"Did you know that Ida had recently had an abortion?"

"Yes. That was one of the things we talked about at that last dinner. It was also one of the things she swore me to secrecy about."

"Have you told the police that?"

"Yes. Your Lieutenant O'Neill called me at home before I had had my first cup of coffee."

"Brett, I have an idea that this whole thing is not at all what we think it is."

"I have a feeling you're right." He paused. "Why don't you invite me home for dinner tonight? I haven't seen Jamie and Martha in a long time."

Claire felt her unreliable heart give another beat. "All right. Come home for dinner. By the way, Jamie told me that he had discussed going to a veterinary school with you."

"Yes, we had a chat about that. I looked up some facts for him and thought I'd let him have the result tonight."

"He never told me."

"As I've told you a boring number of times, Jamie's at the age where he feels the need of male bonding or assertion or whatever the psychiatrists currently call it. Do I have to remind you that he has grown up in a household of women and is, I think, involved in some kind of overcompensation?"

"I suppose not, but the next male who moans about the giggling silliness of adolescent girls is going to be told about what a pain adolescent boys can be."

"I have a feeling that might be me. What time shall I come?"

"Any time. If I'm in the kitchen, then you and Jamie can talk."

Claire sat staring at the phone. She would have to postpone her visit down to the church in the East Village—what was it?—St. Paul's, where Giles Fairmont was rector. Claire knew she should now get up and go home and do something about dinner, which would include one more than she had planned. But a strange sense of unease held her. On impulse, she picked up the phone and dialed Sarah's office. But she was told by someone there that Sarah had left for the day. She then looked up Sarah's home phone in her address book and dialed that number. There was no answer there, and no answering tape to pick up a message.

Claire had barely walked in the door at home when she was greeted by both Jamie and Martha with the statement: "Mrs. Blake called three times and said she's coming over."

"Actually," Martha said, putting Claire in mind of Pen's very English use of the word at the beginning of every other sentence, "she only said that on the third time she called. She just said she wanted to talk to you the first two times."

"She's nuts, Ma," Jamie said from his usual position of lying on his stomach in front of the television set.

"I entirely agree with you. Have you—"

"Yes. I've walked Motley. We even went into the park."

"All right. But what in heaven's name—" She went over and dialed the number of the hotel where Mrs. Blake was staying. After a few clicks the hotel operator came back on. "I'm afraid Mrs. Blake must be out. She doesn't pick up her phone. Can I take a message?"

"Yes. Please tell her that Mrs. Aldington has called and very much wants to talk to her before Mrs. Blake comes to my house." She waited a few minutes. "Did you get that all down? It's very important that she get it just the way I said it."

"I'll read it back to you," the operator said in a resigned voice. And read back word for word what Claire had said.

"D'you think that'll stop her?" Jamie asked.

"Unfortunately, no."

"She does sound crazy," Martha said. "Jamie's right."

"For once," Jamie offered loftily.

"Come off it, Jamie. You're both often right. I think she's crazy as a hoot owl . . ." Claire paused. "That's a very unprofessional statement. What I should say is that for reasons I don't understand, she seems to revert frequently to the age of a three-year-old—a three-year-old in a tantrum!"

"We can bar the door," Jamie said happily. "Like the guerillas in a—"

"I don't think we should descend to her level. Besides, I have one or two things I'd like to say to her, and to say them in front of witnesses, especially in front of Brett."

"Is he going to be here?" Jamie asked. "Great! I have a couple of things I want to talk to him about."

"Homework?" Claire asked.

"I'll do it now," Jamie said, and went off to his bedroom.

"Where's Motley?" Claire asked Martha, who was looking through a notebook.

"In the kitchen with Patsy. I was so afraid that he'd eat her! Now he can't bear not to be with her. I've never seen anything like it."

After brooding a little, Claire decided to fix a rice-and-chicken dish since both ingredients were already in the house. It would take about an hour, she knew, along with making the salad and cooking a vegetable, but she didn't think Brett would arrive before.

Two hours later, the dinner was fixed and ready and Claire herself had had a shower and changed. But Brett was still not there. A little put out, she called his office, only to be told by the same cheerful young man that he had left a good hour before. He was also not at his apartment. She left a message saying, "Dinner's ready. Where are you?" And turned on the television news. "To sum up," the newsman was saying, "There has been a murder at the swank hotel—" Just as Claire heard, with mounting horror, the name of Mrs. Blake's hotel, the phone rang. She picked it up.

"Sorry about not being there," Brett said in a tired, flat voice. "But Cousin Helen has just been found murdered in her hotel room."

V

"*My God!*" *Claire said in horror*. "*Brett, what on* earth—this is terrible!"

"Yes. It is."

"Does anyone know, or have any idea, of who did it, or why?"

"Not that I have heard. The police are milling around. Your friend Lieutenant O'Neill is here. Nothing appears to be missing. And there's no forced entry from the balcony outside the suite, or from the hall."

"How—how was she killed?"

"A blow on the head. She's been dead, they figured, about two to three hours."

"Just a minute, Brett. Martha, Jamie, when did Mrs. Blake call here?"

"Fivish," Jamie said.

"Maybe a little later," Martha added, "like about five-fifteen or five-twenty."

"Brett, did you hear that?"

"Yes. You'd better talk to O'Neill."

There was relative silence, except the sounds of general turmoil and voices, then O'Neill came on the phone. "When was that she called, Claire?"

"My daughter says around five-fifteen or five-twenty. Jamie, my son, thought it was around five. I tried to call her when I was home around six, but the operator said she didn't answer her phone and I left a message."

"I know. I have it here. Claire, I'd like you to come down and talk to us about your dealings with Mrs. Blake."

Absurdly, Claire suddenly found herself thinking of a well-known painting of a Cavalier boy during the English Civil War. He was standing before a panel of judges being questioned. The title of the painting was *When Did You Last See Your Father?*

"When?" she asked the lieutenant.

"How about now?"

"Lieutenant O'Neill, I have been waiting for two hours for Brett Cunningham so we could get on with dinner, which is ready. My children have not eaten. Neither have I. And neither, I must suppose, has Brett."

There was a murmur on the other end of the telephone, then Brett's voice came on. "I'll be there as soon as I can get a taxi. I'll take us to the precinct after dinner. They want to talk to both of us."

"All right."

"I don't know why they want to talk to me," Claire said crossly as they sat down to dinner. "My only contact with the woman—and I'm sorry to speak ill of the dead, but it happens to be true—was to have her rail at me and to insist that I go to see her. When she called at five or so, it was announced to my two children that she was coming to the apartment to see me. You heard the accusations she made against me at Ida's funeral. I think she was—to put it politely—off balance."

"What did she accuse you of, Ma?" Jamie asked, with great interest.

"Of—Of—"

"Of luring me away from her daughter, Ida. Very flattering," Brett said.

"Did you?" Martha asked Claire.

"No, of course not."

"I only asked."

"It's such a stupid and undignified thing," Claire grumbled. "As though we were teenagers."

"It just goes to show," Martha said, "that all those books are right. We're reading *Anna Karenina* in class now and—"

"Neither Brett nor I is married. And I am not contemplating throwing myself under a train."

"What did she do that for?" Jamie asked.

"She felt betrayed and disgraced," Martha said. "It's a wonderful book."

"I saw Ida's picture in the papers," Jamie said. "She was pretty—for a clergyperson."

"I should think the police would be a pleasant change after this conversation," Brett said.

Martha was staring at Brett. "Was Ida in love with you? How exciting! Somehow you don't think of your parents getting involved in madly passionate things like that."

"I thought you just finished saying how wonderful *Anna Karenina* was," Brett said. "She was middle-aged."

"But that was a book and in Russia," Martha argued.

"And besides, the wench is dead," Claire said, and put her hand up to her mouth. "I didn't mean that—at least not in that way."

"But she is," Jamie said.

"Is that a quotation?" Martha asked.

Claire nodded. "Yes."

"Where from? Who said it?"

"The police are looking better and better," Claire commented grimly. "I'll tell you some other time."

"Thou has committed fornication. But that was another country. And besides, the wench is dead," Brett quoted.

"Hey wow!" Jamie said. "Fornication! That's hot."

"Who said it?" Martha asked.

"I believe Christopher Marlowe," Claire said. "Brett— let's leave and go to the police. I need more restful companionship."

"I SUPPOSE IT'S USELESS TO WONDER WHY THEY WANT TO SEE me," Claire said in the taxi. "What with Helen Blake's accusation at me, concerning you, I must figure neatly as the prime suspect."

"Somehow I can't see them thinking you did it. They'd be much more inclined to pick on me."

"Why you? According to Mrs. Blake's script, you're the innocent party, the helpless male, beguiled and seduced beyond your strength . . . I must say that doesn't paint a very flattering portrait of you."

"A rather European one," Brett said, and braced himself as the taxi swung left and then right around the roadway circling Grand Central Terminal.

Claire peered at him in the dark. "How so?"

"The upper crusts of Europe—whom Cousin Helen tended to imitate—nearly always blame the woman when something concerning a couple goes wrong. Men are looked on as creatures unable to control their passions, so if they fall in love and marry unsuitably, it is said the woman concerned took advantage of their vulnerability. You never looked at me in that light, did you?" he asked with mock seriousness.

"Never," Claire said firmly. "Rich, successful investment bankers are not vulnerable."

"I see. In other words, the shoe is on the other foot. The frail and vulnerable in the world must be protected against us."

Something in his voice made Claire reach out and clasp his hand. "I always feel your vulnerability with Adam."

"But not with you."

"No. Should I?"

To her surprise, he suddenly pulled her to him and kissed her passionately. She responded with equal passion.

"Is this the place you wanted?" the cab driver asked. "Or am I interrupting something?" The cab had stopped in front of the police station.

"Yes," Brett said, reaching for his wallet. "You are. But it can't be helped."

"You act like teenagers," the cabbie called after them disgustedly as they walked into the precinct.

Claire turned and looked back at him. "We are. We just aged prematurely."

"YOU SAY MRS. BLAKE CALLED YOUR APARTMENT AT FIVE OR five-thirty, depending on which of your children's stories you take," Lieutenant O'Neill said, "and announced she was coming to the apartment. But when you called back around six the hotel operator said she didn't answer and took a message."

"Yes. In fact, lieutenant, you have the message, or so you said when we talked before."

"That's right."

They were sitting in the lieutenant's dingy office, which was set in a corner of the main precinct room. There was no window and the institutional green of the back wall, now almost dark gray, was cracked and peeling. On two sides were glass, so that the lieutenant could see into the main room. O'Neill was sitting behind the desk and Brett and Claire were on straight, uncomfortable chairs on the opposite side, facing him.

"I do have your message," the lieutenant said. "What I'd also like from you is to have you go back to Ida Blake's funeral and tell me word for word everything that passed between you and Mrs. Blake."

Claire sighed. "All right." She watched O'Neill press a button on a tape recorder.

"Do you mind if we tape this?" he asked.

"What if I said yes?"

"Are you going to say yes?"

"Claire," Brett said, "if you don't want to have your conversation taped you don't have to. If you have any doubts we can get my lawyer down here in nothing flat."

"Why?" the lieutenant put in swiftly. "Does she have anything to hide?"

Claire smiled at Brett. "Thanks. I don't mind. I was just curious as to what the lieutenant would do if I said yes. And he still hasn't answered me."

"I think I'll keep that one shrouded in mystery," O'Neill said. "Now, tell me every word you can remember you and Mrs. Blake said to one another."

With something near total recall, Claire repeated by word and tone the older woman's angry recriminations and accusations and her own replies. When she came to an end, Lieutenant O'Neill said nothing for a moment but sat there watching her. Yet she had the feeling that his attention was not really on her but on something else.

"She just launched into you like that—no preamble, no introduction, no nothing."

"Just like that."

"Let me get this straight. She accuses you of taking Brett Cunningham here away from her daughter and claimed that her daughter and Cunningham were involved with each other and were probably going to get married. That right?"

"Yes, although the marriage part was more by implication."

O'Neill swung suddenly towards Brett. "Is that true? That you and Miss Blake were having an affair and planning to be married?"

"No, Lieutenant, as I have told you not once but at least four times, Ida and I were cousins and friends. She would ask my advice about something over lunch and we'd talk about it. But at no time was I in love with her or she—to my knowledge—in love with me."

"I'm inclined to believe you when you say you weren't in love with her. But how would you know whether or not she was nursing a secret yen for you?"

"Then she would have to have been a powerful actress. A man usually knows that kind of thing. Besides, I'm pretty sure she was in love with somebody else."

"Who?"

"I don't know. She never told me."

O'Neill swung back to Claire. "What was that piece of thirdhand gossip you were going to tell me when you had checked it out?"

"I haven't checked it out yet. I meant to this afternoon, but got waylaid by Althea. I had to take her Dalrymple to the vet."

Brett glanced over. "Who's Althea and who's Dalrymple?"

"Not related to that Letitia Dalrymple in the West Village, is she?" O'Neill asked.

"Don't tell me you know her?" Claire started and then said, "Oh of course, you were involved in that case with her, too."

"I still don't know who Althea and Dalrymple are," Brett said.

"Althea's a bag lady and Dalrymple is her cat. He was sick and she was waiting for Larry Swade to come back to the parish house because she knew he would take Dalrymple to the vet. Only Larry didn't come and I had to sub for him."

"And the other Dalrymple," O'Neill chimed in, "is a psychic. Mad as a hatter, but has been right a couple of times."

"What has she to do with this case?"

"Nothing," Claire and O'Neill said together. Then they looked at one another and smiled.

"Mrs. Aldington," O'Neill said, then his voice changed subtly back to its official note. "What time did you get home this afternoon?"

"As I told you earlier, about six."

"And what time did you leave the office?"

"Around five—well, a quarter to, I think."

"You're not sure?"

"Lieutenant, I don't record every step I take in a notebook. My last client left at four-thirty. What did I do then?"

"Read the papers," Brett said. "You called me right after that in a seething indignation."

O'Neill looked put out that Brett had answered for her. "Let her answer her own questions, Mr. Cunningham, please."

Brett looked back at O'Neill. "Why? You're not trying to tell me that this is anything more than a friendly talk so that you can pick up information from somebody who has helped you in the past?"

O'Neill ignored him and then turned back to Claire. "Did you read the papers then or later, Mrs. Aldington?"

"I read them then. I had the *Times* with me from the morning, but after you told me about what was in the papers—yes, by God, you were the one who did! And here you are pretending you've forgotten that."

"I haven't forgotten, Mrs. Aldington. So where did you get the others?"

"I went downstairs and Darlene—our receptionist—had them, so I read them there, spread out on the desk. And if you don't believe me you can ask Darlene."

"So you left the church at around four forty-five. You didn't get home until six. Where were you in that hour and a quarter?"

"Walking home, window-shopping."

"Did you buy anything? See anybody you knew?"

"No. Are you trying to tell me that you suspect me of stopping by Mrs. Blake's hotel and killing her?"

"Somebody did stop by and got up to her room without anyone in the hotel noticing. And she must have been someone Mrs. Blake knew, because there was no forced

entry of any kind either from the front door of her suite or
the balcony.''

"That still doesn't mean it was somebody she knew,"
Brett put in. "It could have been a bellboy or hotel maid—
or somebody dressed as one—who knocked on her door and
said she had a delivery or order or something.''

"Well, I didn't kill Mrs. Blake,'' Claire said. "And what
motive could I possibly have had?''

"According to what you just told me, she had threatened
you with exposure in the press, claiming to have some
connection there. She certainly got at least part of what she
wanted printed in the afternoon papers. Maybe there was
more, and that was what you couldn't put up with.''

"And what would that be, lieutenant?'' Brett said,
getting up.

"I don't know. But I'll find out.''

Brett touched Claire's shoulder. "Come along. I'll take
you home and we'll call Alan, my lawyer. There's no reason
on earth you should stay here and listen to all this
speculation and fictionalizing.''

Claire got up. "It sounds stupid beyond words to say that
my feelings are sort of hurt, Lieutenant. After all the things
we've been through together, I would have thought you'd
know I was hardly the kind of person who beats old ladies
over the head—however poisonous they may be.''

"Nobody gets let off, Mrs. Aldington. If you can find
anyone at all—a salesperson in one of the stores you looked
in, for example—who remembers seeing you between a
quarter to five and six, it would clear you and be a big help
to me. Just remember: I can hardly say to the police
department and the press that you are innocent because
we've been on cases together and are buddies.''

"DO YOU SUPPOSE HE WAS TELLING ME OBLIQUELY THAT HE
himself believed I was innocent, but was going through the
motions of questioning me this afternoon so he wouldn't be

accused of favoritism?" Claire asked Brett as they walked towards an avenue where they could pick up a cab.

"Probably, but not certainly. You've got to remember that he is first and foremost a police officer. Maybe his superiors were riding him about getting you in for questioning. I'd be willing to bet that he thinks it's a bunch of nonsense, but that doesn't make me any the less eager to have a lawyer with you."

They rode uptown in relative silence. Brett's hand was around hers, holding it firmly.

"I wonder what on earth Mrs. Blake wanted to talk to me about," Claire said. "Until tonight I assumed she was just going to shoot off her mouth again in her lovable way about me luring you away from Ida. But maybe there was something else."

THE NEXT DAY CLAIRE REARRANGED HER MORNING APPOINT-ments and took a bus down to the East Village to St. Paul's Church, which turned out to be on Second Street between First and Second avenues. It was small and looked run-down. Once, a hundred years earlier, it probably served a prosperous congregation moving up from the Wall Street area. Now, Claire guessed, its parish would embrace blacks, Hispanics, Orientals, remnants of the hippies of the sixties and seventies, and today's yuppies, desperate for low rents anywhere in Manhattan. Beside the church was a small parish house.

Claire knew she was taking a chance on finding Giles Fairmont in, but anyone who was rector of St. Paul's would have to be hardworking—he couldn't afford much help. She ran him to earth in the parish house kitchen, where she found him sipping some coffee.

"The front door was open, so I walked in," she said.

Giles Fairmont smiled, lightening his thin, rather austere face. "I try to keep it open, getting across the message that all are welcome, but, of course, given the neighborhood, it also means that I cannot keep anything of the slightest value around."

It was odd to hear that English Public School-Oxbridge accent in the sparse kitchen from a man who wore his clerical collar and black rabat above jeans and sneakers.

"I'm Claire Aldington," she said.

"I know. I've seen you around. Like some coffee?"

"As a matter of fact, I would."

He poured her some from a Silex on the stove. "Milk? Sugar?"

"Milk but no sugar."

He added the milk and then handed her a chipped mug.

"Why don't you take THE chair?" he said. "If it makes you uncomfortable for me to stand, I'll get another one from the study across the hall."

"All right. Or should we go into the study?"

"Then we'd have to bring this chair into there. There are more, but they're temporarily in the basement where we had a meeting this morning. And anyway, I'd rather we sat in here. It's more cheerful. The study window looks onto a graffiti-filled wall. I'll get the other chair."

When he came back and sat down on his folded chair, Claire, seated in the kitchen chair, smiled and said, "Something tells me that life around here is on a very basic level."

He smiled back. "It is, and you'd be surprised how restful that can be, although I think only a bachelor could say that. It would be pretty grim for a family."

"And yet you're a rector, so this parish must be self-supporting. If it weren't you'd be vicar."

"True. But we're only self-supporting because we do live and function at the basic level, and we get donations from various worthy friends." He paused, and then added in the same pleasant way, "Have you come to talk about Ida?"

"Yes. I heard the rumor of a rumor that you and she were—er—going together. Is it true?"

"Was true. Hasn't been for the past about five months.

I'm afraid I lost out to somebody else. But it's no use asking me who, because I don't know."

Claire sighed. "Nobody seems to know."

"Why is that particular question so important? Because of how she was killed?" Claire looked up suddenly. "Yes," he said, "I know she was stabbed and slashed." He smiled. "But that doesn't mean I did it."

"The details of her killing were supposed to be kept secret. They haven't appeared in the paper—at least I don't think so."

"Well, not in the more responsible papers, but they were mentioned on the local TV news."

"Was there an exact . . . an exact description of the slashes?"

"No. Just that there were. I somehow take it that there's more to it than just that."

Claire hesitated for a second. Lieutenant O'Neill had been very explicit about keeping the nature of the slashes secret. "Yes. Sorry. That's all I can say."

"I see. But I take it the part you're not telling me would indicate that her current boyfriend was the guilty one."

"Not necessarily. But if she was going with someone, it is something the police—and I—would like to know."

"Why you, especially? Just in your role as police helper, so to speak?"

There was something in his voice that made her say, "You sound disapproving."

He crossed one knee, then took a cigarette from a crushed pack in his pocket. "Mind if I smoke?"

"No, and anyway, it's your house."

He struck a match, lit his cigarette, then threw the match into the sink. "I've worked in poverty and minority areas for so long that I have lost my middle-class attitudes. I am more inclined to see the police as the enemy."

"I can understand that. But would you want to live in an unpoliced city?"

"No, and I know all the arguments about chaos versus

repression. My feeling is not an intellectual thing—just in the gut."

"I see. Well, I got to know Lieutenant O'Neill originally when St. Anselm's business manager was murdered, and I was enjoying—if that's the word—pride of place as chief suspect.* I've always found him to be extremely fair and—at least as far as I could see—in no way prejudiced against any group."

"I told you. It's not an intellectual thing. I knew your former rector at St. Anselm's by the way—Norbert Shearer. He taught a class when I was at seminary. What an activist he was! He should have been down here with us and the down-trodden. Not up there on the Upper East Side at St. Anselm's."

"With all due respect for the strength and passion of his social views," Claire said drily, "I don't see him down here living, as you put it, at a basic level."

"Perhaps not." Fairmont grinned. "Anyway, we need voices like his among the elite."

"To keep us stirred up and guilty, I suppose."

"Right. If you've got the worldly goods, then you have to have the guilt."

"'Property is theft!' You sound like a Marxist."

"I am. But you'd better not tell your police buddies that, or they'll tell their pals in the FBI and then they'll come and arrest me."

"Considering that avowedly Marxist professors have been teaching quite openly in some of our best universities, I don't think you're in much danger."

"How middle-class you are, Claire!"

"Yes, but as a Christian minister I think you should bear in mind that large portions of Christ's followers came from the middle class of that day. And one of them, Joseph of Arimathea, was actually rich."

"Perhaps." Fairmont's mouth seemed a little tighter, a

---

* *A Death at St. Anselm's.*

little less ready to smile. "Is there anything else I can help you with?"

Claire reflected that she probably should have kept her middle-class views to herself if she wanted any further help from Fairmont. But she decided to try, anyway. "What I'd really like to know is what kind of a person Ida was. I realize that that is an off-putting question, and I may as well tell you that I have been told that (a) she was a thoroughly nice, normal, wholesome young woman, and (b) that she held strong feminist views, but (c) the person who told me that said she didn't feel certain they went that deep. Does any of this jibe with what you knew of Ida?"

Suddenly he stood up. "I'm sorry, but answering your questions has made me feel like the classic stoolie or snitch. I don't like myself in that role, so I think we had better bring this to a moderately civilized end."

Curious, Claire thought, standing up. Those lips were now tightly compressed and there were white patches beside his thin nose.

"In that case," she said, "I'll say good-bye now. Thanks for the help you did give me." She started back out of the kitchen, but paused at the door. "You know, I'd like to remind you, while you're having your ideological spasm, that Ida was murdered, quite horribly. I think she deserves for us—ordinary people and police—to try to find the person that did it."

THE PAPERS AND LOCAL TELEVISION NEWS SHOWS OUTDID themselves in covering Helen Blake's murder. Following so soon after her daughter's violent death, Mrs. Blake's end became the focus of stories, personality pieces, background articles, and general think essays on the growing violence, the irrelevance of the rich, the role and/or vulnerability of the Church in a desperate society and so on, and so on. The viewpoint and bias changed according to the paper or news magazine or commentator.

Claire started getting phone calls from reporters and writers begging for interviews and from at least two publishers suggesting books, all of which she turned down.

"Don't let any of those predators through," she finally told Darlene in desperation. "Just say, over and over if necessary, that Mrs. Aldington is not giving out interviews of any kind. Period."

"What if the Archbishop of Canterbury wants to talk to you?" Darlene said flippantly.

"I'd be delighted to talk to him about any matters theological, spiritual, or ecclesiastical—not that I think he needs my thinking on any such subject. But if His Grace the Archbishop wants to interview me, the answer is still no."

"I'd love to talk to you about something theological or—er—spiritual," Darlene said.

"Good. Make an appointment."

After that little interchange, Claire went up to her office to do some much-needed desk work before her next client. But as she started answering letters and making notes for her files, she found herself tense, as though almost waiting for something. What's the matter with me? she muttered to herself. At that moment her phone rang.

When Claire picked up the receiver, Darlene said in a troubled voice, "Look, I know you told me not to let any newsperson through, but this guy sounds threatening—says it would be for your own good. I think you ought to talk to him."

"All right, although I can't imagine what he has to threaten with. Put him through."

"Good afternoon, Mrs. Aldington," the voice said. "I would like so much to talk to you about what's going on. My own investigations have led me to believe that you know more than anyone, including the police. You would be handsomely paid for the interview, I can promise."

"Who are you?" Claire said.

"All in good time. Our interview must be in the strictest confidence."

Claire found herself unable to decide whether the speaker was a man or a woman. Whoever it was had a voice that could be described as either tenor or alto. Every few words Claire changed her mind about it.

"Any reporter from a reputable news agency, whether print or electronic, has no hesitation in saying who he or she represents. So I see no reason why you don't. I certainly would not agree to anything with someone whose credentials I couldn't check."

"As I said," the smooth, genderless voice went on, "you will, of course, know that the moment we come to a firm understanding. However, just to give an extra nudge to my proposition, let me tell you that if I can't talk to you, there's much I know about your life, your family's and Mr. Cunningham's that I am quite sure neither of you wishes to have made public. This will appear if—"

At that pivotal point, there was a click and Darlene's voice broke through. "Sorry, Claire, but Mr. Cunningham is on the other line and he said it was absolutely vital that you talk to him."

"Darlene, I'll talk to him in a minute. Tell him to hold on, but—" There was another click. "Hello," Claire said. "Hello." But she knew she had lost the other phone call. "Damn!" she said aloud.

"Sorry, Claire," Brett's voice said. "But I have to warn you that you may be getting a threatening phone call."

"I was in the middle of it when your call came through," Claire said. "Did he threaten you with some kind of exposure in the press?"

"Yes. He did. But I couldn't tell whether it was a he or a she. It could have been either."

"Yes. I know. I couldn't tell." She paused. "Brett, I find it weird that this person, whoever it is, was threatening more or less the same thing as Mrs. Blake. I wrote her off as an arrogant nut with inflated ideas of her importance to the press, among others. But I wonder if there was something." She hesitated, and when he didn't respond, said, "Is there anything—something or anything—that she knew about you, or this person might know about you, that I don't?"

There was another pause. Then Brett said, "I am afraid there is, Claire darling, and furthermore, I'm going to have to leave it at that."

VI

THERE WAS A SILENCE AT CLAIRE'S END OF THE PHONE.

"Please," Brett said. "I promise you that when I tell you you will understand. And that you will also understand if I tell you that I can't tell you now." After a second he added, "I realize that's a lot to ask."

"It is," Claire said. "Particularly since I seem to be involved in it, whatever it is."

"No, you're not. You don't see that from where you are, but you're not."

Claire found she was suddenly very angry. "You're right, Brett, that is a lot to ask. I'm not sure that I'm capable of trust like that. I'm going to have to think about it."

"Whatever you decide." He hung up.

Claire got up and went over to her window, and stood staring out at the courtyard below. On one side of the court was the south wall of the church. On the other two sides were town houses, some of them divided into apartments.

Down below, the court itself was shared by the church, the
parish house, and the apartments, and there were bushes
and shrubs and in the center a sundial. Normally this was a
sight that Claire found pleasant and soothing. Now she
didn't see it. Her mind was preoccupied by the question:
Why is Brett doing this to me? And found that even putting
the words into a question was enough to inflame her anger.
Her instinct as well as her professional training, both as a
priest and as a therapist, was to try to imagine herself in the
same position. But she could not picture any situation so
fraught or private or dangerous that she was unable to share
its details with Brett.

But then I don't deal in the world of finance, she told
herself, a world where people used ugly weapons for power
and profit.

But nor did she live a sheltered life. Through the outreach
program in which St. Anselm's was involved clients from
every background came through her door. Some had been in
prison. Some were the victims of bizarre and dreadful
crimes. Crime was not limited to the rich and powerful. But
certain kinds of blackmail might be.

Blackmail. She had avoided, even in her own mind,
using that word. But that's what it was. The voice—he or
she—wanted something—what, she wasn't yet quite sure—
and threatened to publish or broadcast something else—
which Brett knew but couldn't tell—if she didn't comply.
What did comply mean? To meet and what—? On the face
of it, the person on the phone wanted information which he/
she assumed Claire had from the police.

But what had that basically to do with Brett? Claire
wondered. Her relationship with Lieutenant O'Neill was
unconnected with Brett. It was something built up in two
previous cases. So, did the threat mean that if she, Claire,
did not inform the caller as to something unnamed that she
might know because of her relationship with the police,
then something else would be broadcast that would embarrass Brett? Or perhaps embarrass her, as well?

"Damn and blast!" she said. The phone rang. She turned

and looked at it for a moment, extremely reluctant to pick up the receiver, and then shocked that she could feel this way. Every client knew that in moments of emergency he or she could call. She could not allow herself to become chary of answering the phone. It rang again. Walking to the desk she picked it up. "Hello," she said, and heard the tension in her voice that some over-sensitive client could easily mistake for rejection. "Yes," she said more gently.

"Claire Aldington?"

"Yes, Pen." She was glad she'd toned down her voice. "How are you? Beginning to get settled in?"

"I've given up setting a date for the great tidiness. As I said last time, every time I get something put away, four more seem to drop out of nowhere. But we are making progress. Douglas swears that he no longer falls over something whenever he comes through the front door. We were wondering if you and Brett could come to dinner tomorrow. It will be just a small gathering—perhaps one more couple. We'd so like to have you."

"I'm terribly sorry, Pen, I'd love to have accepted. But I have Group tomorrow night, and I can't let them down. For all I know Brett could make it, and I'm sure if he's free he'd love to."

"I'm so sorry. Perhaps another evening?"

"Please don't postpone your plan on my account. I'd love to come another time, with or without Brett.

"Oh. Of course. Well, I'll try you again soon."

Claire sat down, wondering how much of her anger at Brett Pen Morgan could pick up from her voice and words. Well, she thought, it couldn't be helped. She found herself unable to face the prospect of an evening with Brett and at the same time being polite and social with Douglas and Pen.

She had pulled another letter to her and was beginning to make inroads with a reply when the phone rang again. Again she forced herself to pick up the receiver.

"Claire Aldington," she said.

"This is Giles—Giles Fairmont. Ever since you left the other day I've been kicking myself and any available surface for my rudeness. There was no reason on earth why I shouldn't have answered your questions. I apologize, and wonder if you'd pour coals of fire on my head by having dinner with me tomorrow night?"

She laughed. "I'm afraid I have Group tomorrow, from six to eight."

"How about a late dinner? If you have Group there, I could pick you up at the church at about eight-fifteen."

Pen's invitation was large in Claire's mind. And with something like wonder she heard herself say. "If you don't mind, I think I'd like to meet you farther downtown in your direction. I have a small errand to do and that would be best for me."

"By all means. Do you like Indian food?"

"Yes, very much, if they have any plates that are only moderately hot."

"Sabu claims that all his plates are positively tepid to fit the uneducated American mouth. And you can get some that are not hot at all. It's at the corner of Second Avenue and Sixth Street. How about if I meet you there around eight-thirty? Will that give you time for your errand?"

"Yes, plenty." Claire was guiltily aware that the errand was a hasty fiction to keep Giles from turning up at the church. The rectory, where Pen and Douglas would be entertaining, was two blocks away, but she still didn't want a personable Englishman coming to collect her after she had lied to the rector's sister.

"See you then."

THAT EVENING CLAIRE CELEBRATED THE EUCHARIST AT SIX, AND found, as she always did, the words and ritual healing and restoring. Behind everything, like a painful wound, lay her anger at Brett. That afternoon she had found her mind returning to it again and again, only to be pushed aside so that she could give her full attention to the person seeking her help and therapy. But during the service she let the pain surface, exposing it to the healing Presence of the ceremony, the words and the Bread and Wine.

"But if only he'd trust me," she found herself saying aloud as she was in the sacristy putting things away.

"Well why don't you trust Me?" The words were placed in her head as though by an outside agency.

"You have a point," Claire said drily. She put her jacket back on and went outside into the chapel. To her astonishment, Althea was standing at the back, looking as much as ever like a gypsy queen.

"I have not been able to talk to the vet today," Althea called from the back as Claire emerged. "I am extremely worried about Dalrymple. Please go there for me."

"What do you mean, you haven't been able to call him?" Claire said.

"I mean his line is always busy, busy, and anyway I have run out of quarters. If you can spare more quarters for me, I'll go outside to the phone booth and keep trying. It's raining." She added the last on a rising note.

"All right, Althea." Claire thought a minute. To promise to call from home was easy enough. But how would she pass on the message? "You can come upstairs to my office and I'll call from there. I have one of those phones that keeps ringing until it is answered."

Althea took a step back until she was standing in the chapel door. "I do not like walls. I do not like to be inside. It is dangerous for me. Enemies lurk there, evil people who will take me to prison. You call and then come and tell me on my cliff."

"I thought you said it was raining," Claire said, succumbing to a moment of irritation. "If it's raining, how are you going to keep from getting wet?"

"I have my tent, of course," Althea said, pointing out the obvious. "You may call and then come out and tell me how Dalrymple is."

"I'll do it tomorrow morning." One way and another the day had been a strain. And the peace that had come with the evening service had now gone.

Althea sank to her knees, holding up her clasped hands. "I implore you—"

"Get up, Althea," Claire said, unmoved. "Those she-nanigans don't have the slightest effect on me."

Althea got up and started to cry. "I know something is wrong with him. I know it."

"How do you know it?"

"I don't know. I just know it."

Claire paused, and as she did, felt the hairs on the back of her neck move. Factual, down to earth, Claire herself had once or twice been swept with a feeling, an intuition, a something that made itself known to her and demanded attention. "All right," she said abruptly. "Wait here. I'll go up and telephone."

Aware of her tiredness, her crossness, her sore feelings towards and about Brett, Claire went back through the church, through the door leading into the parish house and walked upstairs to her office. There she looked up the vet's number and dialed. The receiver was picked up on the second ring.

"Dr. Rosenthal's office," a girl's voice said.

"This is the Reverend Claire Aldington," she said, parading her credentials. "I'd like to talk to the doctor about—about a cat named Dalrymple."

"The doctor's been trying to reach you, Mrs. Aldington," the girl's voice sounded reproachful, "but your line's always busy or you're not there. Didn't you get our message?"

"No. What's wrong?"

"I'll let you talk to the doctor."

"Mrs. Aldington?" The doctor's voice sounded almost immediately. "We found a slight obstruction in Dalrymple's stomach that I want to take out. But I have to have Althea's permission."

Claire rubbed the back of her neck. "She's downstairs in the chapel, or rather at the chapel door, demanding that I call you. When I told her I'd do it tomorrow, she said she knew something was wrong with Dalrymple and begged me to do it now."

"She has some astonishing gifts. Do you think you could

get her permission for me and come back and call me right away? The sooner I can get this thing out the better."

"Is it malignant?"

"Not completely yet. But it's turning. As I said, the sooner we, can move on this, the greater Dalrymple's chances."

"All right. I'll go down right now. I—" A sound made Claire turn around. "It seems Althea's dislike of walls and buildings has been overcome. Here she is." Claire held out the receiver. "Dr. Rosenthal wants your permission to remove an obstruction from Dalrymple's stomach. You talk to him."

For a second Claire sensed the other woman's whole reluctance to be there in the building and to talk on the phone. But suddenly, long skirts swishing, she swept forward. Her graying dark hair piled high on her head quivered. If she were a little less dirty and a little more expensively dressed, Claire thought, she could easily appear on any stage as a dowager.

Claire got out of her seat as Althea took the receiver. "It is I, Dr. Rosenthal," she said dramatically. "You must operate. The goddess has spoken."

There was a silence. "Yes, yes, I have said so. And Mrs. Aldington here has said Dalrymple can stay with her until he is quite better."

"I have said no such thing," Claire muttered, *sotto voce*. Althea's dark eyes looked at her reproachfully over the receiver. "You will take him, yes?"

"Yes," Claire said, thinking about Patsy and Motley, to say nothing of her children.

"He would like to talk to you," she said, rising from Claire's seat and holding out the receiver.

Claire went over and took the phone. "Yes? This is Claire Aldington."

"I just wanted to make sure that you're entirely willing to take Dalrymple for a few days between the time he leaves here and the time he takes up residence with Althea on the street. I know how bullying she can be, so I thought I'd check personally."

"That just about describes the situation," Claire said. "Yes, I'll take Dalrymple for a limited time."

"He really is a great cat," Dr. Rosenthal said. "And I'm not saying that just to manipulate you. He really is."

"He speaks the truth," Althea said from the window.

Claire was perfectly willing to believe that Althea had acute hearing and could make out what Dr. Rosenthal was saying from across the room. Still, it was strange.

When she had hung up she turned to Althea. "Althea, where were you born?" she asked.

"Vienna."

"I don't believe it," Claire said. "If you were born in Vienna, why are you having hallucinations about saving the White Cliffs of Dover?"

"Sometimes one thing seems the truth, sometimes another. Truth is variable." She added proudly, "I saw that once in a Hindu temple over on the West Side."

"If you're talking about the temple I've been in, then you have the quote wrong. It goes, 'Truth is one. Men call it variously.' I remember because I admired it, too."

"Whatever," Althea said in a perfectly ordinary American accent. "You will call tomorrow to see how Dalrymple is faring after his operation?"

"Yes, I will and I must assume you will, too."

"I told you. I have no quarters."

"If the line is always busy, busy, busy, as you say, then you get your quarters returned."

"I have other calls to make."

"Then you can just go to the trouble to do as I have seen you do, hold out your hand and beg. I bet most people give you quarters."

Althea tossed her head. Claire reflected that she had often read that phrase in a book and had never really seen anyone do it. But there was no doubt: Althea tossed her head. "I do not like to beg," she said.

"It goes with living on the streets, which you have chosen to do."

"You have no pity," she said, "I have been evicted."

"And if we find you a home somewhere?"

"I have no money."

"Don't you have disability money?"

"You will let me know what the doctor says about Dalrymple," Althea said, stalking to the door. When she got there she turned. "I was born in Delhi," she said proudly.

"I'll bet," Claire said to herself.

Claire locked her door and followed her downstairs. "Althea," she said, when the woman reached the door. "Is there anything I can do? Other than pick up Dalrymple?"

"You can give me quarters."

Claire sighed, opened her purse, managed to dig out six quarters. "Here."

Althea took them and bobbed a curtsy. "God go with you," she said.

Larry came up behind Claire. "Good night, Althea. Stay dry!"

"I can't figure out how much is fraud and how much is truth," Claire said when the door closed.

"Neither can she," Larry replied.

THAT NIGHT AT HOME, WHILE FIXING DINNER AND EATING IT WITH Martha and Jamie, Claire was acutely aware that part of her attention was preoccupied with the phone, waiting for it to ring. Twice it did, and each time she jumped, but neither time was it Brett.

"What's the matter, Ma?" Jamie asked.

"Nothing. Why?"

"You're jumpy."

"Not exactly jumpy," Martha said. She was engaged in a battle to keep Patsy off the dining-room table. "Like you were waiting for something."

"I am not jumpy and I am not waiting for something," Claire said emphatically and untruthfully. And then, "Sorry, kids. I guess that sounded a bit heavy. Let's just say it's been a day! By the way, in a week or less we're going to have a visitor stay with us for a while."

"Who?" they both asked together.

"Mr. Cunningham?" Jamie said. "That's neat. We can—"

"No. Not Mr. Cunningham."

"Gosh, I only asked."

"This visitor has four legs, a tail and purrs."

"Not another cat," Jamie said with disgust. "I don't know how Motley's going to like that."

"You're going to have to get over that anticat attitude if you're going to be a vet," Martha said.

"I'm not anticat. I was just thinking about how Motley might feel."

"Since Patsy seems to adore him, I don't know why he should mind."

"This one is called Dalrymple," Claire said, "and is coming here to recuperate after an operation, so he'll probably stay in my room. He'll need peace and quiet."

"Why doesn't he go home?" Jamie asked.

"Because . . . well he can't. His owner doesn't have one."

"What do you mean?"

"I mean she's a bag lady."

"You mean she goes around the streets picking up trash?" Martha said.

"No. She sits on a street corner. Dalrymple, who's quite elderly, usually sits with her, or walks with her on a leash. But he's been sick, so the vet said maybe we could take him for a while, until he's ready to go back on the streets with Althea."

"What's been the matter with him?" Jamie asked around a large piece of bread and butter.

"Don't talk with your mouth full."

Jamie swallowed then started, "What's—"

"He had an obstruction in his intestine and the vet has removed it."

"Which vet? Ours?"

"No. A Dr. Rosenthal."

"I read an article by him in a pet magazine. He's pretty cool. I'd like to meet him. Maybe he'd let me do some work there after school."

"Right now you don't have time. And anyway, I'd bet you'd have to be a bit older."

Brett didn't call all evening. Claire didn't know whether she was glad or sorry. She tried to stop thinking about the matter, to stop wondering what on earth was so vital that Brett couldn't trust her with it. Somehow it seemed to her to go back to the days when women weren't supposed to trouble their heads with matters of importance, except for the fact that the men of the world—in the old English phrase, the lords of creation—entrusted to the patronized lesser beings the care of their most precious possessions, their sons. "Just don't worry your pretty head about it" was always a phrase that made Claire grind her teeth whenever she came across it. Was Brett's refusal to tell her whatever it was that Mrs. Blake and now the unknown caller threatened to publicize derived from that?

Claire, tossing about in her bed, thought about it till her head ached, and still could not decide. Blast the man, she muttered to herself, turned over, plumped her pillow yet again and resolved not to brood over it any more. An hour or so later, still pondering the whole dreary business, she finally drifted off to sleep.

Brett did not call the next day. Claire was glad that it was her day for hospital visiting. Talking to the ill and dying and to their families kept her attention focused. It also jarred her sense of priorities. The subject of the tension between her and Brett seemed less crucial. At least, she told herself, I should give him the benefit of the doubt. Getting back to her office, she put in a call to him, but learned from the perpetually cheerful young man who picked up his phone that Brett had left town.

"When will he be back?" she asked.

"I really don't know. He didn't seem sure when he left here."

"Do you know where he is?"

There was a slight pause. "No, I'm afraid not. He was going to call and let us know."

"Thanks a lot," Claire said, all her previous resentments back.

THE INDIAN RESTAURANT WAS EASY TO FIND. CLAIRE WENT IN and saw Giles sitting at a table next to the bay window, reading a magazine.

"Hello," she said, going up.

He put down the paper and stood up. "Sorry. I didn't see you come in." He went around to ease her chair.

"Did it ever occur to you that your manners and your politics make strange bedfellows?" she asked.

"I know. My mother was nearly fifty when I was born, and she brought me up on the manners she'd been taught by her grandparents. The result is a sort of nineteenth-century leaping to the feet combined with raising the clenched fist." He handed her a menu. "The dishes are listed according to hot, hotter, and hottest."

Claire glanced at the big card. "What do you suggest?"

"Well, I'm going to have this beef dish—" he pointed to an item on the card she was holding—"but it's very hot. The lamb curry is good and only medium hot. I often have it. Why don't you try it?"

"All right. The lamb curry it is."

Giles gave the order to the waiter.

Claire shook out her napkin. "Don't you find the combination of your nice Edwardian manners and your radical politics a little muddling—not to say indigestible?"

"No. Unlike many of my fellow radicals—of both sexes—I do not look upon *la politesse* as chauvinistic or degrading."

"You realize, don't you, that many women feel strongly that all of what you call *la politesse* was simply a device for making sure the little woman stayed in her place."

"Yes, but I'm inclined to think that's bunk, a rationalization for rudeness. There was a whole generation of kids, who, when questioned, did nothing but shuffle their feet and mumble. I think they thought it was super authentic. But the result was that half the time you couldn't hear them."

"Man in his pursuit of the perfect idea in its purest manifestation can become a terrible boor," Claire said, and thought of Brett. It was the kind of thing he would say. In fact she might well be quoting something he had said.

"True. But are you saying we should give up having ideas—perfect or otherwise?"

"No. I just wish we weren't so happy to dismember other people who disagree."

Giles grinned. "Spoken like the practical, pragmatic person I'm sure you are."

"Is that bad?"

Giles speared what looked like a hot pepper and put it in his mouth.

"You didn't even wince," Claire said. "Doesn't it burn?"

"Yes, but you can acquire a taste for that. To answer your question, Is being practical and pragmatic bad? In honor of our truce, and only because I like you and feel I owe you an apology, I'll admit to you, but will deny it if you quote me, that no, it's not bad. Countries where the governments keep falling are inclined to suffer from the purity syndrome—as well as from the usual corruption of power plays. No one is willing to compromise. It's better for people to compromise simply because cities can fall apart while idealists argue. But saying that goes against the grain, so please don't quote me to anyone."

"I won't. But why? Why does it go so much against the grain? It's only common sense."

"That least common commodity. I suppose because my father spent thirty years in Parliament, compromising every step of the way. A most unheroic figure."

There was a bitterness in Giles's voice.

Claire said after a minute, "What is your mother like?"

"Like me, a crusader. Wants to take the world and shake it until it's better. However, I'm finding to my dismay that I'm becoming more inclined to stop and think and count the costs before I storm the barricades."

"You didn't sound at all like that the other day. Anybody who had anything to do with the police was a stoolie."

"Yes, well, I worked in some of the inner-city parts of London. My impression there is exactly what my impression here is, that the majority of police will beat up a black or a Hispanic first and ask questions afterwards. But you can have a double murder in some manor house in Locust Valley and my God! the cops tiptoe around the suspects, making very sure that everybody has his or her rights read and all lawyers present."

"You also sound angry."

"After some of the things I've seen, I am."

"Considering that I'm a walking collection of middle-class attitudes and believe in compromise I don't know why you asked me to dinner."

He smiled, and Claire found herself admitting that his smile packed a great deal of warmth and charm. "I told you. Because I like you. Tell me about yourself and how you came to be a walking collection of middle-class attitudes."

"It probably began with my father who was a District Attorney in the Midwest."

"It's amazing, isn't it, about the fathers and the children."

"Yes, but it can work both ways. My father, whom I was very close to, probably had a big influence on me, as yours did, but you rebelled against it."

"You're right. I know that you're a widow, so tell me what your husband was like."

"In his attitudes, like you, but he looked more like a bear." Claire talked for a while about her late husband, Patrick, and her children and her job.

"And are you now engaged or—er—anything?" Giles asked.

"Engaged to an investment banker."

"Next to police, my least favorite people are investment bankers and multinational types."

"I bet you have a private income!"

He looked at her. His flexible and expressive mouth narrowed a little. "What makes you say that?"

"The only other people I've heard say that have private incomes. Well?"

His mouth relaxed and then he grinned again. "As a matter of fact, yes."

"See?"

"Do I know him?"

"His name is Brett Cunningham."

"I was afraid I knew him. He's on some big church board that spends a large amount of time saying no to various of my projects."

"But he says yes to a lot of others, and is trying to expand our work with the homeless."

"So he ought! But I won't fight with you."

And am I still engaged, she wondered? Engaged to be married, to have and to hold from this time forth, in sickness and in health, in doubt and in trust . . ."

"Hey! Hi! Where did you go all of a sudden?"

"I was just—er—taken with a thought. That's all."

"About the investment banker?"

"Yes, as a matter of fact."

"Want to talk about it?"

She took in the clear gray eyes and intelligent face. "Yes, as a matter of fact. How good a listener are you?"

"Wonderful. Always got A+ in the listening department."

So Claire talked for a while. When she got through Giles looked at her for a moment and said, "Either he's the kind of person you can trust or he isn't. That's the thing you have to make up your mind about, not whatever it is that the

crazy Mrs. Blake was holding over his head to tell the
press."

"You make it sound simple."

"It is. Tell me more about this mysterious caller on the
telephone. The one who implies he or she knows whatever
it is your fiancé is not telling you."

"I can't tell you any more. I just had that one phone call,
and it doesn't sound like much, but it made my blood run
cold."

"He sounds like he might be the one who killed Ida and
Helen Blake. And if he is, take care. Whoever it is has
managed to kill two people, one of them in a well-guarded
hotel room."

Claire felt a slight shudder go over her. "Oddly enough,
when it was just Ida, I was sure it was some woman-priest-
hating, antifeminist psycho. But when Helen Blake was
killed, it made me wonder whether or not they were both
killed for something else entirely." She glanced at Giles. "I
don't want to evoke your wrath again, but I'd like to ask if
you're sure you don't know who she went out with after the
two of you broke up. After all, as you've just pointed out,
my life might be at stake, too."

"And you promise me you'll not confide this to the
police?"

"You know I can't promise that, Giles."

He smiled. "Yes, all right. I was just teasing you. And I
can't be of any help because I don't know."

"You don't have any idea?"

"I didn't say that. What I don't have is positive
knowledge. And it's no use looking at me like that. Given
my feelings about police procedure, I'm not going to
subject an innocent person to it unless I am sure of my
indentification. 'And that, said John, is that.'"

"How very like you that you should end up a thoroughly
wrongheaded indictment of the police with a quote from A.
A. Milne." She glanced at her watch. "Ouch! I should be
home."

He got up with her. "I'll take you there."

"No need. Just take me to a taxi and I'll be more than satisfied. You were right about the lamb curry. It was delicious!"

But when they found a taxi Giles paid no attention to her protests and got in with her.

"You don't have to escort me home, you know."

"No. But I want to. And it's not just my beautiful manners."

She gave a snort of laughter. "You're a disgrace to your fellow thinkers."

"I know, and I couldn't be happier about it."

When they got to her door he paid off the taxi, which drove away. But instead of escorting her to the front door, he pulled her away from the lighted lobby to a small darker niche in the side of the building and kissed her. It was a far more ardent kiss than she had allowed Brett a few nights before. She had no intention of letting it go on, but he held his mouth over hers for a while, and despite herself, she responded.

"I told you I was engaged," she said when she finally pulled back.

"I know you did. But I decided to ignore it." And he pulled her to him again.

This has to stop, she thought, aware of his arms forcing her against him. "Hey—Whoa!" She pushed herself back. "Enough already. Thank you and good night."

"How about dinner next Wednesday?"

"I don't know, I have to look in my book."

"I'll call you tomorrow." He laughed, raised her hand and kissed it. "Until tomorrow, lovely one." And then he was walking down the street.

As Claire was heading down the hall in her apartment towards her own room, the door on her left opened and Jamie in pajamas appeared. "Ma, I saw you from the window and I think it's absolutely rotten of you to go kissing that man whoever he is right out in front of God and everybody when you're engaged to Mr. Cunningham."

Claire heard her own words coming out of her mouth with astonishment. "Then you'll be relieved to hear I'm going to become unengaged."

VII

WHEN CLAIRE CAME INTO THE OFFICE THE NEXT MORNING SHE was told by Darlene that the rector wanted to see her right away. Wondering which of the various duties for which she was responsible might have gone wrong, she headed down the hall to the big corner office.

"Darlene said you wanted to see me," she said as she walked in.

Douglas Barnet was looking out the window and said without turning around, "I think watching the passing parade in New York is different from anywhere in the world."

"Agreed. What about it is particularly striking you at the moment?"

"How well dressed many of the people are. How fashion conscious some of them are. How fast they walk. How full of purpose they look. What do you suppose is the purpose that drives most of them? Money?"

"That's the popular view."

He turned around. "Implying that you don't entirely agree with it, I take it."

"Most of those people have the same concerns that people have in, say, Chicago or San Francisco, or even London. I'll agree they're better dressed and look more fashionable—obviously we're talking about the women—but remember, how you look in New York is part of the asking price. If you're mounting the corporate ladder you can't look as though you had been a secretary all your life. The MBA has to show in the suit you wear and how well you wear it. New York is a place where people identify themselves by what they do, not what they are."

"And then there's the alternate-lifestyle look." His voice was grim.

Claire went and stood beside him and saw a street person, muttering to himself, walking back and forth, about six feet each way, in front of the wall of an elite women's club.

"Yes. That, I think, is Nathan."

"Nathan who?"

"Nathan Smith, I believe, although sometimes he forgets and says Nathan Pruitt."

Barnet turned towards her. "Do I take it that he is one of the homeless we feed and/or shelter?"

"Both. He'll probably continue to walk up and down until our doors open and all the luncheoners come in. He sleeps here at night."

"I assume he's mentally ill."

"He says he's a schizophrenic, but he changes sometimes and claims he's a manic depressive."

Suddenly Barnet struck the side of the window. "It is outrageous that these people should be walking the streets like this. They should be taken care of, lovingly, not impersonally. They should have decent places to go to where people look after them—not just shove them in a ward, or out on the streets."

"I agree, Douglas, but doing what we're doing, feeding

them and offering them shelter, is about all we can do under the circumstances. Some of the laws governing their civil liberties would have to be changed before anything else could be done."

After a minute he said, "It's supremely ironic, isn't it? Well, obviously there's nothing I can do at this moment." He turned back to the desk. "We were sorry you couldn't have dinner with us last night."

"I was sorry, too. But short of a major catastrophe I don't feel I can change Group." Claire was more than aware of her sense of guilt. Group had not stopped her from having dinner with Giles.

"Sit down," Douglas said, and sat himself on the sofa under the window. "Smoke?"

Claire shook her head and wondered what it was he wanted to talk about. Plainly he was having a hard time bringing it up.

"I do hope that Pen gets settled in some of the various activities of the church," he said finally. "She's always . . . well, most of the time, been pretty active in parish work in England, and has a high degree of energy."

"I'm sure the various groups will be most eager to have her help."

"Yes," he said, and stared down at the cigarette he'd just lit.

Claire decided to try and give him a little help. "Douglas, are you asking me to take Pen under my wing? You must be, because as you know I have my therapy work and am not that involved in the women's or discussion groups or the Bible studies—probably not as much as I should be. But then I have the two children at home and try not to be away more than a couple of nights a week."

"I certainly don't want you to put yourself out," Douglas said stiffly.

"No—I put that badly. I didn't mean I didn't have time for . . . for Pen. I guess I was just rationalizing why I am not more involved in the day-to-day work of the church. I'll be happy to take Pen around. At least I know who the people are and so on.'' There was a question she wanted to ask, but knowing, or suspecting, Douglas to be touchy she wanted to be sure she was approaching it the right way.

But the silence lengthened, and Claire knew that, given his sensitivities, she'd have to wait to ask her question. "I know Peggy Anderson is neck deep in parish work. Why don't I arrange for the three of us to have lunch, and we can take it from there?"

"Yes. All right."

But Claire had a strong feeling that that was not what he wanted. "Why don't you tell me what you'd like me to do?"

He got up and went behind his desk. "Nothing," he said. "I'd like very much for her to meet Mrs. Anderson. I'll tell her you'll be calling."

Claire knew she was being dismissed. For a moment she hesitated, considering simply blurting out, "What is it you want me to do for or with Pen?" But at that moment the phone rang and it was obvious he turned to it with relief.

He picked up the receiver, glanced over at her with a smile and said, "Thanks for dropping by."

Soon after she got to her office her own phone rang. She picked it up. "Claire Aldington."

"I thought we were going to stay in touch," Lieutenant O'Neill said.

Claire opened her mouth to say that she had nothing new to impart when she heard herself say, "There's something I'd like to talk to you about, lieutenant."

"So talk."

She told him about her caller.

"When did this happen?"

"Two days ago."

"And why in God's name didn't you call me right away?"

"I don't know. I should have, of course. But—well there

seemed to be so much turmoil about so many things, not even counting Althea and Dalrymple, that I just didn't get around to it."

"Are you talking about Letitia Dalrymple, the psychic who lives down in the Village?"

"No, the cat Dalrymple, companion to the bag lady, Althea, of Lexington Avenue, where she sits." Claire hesitated. "You said you'd dealt with Letitia Dalrymple— I've always wanted to know, are psychics ever right? Are they of real help?"

"Yeah, I don't like to admit it, but she's been on target a couple of times."

"Why don't you like to admit it? Does it go against your principles about the universe?"

"Because I'm a good Catholic boy."

"Who is also divorced. Would you call yourself a practicing Catholic?"

"I'm asking the questions here. But no, I wouldn't exactly." There was a pause. "I don't have any explanation for this, and I don't want you to nag me about it, but Letty called here early this morning to say that she thought I ought to get in touch with you. She said, and I quote because I wrote it down, 'That nice woman priest that the girl who used to have the apartment above worked with.' "

"Very nice of her. I wonder why."

"She didn't say."

"And you didn't ask?"

"You don't push psychics—at least not Letty Dalrymple."

"Speaking of Dalrymple, this time the cat, do you know his owner, Althea?"

"If you're talking about the woman I think you are, yes. She looks like a sort of gypsy and wears long skirts and thinks she's defending Britain. I once asked her how she felt about Ireland."

"What did she say?"

"She said that England started going wrong after Arthur."

Claire laughed. "I know some English who might agree." That reminded her of Giles Fairmont. She opened her mouth to say something about him, when she remembered his paranoia about the police. No need to feed that, she thought.

"What are you deciding not to tell me?" O'Neill said.

"Talk about psychics! You're not so bad in the ESP field yourself."

"Just ordinary psychology after twenty years in the police department. Are you going to change your mind and tell me?"

"No. Not right now. And before you get suspicious, it has nothing whatsoever to do with this case. Just a new friend of mine who doesn't admire the police."

"Anybody who doesn't admire the police usually has a guilty reason for not liking us."

"That's pretty sweeping."

"Why doesn't he like us?"

"What makes you so sure it's a he?"

"All right, she."

"Because the person is an idealist who has seen the police kick around minorities. And much as I do admire the police, Lieutenant, you have to admit it has happened."

"Maybe in the past. Not now. Not here." He paused. "Back to your caller. Would you please go over what he said again, and let me check if I have written it down right."

Claire repeated what she had told him.

"And you can't be certain whether it is a man or a woman?"

"I can't. And Brett couldn't, either."

"You didn't tell me that he'd called Brett Cunningham. When was that?"

"I'm not sure. Brett didn't say and I didn't ask."

"What absolutely burns me is that you've let a couple of

days go by without telling me. You and your fiancé,
Cunningham. What do you think we're here for?"

"Does it make that much difference?"

"Yes. It does. I've been trying to reach Cunningham for
the past several days. Where is he?"

"If I knew, Lieutenant, I'd be happy to tell you."

"You mean he didn't tell you where he was going to be?"

"I mean just that."

"You sound pissed off about it."

"I am pissed off about it, if you want to know the truth. A
friend to whom I confided my feelings about the matter said
I should either trust Brett or not trust Brett and I think he's
right. I'm not behaving very well. I'm ashamed. But I'm
still pissed off."

"Everything okay between you and Cunningham? I
thought the two of you were going to get hitched. Weren't
you? Wasn't there some plan for you to be married?"

"There was."

"So?"

"So what. I can't tell you where Brett is. Is there
anything else you'd like to know?"

"Yeah. Who was Ida going out with? We still don't have
the answer to that."

"If I ever find out I'll let you know. I asked Giles
Fairmont who is the rector of St. Paul's—" at that moment
she remembered that it was Giles who disliked the police,
and if she told O'Neill that he had once gone out with Ida,
that would put the police onto him immediately—"but he
didn't know. So we're bact to square one."

"Why did you ask this Giles Fairmont?"

To continue to give offhand answers would only make it
worse for Giles, Claire decided, so she said, "because
once—more than five months ago—he went out with her,
but not after that."

"Why didn't you tell me that along with all the rest you
haven't told me?"

"I suppose I thought you already knew it," Claire said

untruthfully. "As I said, he hasn't been out with her for several months."

"Nevertheless I'd like to talk to him."

Thinking quickly, Claire tried to figure out whether, from Giles's point of view, it would be better if O'Neill knew his antipathy to the police or not.

"Is he by any chance the guy who doesn't like the police?" O'Neill said drily.

"Yes. He is. I feel now that I've betrayed him. He'll be furious."

"Do you care?"

Claire found to her surprise that she did. "Yes. I don't like somebody who has become a friend to think that I'm a stoolie."

"You know better than that, Claire," O'Neill said. "The police are not the enemy."

"No. But then I haven't spent a lifetime working among minorities and other groups who feel that they are."

"The fact that they feel the police are the enemy doesn't make it true. Any more than the fact that certain segments of the population hold bigoted views of the minorities make those views true. Right?"

"Right. This is my week, I think, for being wrong. I'm going to hang up now and get to work with my clients. It may restore some of my self-esteem, which badly needs mending. Good-bye."

CLAIRE WAS GETTING READY TO LEAVE HER OFFICE THAT afternoon around five when the phone rang. When she identified herself, a careful and precise male voice announced himself as Hector Blake, and asked if he could come and see her.

"Yes, of course," Claire said. "I'm so sorry about your mother. This double loss is terrible for you, especially . . . well, especially in the way it happened in each case."

"Yes," he said. "It is. When would it be convenient for you to see me?"

"Any time that you want. Where are you staying?"

"I'm staying with George Bruce at St. Stephen's rectory."

"Would you like to come and have dinner at my apartment this evening? All I can offer, really, is two teenagers and a modest assortment of animals."

She was unprepared for the anger in his words which he almost spat out.

"I have no desire whatever to consider myself indebted to you in any way after what you did to my sister and mother. I would prefer to see you in your office."

After a moment of shock, Claire said, "Do you know, I haven't the faintest idea of what you're talking about. I don't mean to speak ill of the dead, but is your entire family nuts? Your mother accused me of taking Ida away from Brett Cunningham, which as far as I—and Brett—are concerned is off the wall. And I don't remember having any quarrel with Ida whatsoever. I doubt if we had a single conversation amounting to more than inquiries about health and weather."

"That is not the information I and my lawyers have been given."

Claire drew in her breath. "Perhaps I should have a lawyer of my own present in our meeting in that case."

"Do—by all means!"

Claire sat staring at the telephone after she heard him hang up at the other end. Withdrawing her hand, she saw that it was shaking. This is nonsense, she told herself. Then her phone rang again. With absolute certainty Claire knew it was the person—man or woman—who had called her before. Ashamed of her impulse not to pick it up, she snatched it to her ear. "Claire Aldington," she said firmly.

"Ah, Mrs. Aldington. So good to get you again. We now must make an appointment to meet where I can interview you and get your views on all the strange and tragic events that have occurred." The voice was not only genderless,

Claire decided, it was being passed through something that
gave it a mechanical sound.

"Who are you?

The voice laughed gently. "All in good time," he/she
said—the same words and tone that had been said before.
"We will pay handsomely for your information which has
increased since we last talked. Now when—"

"I will not meet anyone who does not identify him or
herself, so you are wasting your time. And no—I will not
listen further." She slammed the phone down. After a
minute she lifted the receiver and dialed. When someone
answered she said, "Lieutenant O'Neill, please."

"He's out. Can I take a message?"

"Please tell him that Mrs. Aldington called. And ask him
to call me back."

Again the phone rang. Hoping it was O'Neill, Claire
snatched it up. "Yes?"

"And if we do not meet," the voice purred on, "well
then I must remind you of what happened to your late
colleague, Ida Blake." And the phone went dead.

Claire did not know how long she had been sitting there
when she picked up the telephone and dialed Brett's
number.

"I'm sorry, Mr. Cunningham is not there," the same
young man as before said.

"This is his fiancée, Claire Aldington. I want very much
to know where he is and how I can reach him. It's urgent."

There was a slight pause. Then, "I am extremely sorry,
Mrs. Aldington, I have the strictest instruction not to tell
anyone where Mr. Cunningham is—not even you. I am
sure—I know—that when he returns and explains you will
understand."

"You can tell him, if and when he calls, no I won't. And
also tell him not to bother to get in touch with me."

The moment Claire hung up she cringed at her childish
behavior, which was without dignity or balance. *I sound*

like a housemaid, she thought, and then, a little ruefully, and a snob to boot.

At that moment she heard steps mounting the stairs, and knew that her first client, a disturbed and chaotic young woman and sometime drug user, was on the way.

"Hi," she said, as the young woman appeared in the doorway.

Gerry was only twenty-nine, but she looked ten years older. Dark eyes looked out over shadowed puffs. She was white faced and thin. Nevertheless she was well dressed in a tailored suit and with shoes that Claire knew were expensive because she herself had once priced them in a Madison Avenue boutique. Despite a drug-ridden past, Gerry had a good job as a writer in a public relations agency and seemed to be doing moderately well there. But she was also chronically anxious, dependent, and angry.

"Hello," she said, sitting down in the chair opposite the desk.

"How are you?" Claire asked.

"Everthing stinks," Gerry burst out.

"What do you mean by everything?"

"Society, the world, politics, the nuclear arms race, AIDS, and so on."

"You left out famine and the greed of multinationals."

"You're making fun of me."

"Yes, I am, because what you say is meaningless. What you really mean is that you feel terrible about something close to you, such as yourself, or something that has happened to you recently. Somebody else could come in and burble on about the beauty of spring, the kindness of people in the street, the hopes of ordinary human beings going to work, the presence in life of love and friendship. Which, therapeutically speaking, is equally meaningless. It just indicates that such a person is happy with himself and with his surroundings. You're unhappy with the same. Why?"

Thus encouraged, Gerry embarked on a long litany of those who had mistreated her, misunderstood her, thwarted

her, prevented her natural rise to professional heights, and
so on.

"Who are these people—literally, I mean by name. Let's
take them one at a time. And, specifically, how did they go
about thwarting you?"

For the next forty-five minutes they worked through her
parents (living in Toledo), several erstwhile boyfriends, one
or two previous bosses, and one or two so-called friends.

"I take it you consider them all universally rotten."

Gerry remained stubbornly silent.

"What is it you want that you don't have?"

Gerry still didn't speak. After a minute, she muttered,
"It's not fair," and got up. "I have to leave early today,"
she said.

"Why?"

"There's a job I have to do at the office."

"That's not true," Claire said slowly. "I mean, you may
have a job at the office to do, but that's not why you're
leaving early." There was something about Gerry that
bothered her. For all her general anarchy and complaining
and tendency to look upon herself as the world's victim,
Gerry had shown distinct signs of getting better. She had
lately even taken some responsibility for some of the things
in her life that had gone wrong. But now she appeared back
to square one. And there was something else that bothered
Claire, but she couldn't put her finger on it.

"What's the matter, Gerry?" she finally asked. "I know
something's gone wrong. What is it?"

"They never leave you alone," she said, and burst into
tears.

Claire said as gently as she could, "Sit down again,
Gerry, and tell me about it."

Gerry shook her head. Claire got up and started around
her desk to try and comfort the girl, but she ran out.

Claire walked back behind her desk and looked at her
schedule. She had one more client, and then had to go to the
outreach program further east where she was due to super-

vise some of the newer counselors in interviewing new clinic patients. I hope I have more success there than with Gerry, Claire found herself thinking. Had Gerry really regressed? Or was it because of Claire's poor handling caused by distraction. Thinking about it brought back Claire's sense of unease.

There was a knock on her door.

"Come in," she called.

Larry Swade appeared in the doorway. "Was the maiden in distress tearing down the front steps your client?"

"Yes, I tried to stop her. I don't know what's wrong with her. She's a lot better than she used to be, that is, she was until today. Something must have happened to her."

"You don't, if I may say so, look too sharp yourself." Larry looked kindly at her. "Anything I can do?"

What she wanted to do, Claire thought, was cry for an hour. But that was hardly a grown-up way of handling her frustrations and her . . . her misery, about Brett. "Being in love is hell," she said. "Even at my age and with my round collar and my therapeutic training, it's just that. And it's humiliating."

"Perhaps you should try a little blind trust."

"If anybody else tells me that I'm going to go home and stick my head in the oven. Have you tried blind trust lately?"

"Well, isn't that rather what we tell people they should have in the Deity all the time."

"Telling other people and doing it oneself are two entirely different things."

"Yes, that's rather the gist of the backtalk given us by the laity from time to time. You wouldn't like an old-fashioned heart to heart, would you?"

Looking at his rotund form, Claire realized that there was nothing she would like better and there was no one whom she could trust more. But she had to be at the outreach program in half an hour and somehow grab a bite before then.

"I'm going to take you up on that, soon."

* * *

TWO HOURS LATER, SHE EMERGED FROM THE GRIMY, OLD-fashioned red brick building overlooking the East River and stood staring at the water swirling between Manhattan and Roosevelt Island. To the left, on Ward's Island, reared the fortresslike Manhattan Psychiatric Center. Claire had made several professional visits there, and she found it depressing beyond belief. Most of the patients, slopping around in blue robes and paper slippers, had seemed to be drugged into apathetic or zombielike states, many of them still hallucinating. Since the deinstitutionalizing of the less dangerous patients, many of those same people and others like them were on the streets, victims of laws passed with the best of intentions.

For some reason, the sight of the Psychiatric Center made her think of Gerry. And that little flutter of—of something occurred again. Closing her eyes she tried to concentrate, to remember what it was Gerry was saying, the words she was using, to effect that quiver in Claire. But her memory went blank. After a moment or two she stopped trying. If the memory came back, it would come in its own time and most likely when she was thinking about something else.

Claire glanced at her watch. Four o'clock. She could go back to the church. Or she could go home. She'd get back to the church just as others were leaving, and she'd get home before Martha and Jamie. Not that there was anything wrong with that. Far from it—usually. But being at home now made her think of waiting for a phone call. She closed her eyes, and decided to walk along the river path for a while. At some point she'd have to climb one of those overhead steps to get back across the drive to the midtown area. But there was a crisp spring breeze blowing, along with warm sun. The water, which was undoubtedly filthy, looked blue and almost clear. It would be pleasant to walk beside it. The trouble was, she was so unused to having an hour or so to spare that she felt strangely nervous, as though a structure had been taken away from her.

Yet she also found she did not want to direct her feet uptown to her apartment. She wanted to direct them downtown to Second Street. Unlike Brett, Giles had been loving and confiding and he obviously liked her. It would be balm to her sore feelings to talk to him a little. He was someone who could be depended on to see things from her point of view.

"And what about Larry?" her mind asked her.

Larry would not necessarily see things from her point of view. He would see things as they were, she reflected, and it was not at all necessarily the same. At the moment what she wanted most was an ally. No questions asked.

She walked south along the river for a while, then, when there seemed to be some kind of a crossway for pedestrians, crossed over to First Avenue and continued on south. It was a long walk, but, uneasily aware that she did not get enough exercise, she was glad of it.

It was when she was walking down First Avenue, past University Hospital, that her mind registered something that seemed out of kilter. But whatever it was lay for a while, just out of reach. As she walked downtown, the cars heading uptown at this, the afternoon rush hour, passed rapidly, and she watched them unconsciously, not aware of any single car until suddenly she realized she was looking at a dark blue sedan with two passengers, both men, in the front seat, that the sedan had slowed so that it was barely moving and that she had seen it a short while before. The men were looking at her, but as she focused on them consciously for the first time, the car speeded up and passed her. She stopped and turned, but the car, weaving in and out of the traffic, had slid through a yellow light and was lost in the mass of other cars.

She stood, for a moment, staring at the traffic. Well what of it? she asked herself impatiently. Two men had stared at her. It was not unheard of. Men had looked at her before. She was far from vain, but in the immortal words of her late husband, Patrick, "With your red hair and elegant legs you could stop traffic." Which was exactly what had happened.

But it was not the same, and no amount of talking to herself could make her think it was.

On sudden impulse she moved to the corner and as soon as the light changed in her favor, crossed the avenue and started across a side street west to Second Avenue. When she got there she turned south again and started down Second Avenue. At least the traffic was not coming towards her, she told herself. But what she had not taken into consideration was that it flowed with her. That car, any car, could simply follow her.

Rubbish! she told herself. They were two boors who were attracted (maybe) by the combination of red hair and round clerical collar. Maye they just didn't approve of women priests.

Of themselves, her feet slowed. Then she swung around. The cars pelting down Second Avenue were so tightly packed that they looked sewn together except for a maverick or adventurer here and there who darted into a vacuum and then shrieked to a stop when it was obvious that the vacuum was behind some stationary vehicle and it was now worse off than it had been before.

But whether the blue sedan was there or not, Claire felt exposed, the insinuating, sexless voice on the phone sounding in her head. The precious ingredients of a walk in the city—the anonymity, the freedom—were gone. She gazed back to see if a bus was coming. There was one about four blocks away. The blinking yellow traffic light had already changed to red when Claire scooted across the avenue, counting on the safety of that fraction of a minute when both lights were red. As she did so, a horn blared behind her.

"Watch out," somebody yelled. She felt herself hauled towards the curb.

"What's the matter, lady? Tired of life?" her rescuer, a

black man in a business suit, said. And then, "Look at that car. He ought to be arrested."

Claire swung around. Because it was, for a moment, caught by the traffic, she could see the back of the blue sedan and of the heads of the two men sitting in the passenger seat. Then it speeded up and was gone.

VIII

PEOPLE IN NEW YORK WERE MUCH NICER THAN THEY HAD THE reputation for being, Claire thought, as the various individuals waiting for the bus offered her condolence, sympathy and a few choice epithets for those who drove like maniacs. She managed to thank them and put on as much calm as possible as she got on the bus and found a seat. Underneath she did not feel at all calm, and for the length of the bus ride did what she would probably have rebuked a client for doing: she carefully did not think about what had just happened and about the life she might have lost.

When she got off, her knees felt odd, and she stood on the curb for a moment to make sure they knew what they were supposed to be doing.

She had not called ahead and had no idea whether Giles was in the parish house or not. But, after making sure there was no blue sedan in the vicinity, she crossed the street and rang the parish house bell.

A tall young Hispanic opened the door. "Yes?"

"Is Mr. Fairmont in?" she asked.

"He's in a meeting." The young man stood in the door. There seemed to be no way that Claire could squeeze past him.

"Well, will you tell him that the Reverend Claire Aldington is here, please?"

"Is he expecting you?"

"No."

"Like I said, he's real busy."

"Please take him my message—immediately. Or, better still—" Claire had once been moderately good at athletics. And the advantage was on her side. The gatekeeper was tall and strong, but he wasn't expecting any physical opposition. Putting out one hand and arm, she swept him aside before he had time to take in what she was doing.

"Look lady—"

But she kept on going and burst into the kitchen. Giles was there with three other young men, one white, one black and one Hispanic. The black and Hispanic were young. The white, who looked to Claire like an aging hippie, was much older. "Well times have changed," the black was saying, then they all turned towards her.

"This is a private meeting," the tall, shaggy-haired white said.

Claire ignored them. "Giles—"

"Lady—" the white man started.

Giles had been studying a piece of paper in his hand, but he glanced up. For less than a second he looked put out. Then he put down his paper. "Hold it, Jesse! Claire! How delightful! Sorry you walked into the middle of all this. We'll be through in a moment and then I'll be with you. Ignacio, please see Mrs. Aldington to the front."

The young man who had admitted her took her by the arm and led her to the living room. "Told you he was busy. He don't like people running in on him like that." With that, he all but pushed her into a chair and then went back towards the others.

Claire's knees were shaking quite badly at that moment. She looked down at her fingers. So were her hands. Suddenly she felt an overwhelming urgency to be sick. Where was the bathroom? Coming out into the hall, she encountered Ignacio. "Where is a bathroom?" she asked.

"Behind the kitchen and you can't go in there right now, I tell you."

"But I—" She knew she couldn't move him, and the door into the kitchen were Giles and the others were was shut. Turning, she fled to the front door, yanked it open and managed to reach the small courtyard in front before she was violently sick. After several heaves, she found a tissue and wiped off her mouth. Fascinated watchers stood on the sidewalk at the edge of the yard.

"You bin drinkin'?" a teenager asked, not unsympathetically.

A couple giggled.

Getting away now, before that wretched meeting would break up, was more important than anything else. Unbearable, unthinkable, was the possibility of Giles coming out here now. Putting the tissue away, she all but ran to the street, dodging the watchers. Then she went to the curb and her heart lifted in gratitude as she saw an empty cab cruising down near her. Just as she got in she thought she heard a shout behind her. "Keep going," she said. "Then turn west as soon as you can. I'm going back uptown."

Only when they had slipped into a side street and then onto Third Avenue did she look back, almost as though she expected Giles to have run the full block between the two avenues in pursuit.

"Somebody chasing you?" the cab driver asked.

"I'm afraid so," Claire replied, reflecting that she was referring to more than one pursuer.

"Don't worry! I'll lose 'em!"

JAMIE LOOKED UP FROM HIS FAVORITE STANCE, BELLY DOWN, IN front of the television set. After a moment's examination he said, "You okay, Ma?"

"Yes," she said, fighting an overwhelming desire to cry.

Jamie got to his feet. She had never really thought of him as someone of exquisite perceptions, but she knew she had underrated him when he came over and gave her a hug. "Whatever it is, it's okay. We love you. Don't we, Motley?"

Motley barked. Claire burst into tears. The phone rang. Martha came out of her room. "What on earth's the matter?"

"Something's happened to Ma," Jamie said. The phone went on ringing. As Martha moved to answer it, Claire sobbed. "I'm not here. You have no idea where I am or when I'm coming back—that is, unless it's Brett."

"I'm afraid she's not here," Claire heard Martha say in her coolest, rising-young-urbanite voice. "No, I don't know where she is. I'm afraid she didn't say when she was coming in. What? I'm sure you're speaking of the wrong person. My mother would never be sick in front of a church." And she hung up. "Mom, that was Giles somebody. He said you were sick in front of a church. I told him you'd never do that. Did you?"

Claire, who now seemed afflicted by the hiccups, nodded.

"Are you ill?"

"No. Just angry and abandoned. Jamie, this does not refer to you. But *men are no good*. That statement should be mounted in lead on every male's forehead."

"What'd Brett do now?" Jamie said.

"He hasn't called me, and he isn't telling me something important, something he told Ida Blake. He trusted her but not me."

There was silence as her children looked at her. Finally Martha asked, "What would you say if you were your client?"

Claire gave a watery grin. "I would counsel patience. I'd ask my client if she had had any previous reason to distrust her fiancé. I would suggest that she write a letter. I would also suggest that she try and put it out of her mind—no, I

wouldn't do that. Only old-fashioned klutzes go around
telling people not to think about what they can't help
thinking about. I guess I'd just tell her to hang in there."

"Hang in there, Ma!" Jamie said.

"Thank you, darling. I'll try. And thank you both. You're
wonderful."

"Who's Giles?" Martha asked.

"He's the rector of St. Paul's Church, in front of which I
was sick."

"What happened to you? Why were you sick?"

The true answer, she thought, would have been because I
believe someone is trying to kill me. But that was not a
burden to put on children. "I almost got run over," Claire
said. "And it shook me up. I'm a little ashamed of myself. I
guess I was more scared than I thought. And then that awful
young man—"

"Ma—you're going to have to watch this thing you have
about men. After all, I'm a man!"

"Yes darling." Claire put her arms around Jamie. "And
you were wonderful a while ago. You know I'm sure that
men probably say the same kinds of things about women
when there's a great spasm of un-understanding all around.
Despite what it's fashionable to state, I still think there're
some profound differences in the way the sexes deal with
things. And when that's going on, hackles rise, feathers fly.
I'm sure Brett is thinking right now that I'm being difficult
and demanding and behaving like a woman. Which I am.
And I am now going to bed. Good night, loves."

She was almost asleep when she became dimly aware of
some sort of heated discussion going on in whispers near the
front door. I ought to go out and see what it is, she thought,
and then sleep enveloped her.

SHE WAS RUNNING DOWN A LONG HALL, PURSUED BY TWO MEN IN
dark suits. The trouble was, all the doors she tried in the hall
as she passed were locked. She couldn't go back. There was
only one other door in front of her. Finally she reached it,

only to discover that that, too, was locked. She turned to face the men—and woke up, her heart pounding.

Turning on the light, she sat up in bed. It was only a dream, she told herself. And she didn't have to dig too deep to know what the dream was about. Those were the men in the blue sedan, earlier in the day. Probably the most unpleasant thing about their pursuit of her in her dream was that they were laughing.

Getting up, Claire went into her bathroom and put cold compresses on her temples and wrists to make sure she was thoroughly awake. Better a spot of insomnia than to have that return when she woke up. Fifteen minutes later, now thoroughly awake, she became powerfully aware of the fact that she'd had no dinner. Creeping down the hall to the kitchen, she went in and closed the door.

She made herself a sandwich, poured a glass of milk and sat down at the kitchen table. She could, of course, go into the living room or back into the bedroom to get something to read. But she wanted to avoid anything that might wake Martha up. Jamie slept the sleep of the just and the young and healthy. Martha had always been a light sleeper, and one unnecessary set of footsteps passing her door might do the trick as far as she was concerned.

So Claire sat there and tried to analyze what had happened and why it had happened, with the idea of finding any common link. Because she was without pencil and paper, she had to make do with a mental list:

A voice that could be either male or female had called her twice on the phone, demanding to see her and offering threats of exposure for her and for Brett and for Brett's son, Adam, if she didn't comply.

Comply with what?

Comply with letting herself be interviewd by G.V., the genderless voice.

Why did he want to interview her?

Because he thought she knew something through her association with Lieutenant O'Neill?

Did she?

Only the nature of the slashes on Ida's body.

Why would he want to know that?

Because he was the killer and wanted to see how close they were to catching him? Because in some way it would give him power over something or somebody?

The answer could be any of the above or something totally different.

Was he one of the men who were in the car that tried to run her down?

Why did anyone want to kill her?

Claire picked up the second half of her sandwich. What else was there to try to figure out?

Plenty. For example, who killed Ida? Why?

Who killed Mrs. Blake? Why?

Was there a connection?

What did Mrs. Blake want to see her about?

Was it the same thing—information—that the sexless voice wanted? To learn something they were both convinced she knew? Or something else?

Was that what the Reverend Hector Blake wanted, too?

Claire put down the last quarter of her sandwich and held her head. Was there any connecting thread there at all? The trouble was, the more she thought about it the less there seemed to be, the less sense any of it made. But the questions in her head ground on.

What was it Brett refused to tell her but told Ida Blake?

Why did it bother her so much? Wounded vanity? Wounded feelings?

Did she trust him?

She was, curiously, unable to answer that.

All of which made her feel infinitely worse than she had when she went to bed, and boded ill for her getting back to sleep.

"Hi, Mom! Can't you sleep, either?" Martha, in her blue robe, was standing in the doorway.

Claire raised her head and smiled. "I didn't mean to wake you up. I'm sorry."

"I wasn't really asleep. I was dozing, and I heard you

open your door about half an hour ago. I decided to get
something to eat."

"I'll make you a sandwich."

"No, I can make my own." Martha went towards the
refrigerator, removed some cheese, bread, the remains of a
chicken, and mayonnaise, which she put on the table.

"You know that Giles that called you," she said, laying
slices of cheese on a piece of bread. "Well, he showed up
tonight after you'd gone to bed. Rick, the doorman, called
from the lobby and said he insisted on coming upstairs, and
a few minutes later there he was."

"I'm surprised Rick let him up."

"It was the clerical collar, I think. He wouldn't have
otherwise."

"I guess that was the noise I heard at the front door right
before I went to sleep."

"I'm sorry you heard it. He was not easy to get rid of. He
acted like he had some right to come charging in on the
grounds that you weren't well. I told him we knew you
weren't well and didn't want you bothered. It took him a
while to take no for an answer."

"Well," Claire said, gathering up the last crumbs of her
sandwich, "as you know I gave my all on the pavement
outside the parish house—just thinking of the whole thing
fills me with shame."

"That's what I got up to talk to you about."

Claire looked at the slender, dark-haired girl, who
resembled her own natural mother, Patrick Aldington's first
wife, but had her father's brown eyes. "What is it you want
to talk to me about?" Claire asked.

"About what really happened. Anybody can be suddenly
sick, and I'll grant it's pretty embarrassing. But I don't think
it was just that that you were so upset about when you came
home, was it? That Giles something said that somebody
who worked around the church had insulted you in some
way, without his knowing it, and he felt terribly responsible
for the whole thing. Is that true? Why would anybody insult
you? The whole thing sounds pretty off the wall to me. And

it doesn't—any of it—sound like you, Mom. You've always handled people well—they've never thrown you. What's going on?"

Claire sighed. "I was upset because Brett and I seem to be having problems long after I thought we'd ironed them out. And there are the murders, Ida Blake and her mother, which are upsetting everybody. And then I nearly got run down . . . I guess it's accumulation."

"Did the person who ran you down do it deliberately?"

Claire looked up at her suddenly. "Why do you ask that?"

"Because a couple of days ago, when Jamie and I were in the park walking Motley, this creepy-looking guy comes up and says, " 'When's your mother home, kids? Tell her we have to talk.' "

Claire felt as though her heart had stopped. "When did this happen, and why in God's name didn't you tell me?"

Martha shrugged. "Well, nothing else did happen. Jamie said, 'Go get him, Motley!' Motley just took one leap at the man and he ran so fast he was out of sight in three seconds. Jamie was absolutely thrilled. He said he'd been training Motley to be a guard dog, and wasn't he wonderful? I told him I thought the whole thing was scary, but he said it was probably just one of your crazy clients."

"They don't come that crazy."

"Well I don't know. Weren't you talking about a bag lady and her cat the other night. By the way, how is her cat?"

"I haven't asked lately," Claire said. Then she got up and clasped Martha's arms. "Listen honey, something weird's going on, beginning with the deaths of Ida and her mother. I don't know why somebody seems to think I know more than I do, but . . . but there have been threats—"

"Mom, have you told the police?" Martha protested.

"Yes, I have. And don't worry about it."

"You're telling me not worry about it when somebody threatens you and then nearly runs you down? Of course I'm going to worry. What did the police say?"

"Not much. There wasn't much to say. I described the

call and the voice, but that's all I could do. Martha, believe me, there's nothing more I can do, so don't go adding to my worries by getting worried yourself. I'll take all the care of myself in the world."

"Like you did this afternoon?"

"I didn't know somebody was—er—physically out to get me until this afternoon. I promise you I'll be careful and on guard."

"And don't go meandering about the East Village that way. Anybody can tell you that some pretty crummy types are down there."

"No, ma'am. I'll make a bargain with you. I'll stay in safe, crowded places if you and Jamie will too and if you'll try not to worry."

"Okay."

"Do you think that Jamie's upset? He doesn't always spit out what's in his mind. He used to, but not so much any more. I guess it's part of growing up."

"I wouldn't be surprised. He seems to be keeping much more of an eye on you." Martha hugged her. "We both do."

CLAIRE WASN'T SURE HOW SHE FELT ABOUT GILES AND HIS unorthodox visit the night before. Her wounded feelings were a little salved by his belated concern, but then it wasn't Giles himself who had been so obstructive. And she didn't much care for that unhelpful young man. Of course, he might have been acting out of consideration for Giles and Giles's interests . . .

The next morning she got to the early Eucharist service at seven-thirty. At one time, she reminded herself, she had attended every day. Then life and a busy schedule and not enough time to sleep had interfered, and she attended only when she was the celebrant and was much the poorer for it. Sitting there in the second pew of the chapel while Larry Swade celebrated the liturgy, she marveled how she could have let slide anything so necessary to her peace of mind. What meditation was to Eastern adepts, she decided, the liturgy was to her. She had tried orthodox meditation on more than one occasion and the only conclusion she had emerged with was that there was nothing in the world easier than not to meditate. But to hear the great words of the Book of Common Prayer slide through her mind and consciousness served for her the same purpose. ". . . .Almighty God, unto whom all hearts are open, all desires known, and from whom no secrets are hid . . ."

There was great relief in knowing that her secrets, however paltry and discreditable—such as childish jealousy—were no secret at all to the Mind that was in and around her, in Whom she lived and moved and had her being . . .

"Nice to see you," Larry said, after the service. "How're things?"

"Not too great at the moment."

"Come to the cafeteria and have some coffee with me. I haven't had any breakfast."

"All right." She glanced at her watch. "But I have to be back for a client at eight-thirty."

While Larry munched on an English muffin and they both drank coffee, she outlined for him all the questions and imponderables she had listed to herself the night before. "Sorry to throw all this at you," she said when she was finished. "But it's your fault for being such a good listener and counselor. And it's beginning to curdle my peace of mind."

Larry put down his coffee cup. "To deal with first things first, I think you ought to call your policeman pal the moment you get upstairs and tell him about your unpleasant little adventure on Second Avenue and Martha and Jamie's encounter in the park. You're not helping anybody by not telling the police and allowing them to take sensible precautions."

"All right," Claire said. "I think the trouble is, I was so scared that I didn't want to act like a panicky female. Also, I don't have absolute proof that these thugs were trying to run me down."

"I didn't say produce a photograph for the police's

benefit. I just said tell them. And you should be happy to have all the help you can get with your children."

"I am."

"Second," Larry polished off the last piece of muffin, "I think you ought to get in touch with Brett."

Claire almost exploded, "I've tried. But that wretched aide or whatever he is in his office talks to me as though I were trying to collect a bad debt. He has been instructed that no one is to know where Brett is, and I'm told that that includes me. I've left my name. Why doesn't Brett call me?"

"How did you leave it when you last saw one another?"

"Not well." She paused. "He seemed to feel that if I didn't trust him, then that was my lookout."

"Isn't it?"

"Et tu, Brute?"

"I take it somebody else has said that."

"Yes. Giles Fairmont."

"I didn't know you knew him."

"I went down to talk to him because he used to go out with Ida Blake, and Lieutenant O'Neill had sent me out bird-dogging that. Do you know him?"

"I've met him," Larry said cautiously.

"Does one gather you didn't altogether like him?"

"He's an idealist."

"From anyone else that would be a compliment. But from you, obviously it isn't. What do you have against idealists?"

"Only that a large number of them feel so passionately the world should be a better place that they'll sacrifice any number of other individuals to see that their plan goes through."

"You sound like the total pragmatist. But I would have called you an idealist."

He winced. "Please don't. I like helping people. I'm not interested in theorizing what they ought to be doing. Or what other people ought to be doing about whatever it is."

"Is that what Giles does?"

"It's what he used to do. He once had a sort of sanctuary for every kind of revolutionary group going—like other churches now have for Salvadorans and Guatemalans, only he had them for Black Panthers and the People's Revolutionary Army and that sort of thing. Some of them had blown up all kinds of innocent types on their way to a better world and I wouldn't have given them house room. But Giles did when he was assistant rector of some church out West."

Against her better self, Claire instantly envisioned the young men she had seen down at St. Paul's the day before. Then she reproached herself fiercely. She had no reason to think they were revolutionaries.

"You're looking guilty," Larry commented sardonically. "Why? Have you seen lurking revolutionaries around St. Paul's?"

"I have no reason to think they were revolutionaries."

"But they occurred to you immediately when I mentioned the word. Who are they?"

Claire told him about the meeting she bumped into. "It's funny, I didn't think about its being a private meeting before and it almost certainly wasn't, or if it was, it was a private meeting about how to enlarge the parish budget. But it did strike me as, well . . ."

"Secret?"

"Sort of. And then there was Ignacio, who escorted me out of the meeting as though I were an FBI spy and wouldn't let me go back when I desperately needed the bathroom. That's why I was sick on the pavement outside."

Larry stared at her. "Good heavens! That doesn't sound revolutionary, it sounds demented. If Ignacio were a helper of mine I'd give him what for. That's inhuman."

"Thank you."

"And you threw up on the pavement?"

"Outside the parish house."

"Was this flu or trauma?"

"Trauma. I was shocked and scared. As I've already told you somebody almost ran me down in a car."

"I repeat, tell O'Neill at once. If you haven't by the end of the afternoon, I will."

"Do you think the two murders are connected?"

"Certainly the two victims, mother and daughter, are, by blood, but other than that the two crimes are quite different, which would argue different criminals." He drank down the rest of his coffee and then said, "I'd like to return for a moment to the subject of Brett. Why aren't you willing to extend trust to him? As I told you once, he is one of the most trustworthy people I've ever known."

"For one thing—that's a man's point of view. For another—are you talking about blind trust?"

"Is there any other kind? I mean, would you say there's thirty percent trust and seventy-five percent trust and then a hundred? Surely there is all or none."

"The man you admire so much, Giles Fairmont, said the same thing."

"Nobody can be wrong all the time."

"You're both men and you're both trying a typical male ploy—making me feel guilty."

"So ignore us!"

Claire got up. "I will."

Larry got up, too. "I know of a great spiritual leader who said it is a universal maxim that when we're upset with somebody, the problem lies within ourselves."

"I bet he was a man."

Larry grinned. "But it's still true!"

Claire suddenly glanced at her watch. "Oh my God! My client will be there."

GERRY WAS SITTING ON A CHAIR IN THE LOBBY WITH A LOOK ON her face of angry long-suffering.

"Sorry to be late," Claire said. "Let's go upstairs." She glanced over at Darlene. "Hold all calls, Darlene please, until I let you know."

"Here's a couple that have come in already." And Darlene held out some pink telephone message forms.

Claire went over to the reception desk and took them, glancing at them as she went back to Gerry. Two were from Giles, one from Pen Barnet, one from Letitia Dalrymple, one from Lieutenant O'Neill, and one from Brett. There was no telephone number on the line under the name. Claire stopped in her tracks and turned back towards Darlene. "I take it Mr. Cunningham didn't leave a number where he could be reached."

"He didn't give any."

"Did you ask him for one?"

Darlene shook her head. "I didn't think it was necessary. I mean, after all, you are engaged."

Claire's elation when she saw the name turned to frustration. "Darlene, always, always, always get the number. You can't make a judgment like that."

Darlene's features collected into a sulk. "Whatever you say."

"Will I get my full session?" Gerry asked as they went into Claire's office and closed the door.

"Yes. Why do you ask?"

"Well, you were late. And I just thought you might have to cut me short because of somebody else coming in at the end of my session."

"Gerry, think hard, have I ever short-changed you before?"

"No."

"Then why do you think I might now?"

"Well, you were late and—"

"You do nurse grievances, don't you? Think how much of your life and energy you'd have left with which to conquer the world or write a book or discover a new continent if you stopped feeding and watering your resentments."

Gerry sat down. "There aren't any new continents."

Claire's irritability changed to amusement. "And you

think they were all mapped out and discovered before you were born just to frustrate you."

Gerry suddenly shouted. "You're making fun of me again."

"Yes, a little, because I think you're well enough to take it. You hold down and do well at a good job, and it's time to shed the self-pity and the alienated-from-society stance."

"Society stinks."

"Oh, why?"

"I told you—the world, nuclear war, politics . . ."

"Famine, disease, and death. That's just a cop-out and you know it. Besides, we went through the Four Horsemen before."

They sat there in silence for a moment. Then Gerry got up. "I guess I better go."

"No. Not this time. Gerry, sit down. There is something more going on. You were beginning to do well, take responsibility for your own life. Now you're backsliding. Why?"

Gerry, standing rigid in the middle of the floor, said nothing.

Claire got up. "Let's start again. I'm sorry I was late. And I don't blame you for being upset, especially if there is something on your mind. And I will keep the next client waiting so that you will have your full time." She paused. "Okay?"

The tension quivered for a moment. Afterwards, Claire often wondered if the course of her life in the next few weeks would have changed if the telephone hadn't rung. But it did. Claire glanced at it.

"You have a phone call," Gerry said.

"Never mind it. Let's talk some more."

The phone rang again.

"It must be important," Gerry said.

Claire went and snatched up the receiver. "Darlene—I told you . . ."

"I called to see if you're all right," Brett said.

Relief washed over Claire. "Brett how are you? *Where* are you?"

"Out of town."

Claire recalled Gerry. "Can I call you back?"

"I'm afraid not. Sorry I interrupted you. Are you all right?"

"Yes, I'm fine. Look, let me know where I can reach you."

But he had gone. She turned. So had Gerry.

IX

CLAIRE CLOSED HER EYES AND SAT THERE FOR A MOMENT, WHILE a profound wish to go to the South Sea Islands or the North Pole or the Amazon for the foreseeable future washed over her. "Perhaps Tahiti," she murmured aloud.

"Overrated," Larry said from the door.

"How do you know? Have you been there?"

"No, but I know people who have. I take it that was your client departing in tears."

"That was indeed my client, Gerry. And although I could shake her, I think this time I let her down."

"That's most unlikely. How?"

"I committed the therapist's great sin—I let myself be distracted by the *Sturm und Drang* of my own life. And then when Brett called—"

"He called?"

"Yes. And when I asked if I could call him back, he was gone. And when I looked up, Gerry had gone, too."

"I'm sort of surprised that Darlene let the call go through."

"So am I. He must have been very persuasive."

"Even dictatorial." Larry grinned. "I'm glad to hear that all communications have not ceased, but I could wish you'd have had more time to talk."

"So do I. Larry, what on earth do you suppose Brett is up to? He sounds like an agent of the CIA, checking in from phone booths. It's all like a bad movie."

"Well, since Brett isn't given to self-dramatization and overreacting in general, I must give him the benefit of the doubt and suppose that he's doing what he's doing for a good reason."

"Meaning, so must I."

"You'd be happier, wouldn't you?" When Claire didn't answer he said, "You know, all this doubt and suspicion is not like you—at least not like the way you've been with other people. I grant you that being in love is a license to general pottiness and paranoia. The most sensible people go off the rails when they get bitten by The Bug. But I didn't expect it to apply to you, or at least, not so totally. Do you have any idea of why you're behaving the way you are vis-à-vis Brett?"

Claire said slowly, "I've been thinking about that, especially in light of what appears to be a unanimous opinion that I should have blind trust. I think my capacity for blind trust got dented—if not annihilated—partly by an affair I had when I was still in college, and partly by marriage. In both cases I had all the blind trust in the world, and in both I got taken. The first was an instructor at Stanford. It was the first time I had ever fallen in love—and I guess, until Brett, the only time. Anyway, we had this ardent affair, and come summer, were supposed to meet for a slow, romantic journey through Europe. I got to London first, and when I arrived at the little hotel we were supposed to stay at for the beginning of our tryst, I found, instead of my lover, a letter from him. It seemed he had been married all along, but that during our interlude, he had been separated. Now he and his wife had decided to give the marriage another chance. 'I'm so sorry and good-bye, et cetera, et cetera.' " It wasn't so much, she thought now, that she was still bitter. What was powerful was the memory of her devastation at the time.

"And in your marriage?" Larry asked gently.

"I discovered that Patrick was having an affair with one of the parishioners."

"I can see why you retain a certain skepticism. It's highly understandable. But it's also too bad, because in this case I think you're wrong. However, my saying so isn't going to convince you. What I came up for was to ask if you had called Lieutenant O'Neill."

"I was just going to."

"Good! I'll just hang around and make sure you do."

Claire pulled the phone towards her and dialed. Secretly she hoped that O'Neill would be out, more out of pigheadedness than a reluctance to talk to him. But he was in.

"This is Claire Aldington," she said. "I have something I want to tell you, and I have here also a colleague who refuses to leave my office until I do."

"Shake him by the hand for me. Okay. Tell me."

So Claire told him all the events that had occurred the day before.

"And you waited this long to phone me? Why?"

"I take it you think the men really were out to run me down."

"What do you think?"

"I guess I think so. I just don't want to think that."

"Who can blame you? Now, what do you link this to?"

"I suppose to whoever it is who has called me and said if I didn't see him or her and grant him an interview, then I could consider myself threatened."

"Let's cut out the fancy footwork. I'm not sure I believe in that phone call—No," he said hastily as Claire started to argue, "I don't mean those calls didn't happen. I just think they were some kind of a smoke screen."

"For what?"

"I don't know. But I'd guess that somebody thinks you know something you don't, and wants to get you scared enough so that when he, she, or it turns up and demands information, you'll be so scared you'll give it. That would also be the purpose of whoever it was who approached your children."

"Jamie said he sicced Motley—that's his dog—onto the man, which is what saved them."

"Well, maybe. But big-time hoods wouldn't let themselves be pushed around by a dog. They'd shoot the dog."

Claire shivered. "You make them sound—sadistic."

"Believe me, I think they are."

"Well, what can I do about it? I'm not going to stop working or going about my business. What does worry me, though, is Martha and Jamie. They're totally vulnerable going to and from school."

"Could you take them there?"

"They'd fight like tigers if I tried to. Adolescents consider adult accompaniment an insult to be avoided at all times. And Jamie would see it as a feminist plot against his masculinity. I honestly think he'd rather leave home."

"Well, talk to them. Will they listen to you?"

"Yes. They really do—at least, most of the time."

"You don't have to scare the daylights out of them, or of yourself. After all, they're not small children. By the way—how old are they?"

"Martha's eighteen and Jamie's twelve."

"Maybe they could just make it a point for a few weeks of always going with friends. Don't they have friends they go to school with?"

"As a matter of fact, Martha is always picked up by a girl called Jennifer Bernstein who lives two doors down. Jamie goes with a couple of his pals who live on our block."

"I suppose you wouldn't like to call their parents and enlist their help?"

Claire had a sudden picture of herself trying to explain to the mothers concerned why it was important that their offspring should act as honor guard to her two. "My strong feeling is that if they had the remotest idea my children might be in any danger, their first thought would be to keep their own as far away from it as possible."

"Is that how you would react?"

"Yes. In certain circumstances, it is. I'd do everything I could to persuade the parents to get protection for the children, but I wouldn't be eager to have my own in a position where they could be hurt or kidnapped."

"I guess not. I'll tell you what. I'll try to detail a couple of men to keep an eye on them when they're going to and from school."

"What about if they're just going out? Both Jamie and Martha sometimes stop at the houses of some of their friends, or they all go to some ice cream place before coming home."

"We'll do our best. But it's a limited best. We don't have enough manpower. You tell them to travel in bunches whenever they can. Okay?"

"Okay."

"And I don't have to tell you, do I, to caution them not to talk to strangers?"

"No. I have hammered that lesson home as much and as hard as I can. But I'll talk to them again about it."

"Do you have any idea at all what they—the people who called you and tried to run you down—might think you know?"

"None. But whatever it is, I think they think I know it because of my association with you."

"Hmm. Well, if anything occurs to you, let me know."

"Of course."

Claire hung up and looked at Larry. "Shall I repeat all of that to you, just so you can be satisfied?"

"I pieced a lot of it together from your end of the telephone, so I think that's not necessary." He paused. "Claire, please, please, do what the lieutenant says. I must remind you that Ida Blake was murdered and so was her mother. Whoever is out there is ruthless. I don't think killing another woman priest would faze him at all."

"I promise, Larry. I am not a hero. I have no desire to die. And I certainly don't want my children to. So I shall take all the care in the world."

"Good!" He paused. "I actually came up for two purposes: to make sure you called the lieutenant but also to repeat something Doug Barnet said. We were chatting about one thing or another, and when the subject of his sister, Penelope, came up, he asked me if you had said anything to me about her. I told him no. I wasn't even aware that you had met her. I take it you have."

"Yes. Brett invited Doug and Pen to a dinner at his club and I was along for that. Then Pen called and asked me to have dinner with them at their flat. I had to refuse because of Group."

"When was that?"

"Last Wednesday." She glanced at Larry. "I might as well tell you that that was the night I met Giles for dinner. I felt slightly guilty about it, although I could hardly expect Pen to delay her dinner until I had finished with Group."

"Don't see why you should feel guilty, unless, of course, you had other reasons for turning her down."

Claire sighed. "Such perception! I refused because she invited Brett and me, and at that moment I was at the peak of my mad at Brett. I was too angry or too something to face spending an evening with him, even when buffered by the presence of Doug and Pen. But I do think it's odd that Doug should ask you if I'd said anything about his sister."

"Yes, so do I." Larry heaved himself to his feet. "Take care and all that."

Claire looked at her desk, eyeing all the things that lay there waiting to be done when she had a free moment. Then she picked up the phone and dialed the rectory residence.

"Hello," Pen said. "St. Anselm's Rectory."

"Hello, Pen. This is Claire Aldington. I've been planning to set up a lunch with you and me and Peggy Anderson, and I thought I'd check to make sure what days you're free. Peggy, by the way, knows more people in the church than anyone else and there isn't a committee she hasn't been on."

"My dear—how nice of you! I'm free pretty much any time since I'm still here at the flat, trying to bring order out of anarchy!" She laughed cheerfully.

"Good, let me call Peggy and see when she's able to make it, and I'll call you right back!"

But Peggy Anderson, that redoubtable lady with a finger in every church pie, was, in two days, going to California for three weeks to lend support to her daughter who was about to have her first baby.

"Oh Lord," Claire said. "I should have called you the minute I talked to Doug so we could have fit it in. He seems eager to have Pen get involved with some of the church groups and I thought you were the best person to help her with that. You've served on every committee and you know everybody."

"Yes," Peggy said thoughtfully. Then, "By any chance, would the two of you be free today? Somebody just cancelled on me."

"Yes," Claire said immediately. "We are. That's wonderful! I'm free from twelve to two. I can pick Pen up. Tell me where."

"How about the Academic Club at twelve-thirty? George is always telling me I don't use it enough, so since I'll be near there anyway, we might as well take advantage of it. The Ladies' Dining Room at twelve-thirty."

"Fine," Claire said. "See you there then, and thanks so much."

Shades of Ida, Claire thought, as she dialed Pen's number. The Academic Club was, like Brett's, one of the most prestigious of the men's clubs and to Ida and her fellow thinkers a constant irritation and reproach.

When Pen answered, Claire explained about the last-minute invitation and Peggy's projected trip, and offered to pick Pen up a few minutes after twelve.

"Nonsense," Pen said. "I'll meet you in the front hall of the parish house. The club is nearer to you than to me."

SITTING IN THE PANELLED SPLENDOR OF THE LADIES' DINING Room of the Academic Club, Claire reflected that she could not have brought together two more different women. Yet, if asked, she might have a hard time expressing where the difference lay.

Peggy Anderson was of medium height and build and exuded both kindness and competence. Her gray-brown hair, direct blue eyes and well-cut tweed coat and skirt proclaimed her for what she was, an upper-crust WASP and a descendant of many others. Her voice, Claire decided, suddenly aware of her own Midwestern tones, was Smith College out of Locust Valley. And Pen's was the English equivalent, unmistakably Country and Oxbridge. In short order they had arrived at a language they both understood, the recognized needs of the poor and unfortunate and the obligations of the upper levels of society to meet those needs. Claire, listening while they discussed volunteer agencies, aid to children, family planning, minority tutoring, and so on, thought of her own parents. What did they and their friends talk about? The work ethic, the need for self-help, the merit system, how to get ahead, the snobbery and patronizing manners of those above, the laziness of those below.

Her father, who had gone through college and law school on scholarships, always contributed part of his salary every year to a scholarship fund. What he had been given, he believed in giving back—but not to those who, in his view of life, did not deserve it, who wanted it the easy way. To him, the societal shorthand these women were talking would have been anathema.

To Patrick, it would have been familiar and praiseworthy. Her father had always had an ironic phrase: "Find the enemy. Find a man's enemy, Claire, or who he thinks is his enemy, and you'll know everything you need to know about him."

Who was Patrick's enemy and the enemy of these women? The middle class and its passionate belief in meritocracy.

Who was her father's enemy? Those people who, having been born with everything, had no respect for those who had earned it and, furthermore, despised them for not wanting to give it away.

And what about Giles?

Suddenly Claire found herself thinking about him. Where did he come into all this? By voice, he was similar to Pen. By attitude? To Patrick, except there was a hard note of anger in his voice that had never been in Patrick's. In the last analysis, Patrick's guide was compassion. Somehow, Claire could not believe that compassion played that much of a part in Giles's convictions. And Brett? Who was The Enemy for him?

Theorists. Theorists who wanted to tell other people what to do with their time, feelings and money.

"Good gracious, there's Douglas," Peggy said, snapping Claire out of her musings. She was looking past Pen's shoulder. "Who is that he's lunching with?"

Claire half turned and became aware of her own mild surprise. "Sarah Buchanan."

Pen turned right around. "Oh, that's who she is. I was wondering."

Peggy smiled. "You must have seen her when we came in, then, because they're sitting directly behind you."

"Yes, I did. And I know they were on the phone about one or two matters."

"Did you know Douglas's wife?" Claire asked, following an obvious train of thought.

"I only met her once, when they came to England on their honeymoon."

"Was she nice?" Peggy inquired.

"As much as I let her be." Pen gave her cheerful, almost boisterous laugh. "You have to understand that I was half mad with jealousy. I had always been the raggedy half sister trailing after him adoringly and making a general nuisance of myself.''

Peggy glanced at her watch. "I hate to run like this, but if I don't keep to my schedule, I'll have a nervous breakdown before I ever get to the plane. I'll call Mrs. Wood before I go, Pen, and tell her about you. I know her committee is desperate for bright, hardworking women and I think you'd be perfect. You'll be hearing from her. Now you two stay here while I dash. It's been wonderful meeting you. Claire, I'll see you when I get back.''

After she'd gone, Claire looked at her own watch. It was one-twenty and time she herself got back to her clients. "I think we ought to be getting along, too," she said, finishing her coffee.

"Of course," Pen agreed, pouring herself some more coffee from the pot placed on their table. "But I would just like to finish this. Tell me what you think about the committee work that Peggy suggested.''

"I think it's a worthwhile group of women doing a necessary job. As a matter of fact, if the volunteer agencies among the churches and other organizations in New York ever stopped, the city would be in a big mess.''

"Ida Blake rather disapproved of them," Pen said.

Claire was surprised. "I didn't know you knew her. I thought you arrived after . . . after she died.''

"No. We met once or twice before that horrible tragedy. I remember one time she and Douglas and I talked about the enormous amount of volunteer work that the Church does. She felt that women did most of that kind of work and should be paid for it.''

"And how did Douglas feel about that?''

Pen smiled. "Ida was extremely pretty, and Douglas is very vulnerable there. He probably didn't even listen to what she was saying.''

Claire tried to picture Douglas in the role of the easily enamored, and failed. But then, she thought, she hadn't seen him around other women and had nothing to go on. She decided to ask Brett about it. Brett—where was he?

Suddenly, and for no reason that she could think of, she said, "Do you by any chance know Giles Fairmont? He's English, too."

"Of course. He was a great friend of a friend of Daddy's. They couldn't have been farther apart in their view of the mission of the Church, but his family and Daddy's friend's family had all been in the same part of the country for ages." Pen looked at her. "How do you know him?"

"I went down to see him because someone—it may have been Sarah—told me that he and Ida had gone out together. And I was trying to track that down."

"Why?"

"Well, Lieutenant O'Neill asked me to. The case is still open, of course, as is Mrs. Blake's. I don't know how much more has been discovered about Ida. But Lieutenant O'Neill wanted me to find out who it was Ida was going out with and I went down to see Giles to ask him."

Pen poured herself a third cup of coffee. "And did he tell you?"

"No. He says he once went out with her, but since then she had acquired another boyfriend."

"And they think the boyfriend, if there is one, might have done it?"

"It's a possibility."

"I think Giles was pulling wool over your eyes."

"Why?"

"Because he was still very much involved with her. After all, he'd made her pregnant." She looked up, her almost azure eyes brilliant in her angular, handsome face.

Claire was startled. "How do you know that, Pen?"

"I told you. Douglas and I saw her more than once. She was very candid about her affairs, perhaps because of my knowing Giles's family back home."

"Look here, Pen. I think you ought to talk to O'Neill yourself. He'd certainly be grateful for any lead you could give him."

"Oh, I don't think it would be suitable for me to talk to him. You tell him for me. After all, Douglas is my brother, and I don't want any more publicity to come to the church because of me. Heaven knows it's had enough."

That that was directed at Claire herself, she had no doubt. But she was astonished. The only quality she hadn't been aware of in Pen was hostility. And yet it was an extremely hostile comment.

"And now I really must go," Pen said, gathering up her gloves and bag. "Can I give you a lift back?"

"Just a minute, Pen," Claire said. "I had the distinct feeling that that last comment was directed at me, and I'd like to point out that I have not sought any of the publicity that has come my way. If I had it before, when . . . when our business manager was killed, it was because I was a suspect myself."

"Really, Claire, you Americans do take things personally! I certainly did not have that in mind." She stood up. "Bye, bye." And was gone.

"It's like that game we used to play," Sarah Buchanan's voice said behind Claire. "One by one they all steal away. Why are they deserting you?"

"Pen seemed to be in an awful hurry," Douglas Barnet said, coming up to Claire's table.

Claire got up. "I'm beginning to feel a little like Typhoid Mary. Or that I have some unmentionable problem."

"She probably suddenly remembered that somebody was delivering something at the apartment, or coming to do some renovating," Douglas offered.

"I don't think so, Doug," Claire decided it would be better to get this out in the open. "We were talking about Ida and Pen said that you and she knew her, something that hadn't occurred to me, because I thought Pen had been here only a short time. Anyway, I suggested that she talk to Lieutenant O'Neill of the New York police, who is trying to find out what happened to Ida and why. I did so because she implied she knew something about Ida's . . . Ida's social life."

"I'm sure she doesn't." Douglas spoke almost brusquely. "She may have met her once or twice. That's all."

"But if Ida said anything to her—"

"As I have just finished saying, she didn't."

Claire stopped. "I see. Well, you seem to be having the same reaction. In her, it took the form of accusing me of bringing unwanted and unnecessary publicity to the church. As I told her, when our business manager was killed I had no choice. I was the chief suspect. I'm sorry both of you seem to think it was a bid for notoriety. Believe me, I could have done without it."

"Of course! I'm sure you could. No harm intended. Sarah and I are treating ourselves to a taxi. Would you care to join us?"

"Thanks, but I think I'll walk." And Claire turned and left the dining room.

It was a beautiful spring day and when Claire reached the park entrance on Fifty-ninth Street she decided to take a slight detour and walk in the park to Seventy-second Street and then back down to the church.

Having ended the lunch on a somewhat unsettling note, she tried to let her mind drift, her ancient remedy for anxiety. Every time her attention was drawn back to Pen's (and Giles's) acerbic references to her association with Lieutenant O'Neill, she made a conscious effort to pull it away onto some other subject. Brett's strange and mystifying absences were hardly less unsettling topics to consider, but they seemed to be an ongoing state, whereas Pen's hostility and Douglas's brusqueness and evasion had just burst out of the blue.

Is something wrong with me? Claire questioned herself. Did I say something, do something, imply something wrong?

Then she smiled. That was a reversion to childhood with a vengeance. If it snows, is it my fault? How Pen and Douglas behaved had more to do with them than with her. Remember that! she counselled herself severely, as she abandoned the main path for one that slanted up among trees and bushes.

At some point later, she was never quite sure when, she

became aware that a set of footsteps had been maintaining
an even rate behind her. The conscious thought washed like
a chill over her. The men in the car sprang to her mind as
vividly as though she had turned a movie on in her mind.
Deliberately, suddenly, she stopped. So did the footsteps.
Swiftly she wheeled around. The path she was on turned
and wound. All she could see to the next turning were the
bare limbs of trees and bushes, and the evergreens with their
leaves.

Then she turned back and looked ahead. The path wound
on. She could not be sure where it rejoined the drive. For a
moment panic struck. She could feel her body break out into
a sweat. Her heart was pounding. Deliberately, slowly, she
took a deep breath, standing there. Then without haste she
resumed walking. Her mind slid to Ida's body which had
been hidden in the undergrowth beside a path similar to this.
How on earth could she have forgotten that? Or forgotten
Lieutenant O'Neill's warnings? True, he had told her that
Ida had been killed elsewhere and brought here. But at the
moment those were merely words. The pictures in her mind
were of Ida, lying there mutilated, with the terrible empty
look on her face that death brought, a look that in itself was
a mutilation . . .

A few minutes before, Claire had been strolling, time-
less. Now time stretched out, a deceptive entity in itself, as
she kept making more and more turns on a path that seemed
endless, as though it were in some forest, not in Central
Park in the middle of Manhattan. The footsteps had started
again when she had. Could they be an echo? Claire had an
overwhelming urge to turn and yell, Who's there? But if she
did that, she couldn't help but give away how frightened she
was.

But Lieutenant O'Neill had said that whoever was calling
and following her was more likely to be doing it simply to
scare her and make her more amenable, not necessarily to
kill her. But then Ida might have thought that. Or Mrs.
Blake, and they were now dead . . .

Quietly, slowly, not mouthing the words but saying them

in her head, Claire prayed. She prayed for her children, for herself, for Brett, and finally, although it was a struggle, for whoever was following her. Once, an Eastern guru had referred to the rosary as said by Roman Catholics as a mantra, a meditation discipline. That was the way Claire now used praying. And then suddenly, when she least expected it, a noisy party burst onto the path, coming towards her, and Claire saw she was only a few feet from the drive.

Gratefully, she plunged down towards it. The ordinary New York people moving towards her and coming along the drive back of her looked more beautiful than she would have believed possible: men and women, black and white, adults and children, rich, middle-class and poor, dressed in designer clothes or in rags, fat, thin and medium, she could have embraced them all.

Her courage returned, she grasped the back of a bench and turned towards the path and waited. After a while two young people, hands locked and swinging, came along. Then an elderly couple. After ten minutes Claire gave up and walked out of the park at Seventy-second Street. Either she had imagined the whole thing, or whoever it was had turned around and gone back the other way, or had hidden among the bushes that, even with some leafless, were surprisingly thick for this time of year.

Walking past the classic grace of the Frick Museum, Claire turned into Seventy-first, walked over to Park and then quickly down to St. Anselm's, arriving ten minutes before her first afternoon client.

Back in her office she dialed Lieutenant O'Neill's direct line. "I was followed a few minutes ago," she started. "I was coming back through the park on one of those rather solitary paths and, after a few minutes, became aware that someone was following me. When I stopped, he stopped. When I went on, he went on."

"I'm surprised you didn't call out, 'Come here. I'm waiting, come and get me.' I mean, that was a really dumb thing to do. Even for you."

"I thought you said whoever it was was just trying to scare me."

"That was my theory. It may be true. Equally, it may not be. What in God's name made you walk through the park? You know your friend Ida Blake's body was found there. You want your body to be there, too?"

"You told me she had been moved, that she hadn't been killed there."

"If you think it was a perfectly okay thing to do and there's no danger, then why are you calling me?"

"I just thought you ought to know."

"Thank you. And you weren't scared at all."

"I was frightened half out of my wits. I broke out into a sweat and then started to shake."

"Serves you right. Now stay out of the park. Stay out of the subway. Walk in decent parts of town where there are plenty of people. It's true, I think all this following you is possibly—not probably, mind you, but possibly—a device to get you frightened enough to be pliable. But that's only a theory. Those two dead bodies are not theories. They're dead bodies. I don't want you to join them."

"All right. No more strolling in the byways."

She had no sooner hung up than her phone rang. "Claire Aldington," she said and, seeing her next client come into the door, waved her to a chair.

"In God's name," Giles's voice said. "Will you please let me talk to you. This must be the third time I've tried."

"Giles, I have a client waiting here and I can't talk to you now. She walked in just as I picked up the receiver. I'll call you back later."

Curiously, she thought, as she put the receiver down, her shaking had started again.

X

SHE FINALLY CALLED GILES BACK ABOUT FOUR-THIRTY, WHEN SHE had a free moment.

"How are you?" he asked.

"I'm fine. Really."

"You mean really fine? Not just suffering in silence?"

"I don't suffer in silence. When I suffer I make a loud noise."

"Good. First of all, I want to apologize for Ignacio's boorish behavior. He's spent most of his life in reform schools, juvenile court and a few foster homes. None of the above specialize in good manners and his are on the rough side."

"I'm not a hothouse plant, and I have come across rough manners among some of my own clients. What I got from him was not just the diamond-in-the-rough ambiance. I felt real hostility, and I didn't know why. But such was my state at the time that I couldn't ask him."

There was a slight pause. Then Giles said, "Ignacio, and the others that you saw in the kitchen, have all been in prison. Being in prison makes for paranoia—even if there wasn't any there before. You come in looking like the establishment, an obviously middle-class person from a middle-class background, and their suspicions multiply. Their natural inclination is to be convinced you're there for reasons that bode no good for them. I blame myself, because if we hadn't been in the middle of a rather important discussion, I would have greeted you myself and made introductions. I'm fearfully sorry."

"Giles—you didn't exactly grow up on the breadline, and while that particular group probably doesn't take in the fine gradations of English accents, everything about you breathes money and background. They may be minority, poor and ex-convicts, but they're not stupid, as I'm sure you'd be the first to agree. So their anti-middle-class prejudice is selective."

"I've spent a lot of time persuading them I'm on their side—not the law's and not society's. It took me a while to establish my credibility with them, but I finally succeeded. Now they trust me." Under the careful English understatement, he sounded, Claire thought, as proud as though he had won the Nobel Prize for Christian intermingling. "Anyway," he went on, "let me apologize again. To be forced to be sick on the sidewalk instead of your friendly neighborhood bathroom is beyond bearing. Incidentally, I trust it was a passing thing. You sound all right. You're not ill or anything, are you?"

"No. But I had had a bad scare. When I was on my way to see you, I almost got run down by a car and it shook me up."

"Accidentally, I trust. I mean, it was awful, but are you saying that somebody was deliberately trying to kill you?"

"I don't know." Saying the words now to Giles made the possibility frighteningly real, as though whatever shadowy enemies were around her had taken a step forward. Talking to O'Neill had always had the opposite effect. His insistence that she might be in danger and her counterbalancing skepticism had made the danger seem exaggerated. Now it had the dimension of fact.

"But why on earth—"

"I don't know, Giles. Why on earth would anybody kill Ida? Why would somebody kill Mrs. Blake?"

He said slowly, "Somehow, with Ida, I always assumed it was something personal—an outraged lover, perhaps."

"I was told today at lunch that you had made her pregnant. I'm sorry to be so flat-footed about it, Giles, but is it true?"

"Are you asking as the friend of the police, or as the friend of Ida?"

"Both. And as the friend of me. She was a woman priest. I'm a woman priest. If there is any connection there to the profession, then it is very much my concern."

"And what would the relationship between Ida and me have to do with that?"

"It might at least make clear some aspects of her life. The more that is known, the easier it will be to find out who killed her."

"Scotland Yard or the NYPD could hardly say it better. All rght. I'll answer your question. Yes, we did have what is now called nauseatingly a meaningful relationship. But whether I was the father of her embryo I don't know, because I don't know who followed me. Anything else?"

"You know," Claire said, "with no effort on my part that I am aware of, I seem to be making enemies the way other people make cookies—in batches. The hostility in your voice would freeze a stone; Pen Barnet ended our lunch today accusing me, as you have done, of seeking out publicity for myself in trying to help the police clear up this murder; and Mrs. and Mr. Blake—the Reverend Hector Blake—have accused me of doing something—I don't know what—to damage Ida. And all this as I trot through my daily round, my common task." And, she thought,

Brett's distancing himself, too, but that was different. In her saner moments she realized it was her own fault because she had not behaved well.

"All right. I'm sorry. I'm a holdover from an earlier and better day when all right-minded people called the police pigs. I'll take your average criminal any day before your average cop. The first usually commits his misdeeds out of need or anger. The need shouldn't exist and the anger is understandable."

"Does that include all those heroic types who maim and kill old people afraid to leave their homes to cash their Social Security checks?"

"The people who do that have been spiritually and socially maimed. They're reacting. The society that created them is responsible."

"Bunkum! For heaven's sake, Giles, that's a pretty odd thing for a priest to say. I grant social conditions have to be factored into crime, but what does that say about the huge majority of the poor, the minorities, and so on, who do not steal, rob, rape or kill? Have you ever heard of Thou shalt not kill? Thou shalt not steal? What do you preach down there on Sundays? How to make Molotov cocktails?"

"Well I certainly don't preach how to be subservient to the self-serving middle class. Nor do I teach them to betray one another to the police. Down here we believe in sanctuary, in its oldest sense. Probably the only people who can find sanctuary at St. Anselm's are the chief corporate officers of most of the thieving multinationals."

Claire, realizing she was gripping the phone as though it were going to be snatched from her hand, made a deliberate effort to relax. "Okay, Giles. What did you call me about?"

"To find out how you were, and, eccentric as it may seem at this point, to invite you to another dinner down here."

"I'll take a rain check. But thanks." And she hung up.

Suddenly and overwhelmingly she wanted to talk to Brett. Not for the first time she realized his calming effect on her. She was sitting there, her hands on the desk, when the phone rang again. The temptation not to answer it was so strong that she made herself pick up the receiver before she could decide not to.

"Claire Aldington," she said.

"Dr. Rosenthal here. Dalrymple is ready to go to his temporary home. Could you pick him up tonight? I've already talked to Althea and she knows he's going home with you. She says—and I quote—'Thank you from the heart.'"

Claire laughed. "I can hear her. All right. I'll pick Dalrymple up in about an hour."

She was putting on her coat when the phone rang again, and she stood there, staring at the instrument as it rang a second and then a third time. The thought that it might be Althea made her move over and lift the receiver on the fourth ring. "Claire Aldington."

"There's something I'd like you to do," Lieutenant O'Neill's voice said.

"I've been getting into trouble about you," Claire said. "The most surprising people resent our association."

"Like who?"

Claire paused. "Church people," she said finally. "Those who, I would have thought, would be outstanding upholders of law and order."

"Depends which church in which denomination in which neighborhood. Anyway, anybody in particular giving you a hard time?"

"I've been accused twice today of practically being a snitch, so I think I won't answer that. What is it you want me to do?"

"I got hold of the keys to Blake's apartment. The police have been over it many times. Everything has been dusted and printed and photographed. But it occurred to me that you, being in the same profession and knowing her, might see something that might give you an idea and help us find the killer."

"Like what?"

"How the hell should I know? It's a shot in the dark. We're not getting very far, you know. And I could use all the help I can get. Or have your clerical friends brainwashed you into thinking of us as pigs?"

It was so on the nose that Claire jumped. "Er—no. When do you want to do this?"

"How about now?"

"How long do you think it would take?"

"Couple of hours at most."

"All right. Where shall I meet you?"

"By the gate of her apartment house on West Twentieth Street. In an hour. By the way, have you been to the apartment before, when Blake was alive?"

"Yes. Once, when she had a few of us over for sandwiches and coffee before a lecture at the seminary across the street."

"Okay."

Claire called Dr. Rosenthal back and postponed her collecting Dalrymple until seven. "Will that be all right?"

"Sure. We have office hours tonight. See you then."

IDA'S APARTMENT WAS BETWEEN NINTH AND TENTH AVENUES ON West Twentieth and was on the third floor of one of the Greek Revival houses that faced the campus of General Theological Seminary, the oldest Episcopal seminary in the country.

Lieutenant O'Neill had the keys and let them into the front door. Claire had forgotten how graceful the house was inside. Built in the 1840s, it had been a single private house before being converted into apartments, and the stair curved pleasantly from floor to floor.

Ida's apartment on the third floor consisted of a bedroom, a living room, a study, bath and kitchen. The front looked towards the seminary chapel set back behind a wide green lawn; the back confronted a looming housing project that had gone up on Nineteenth Street. But between Ida's windows and those of the project were large trees, now bare, but in summer thick enough to give the house the illusion of total privacy. The ceilings were high, and there were fireplaces in both the bedroom and living room.

"People forget there are places like this in New York," O'Neill said, looking around the living room. "According to the landlord, who lives above, Blake was paying eleven hundred and fifty a month for rent. But the previous tenant lived in it under rent control, so that ten years ago, she—the previous tenant—was paying one hundred and sixty-nine a month. How's that for inflation!"

"Yes, but if all the apartments in this building were still under rent control, it would be an abandoned wreck. You couldn't run it on that, and pay the taxes and heating bill. On the other hand, according to Ida, it's a landmark house, so you couldn't tear it down. And it would be a crying shame to, anyhow."

They walked through to the front and looked out the study window. From this height, it was possible to look into the campus opposite.

Claire said, "Did you know that Clement Clarke Moore, who wrote *The Night Before Christmas,* taught over there?"

"No kidding? How'd you know that?"

"Ida told me."

They turned away from the windows.

"What do you want me to look at?" Claire asked.

"Anything you want. All her stuff, her correspondence, letters, bank statements and so on are where they've always been. I'd just like you to look around, look in the drawers, wherever you want. If anything strikes you as odd, tell me."

"I feel impelled to remind you again that I didn't know her that well. Sarah ought to be here."

"Sarah who?"

"Buchanan. She knew her a lot better."

"Want to call her? Ask her to come down?"

Claire hesitated. "Maybe I'm being a coward, but I don't want yet another person to give me the cold stare because

I'm helping the police, and I have an odd feeling that Sarah might. If I don't come up with anything, I'll leave you to call her."

"All right. If that's the way you want it. But I'm surprised that a bunch of clergypeople should get so high-minded about your helping the police. After all, we're the servants of the public and in the name of the public are supposed to get murderers, among other miscreants, off the streets."

"No, you're not surprised, Lieutenant. You're too experienced for that. You're just trying to make me feel bad."

O'Neill grinned.

Claire stood in the middle of the little room, wondering where to begin. Finally she went over to the small desk and opened the first drawer.

At the end of an hour she had found nothing that meant anything to her whatsoever. "Let me try the living room," she said.

Twenty minutes later, while looking through a photograph album in the top drawer of the chest in the living room, she stopped. The snapshot she was looking at had to be ten or fifteen years old. A teenage Ida was standing by a swimming pool in somebody's garden. Both she and her companion were squinting into the light. Ida's small figure showed forth to considerable advantage in a bikini that would hardly have covered a teacup. But it was the man standing beside her, in jeans and shirt, that held Claire's attention. Where on earth have I seen him before, she wondered? She stared so long, trying to locate the man in her memory, that O'Neill strolled over. "Found something?"

"I don't know. I think I recognize this man, but I can't remember from where."

He reached out and slipped the picture from its holders pasted on the page. Taking it over to the window, he examined it carefully. "Do you think you might recognize him if I had this snap blown up?"

Claire shrugged. "I really don't know. When I stare at the face it—the resemblance—gets less, not more. But when I come back again and look at it, then it hits me all over again."

"Anything else in the photograph album?"

"Not of interest to you."

"But of interest to you?"

"Well, there's a photo here of Brett, taken about twenty years ago." Claire turned back to the picture in question.

"He looks younger—naturally enough," O'Neill said.

"Yes." But what had struck her was how vulnerable he looked—so different from the guarded man she had come to know.

"Anything else you want to look at?"

"Only the books. Have your men looked at them?"

"Only their backs."

"Well, I don't know what I can do about them. I certainly don't have time to look in all of them."

"Just take a few at random. Any book, say, that strikes you as out of character, maybe."

"And what would that be?"

"I don't know. I'm hoping you'll tell me."

Impatient with what she thought was a fool's errand, Claire went over to the bookcase and ran her gaze over the titles. It was when she was on one of the lower shelves of a bookcase on one side of the fireplace that she came across books that did surprise her.

"I didn't know Ida was into the occult."

"Wouldn't you call it a related subject?" O'Neill asked, so dead-pan that it took Claire a moment to realize he was gently needling her.

"I know some clergy who might, but I'd never have thought Ida was among them." Without thinking she pulled some of the books out. A folded piece of paper slipped from one of them. Opening it, Claire saw a horoscope chart. "Well, well."

"Do you understand any of that?"

"Not really. But I suppose I could find somebody who does. For heaven's sake!"

"What?"

"Didn't you tell me you knew Letitia Dalrymple down in the Village?"

"I did. Why?" O'Neill came over. "Did she draw up that chart?"

"Yes. Here, look. Her name is on it."

O'Neill examined the huge wheel with its zodiac signs and cryptic words. "I ought to call Letty and find out what this means." Moving over to the desk, he pulled the telephone near him and, looking up something in an address book he pulled from his pocket, dialed a number.

"Miss Dalrymple? This is Lieutenant O'Neill of the New York Police. Fine, thanks. How are you?" After a few such exchanges, he said, "Let me tell you why I called." He told her about the chart falling from one of Ida Blake's books. "We'd like very much to talk to you about it. Do you think you could come over? A colleague of Ms. Blake's is here. She's the one who found it." There was a pause. "Yes, her name is the Reverend Claire Aldington." Another pause. "All right. The address is 116 West Twentieth Street, across from the seminary." Then O'Neill held out the phone. "She wants to talk to you."

By this time Claire was guiltily remembering that she had failed to return Mrs. Dalrymple's call for no better reason than that she was always busy and rushed and sometimes things dropped between the cracks.

"Mrs. Dalrymple," she said. "I'm so sorry not to have got back to you on the telephone. No, it's not all right. I owe you a large apology." There was a silence. Then, "Oh," she said.

"What's she saying?" O'Neill asked.

Claire waved her hand, indicating she was listening. After a longish while Claire said, "All right. We'll wait here."

"Now what?" O'Neill asked when she hung up.

"It's sort of spooky, but she said she was glad she was coming here to talk to us, because she had felt that Ida was in danger, and as a matter of fact, tried to warn her."

There was a silence while O'Neill strolled around the room with his hands in the pockets of his raincoat.

"If it weren't Letty, I'd say that sounded like a lot of mumbo jumbo double-talk. Cross my hand with silver and you'll meet a tall dark man, or in my case, a luscious redhead."

"The trouble with you, Lieutenant, is that even if you did meet a luscious redhead, you'd never be able to do anything about it because it would interfere with your work."

"You sound like my ex-wife."

"It sounds like a whole bunch of ex-wives."

"Yeah, but if you start taking days off to go to the beach, then they think you're not ambitious about getting ahead and making more money. In other words, you can't please them."

"I'll eat my collar the day you prove to me that you started taking unauthorized time off. Not you."

"Well, who knows. Anyway, is Letty on her way over?"

"Yes. She said she wanted to feel the place."

While they were waiting, Claire went steadily through many of the other books, shaking them, flipping them open for any writing in the margins or significant underlining. "Humm," she said after she'd opened one book. "That's odd."

"What's odd?" He was still looking at the horoscope.

"The book here has Douglas Barnet's name in it. I don't suppose that that's really odd, except that it's surprising. Pen did say that she and Doug had seen Ida once or twice. Certainly if he had a book that he thought she might enjoy he'd lend it to her."

"What's the book?"

"*The Place of Eros in Catholic Christianity,* by William Smith. Never heard of it."

"I wonder what my parish priest would think of it," O'Neill said. "I can just imagine his face."

Claire turned the book to the spine. "And I never heard of the publisher, either." She flipped through to the title page. "They're in Oakland, California."

"Along with all the other nuts. What does the book say?"

Claire opened to the first page, read a little, skipped a few pages, then read some more. "What I think it says would have shocked my District Attorney Methodist father no end."

"I thought you were an Episcopalian?"

"My father, I said. Not me. My mother was Catholic, my father Methodist. So I went for what one of my colleagues once called the Elizabethan Compromise—i.e., the Episcopal Church."

"I'm surprised your Catholic mother allowed that."

"She wasn't into religion very much. Hardly ever went to mass. My father was much more devout."

"So why didn't you go for the Methodists?"

"Because I married an Episcopal priest and went into the Church with him. Then, after he died, I decided to do what he had been urging me to do, continue my therapy work as an ordained priest." Claire read some more pages. "What surprises me about this is that Doug would have given or lent Ida the book. I know there are priests who feel that the Church's stand on sexual matters is hopelessly outdated and that it got put on the wrong track by the puritanical Paul. But I wouldn't have said Douglas, who sounds to me quite traditional, not to say Anglo-Catholic, was one of them."

O'Neill turned around. "He's not married, is he?"

"No. But he was. His wife died."

O'Neill shrugged, then went over and took the book out of Claire's hands and looked at it. After a moment of looking he whistled softly. "Now I'm shocked. Do you suppose he had a thing for her?"

"I don't know. I didn't think he and Pen even knew Ida. He said they'd only met her once or twice."

"My, my. Who'd have thought—" He put the book down as the bell in the front hall rang. "That'll be Letty."

He went out to the hall, pressed the bell that would release the lock two floors below, then went out of the apartment onto the small landing. A few minutes later, Claire heard soft footsteps on the carpeted stairs. Then she heard O'Neill's voice. "Hello Letty. Come in."

Claire was not very sure what she expected Letitia Dalrymple to look like. But the reality was far different from anything she'd vaguely imagined. What she saw was a slight figure with a cloud of curly white hair, a fresh-skinned face and periwinkle blue eyes. Underneath a raincoat, Letty was wearing jeans and sneakers.

"Sorry about the appearance, but I don't think that's too important in matters of urgency, do you Mrs. Aldington?"

English, Claire found herself thinking. The clipped vowels had remained intact.

"No, I don't. How do you do? Thank you for coming over. And, once again, I'm sorry not to have got back to you. I hate it when people do that to me."

Letty cocked her head on one side. "It's quite all right. There's an awful lot going on with you, isn't there?"

Claire felt an odd, unexpected sting at the back of her eyes. Letty was the first one who had made a sympathetic comment about it. "Yes. You're right. There is."

"All right, Letty," O'Neill said. "You said you wanted to get a feel of this place, now go ahead. See if you can tell us something we have overlooked."

Letty unbuttoned her raincoat and walked slowly around the room. After a moment she said, "You know there was something a little bent about her."

O'Neill who had been looking back at the book, glanced up and stared. "Bent? What do you mean by that?"

"It means wrong, distorted in some way."

"You know," Claire said, "I've never been able to get a sense of the kind of person she was. I didn't know her well, and when Lieutenant O'Neill here asked me to find out if I could what kind of person she was, I had a hard time. I asked a colleague of mine who knew her better, and I got a double answer, but the two sides didn't fit. I knew she belonged to some of the more militant of active feminist groups in the Church, but then, when I mentioned this to my colleague, she implied, without actually saying, that she didn't believe that with Ida it was passionate conviction. This same colleague, a woman priest named Sarah Buchanan, said she thought that Ida, rather than being a militant, was . . . was sort of putting it on, but why, she didn't say. She also said Ida was very much the wholesome nice girl next door." Claire paused. "And then we see this—" She pointed down to the shelf of occult books.

"That isn't a blot on her character," Letty said mildly. "I have those."

"Sorry, I didn't mean it to sound that way. It's just— well—unexpected, with Ida."

"Perhaps no one knew her very well," Letty said.

"Ça va sans dire," Claire said.

"That's French," O'Neill stated.

"It means," Letty said, "That goes without saying."

"Umph." He turned to Claire. "Did you get anything out of that clergyman downtown who was once her boyfriend?"

"No," Claire said unhappily. "He still seems to feel that to help the police is letting down the coming revolution."

"What's his name?" O'Neill asked.

Claire said nothing. She did not agree with Giles in any aspect of his feeling about the police. But, since he did feel that way, she couldn't bring herself to name him.

O'Neill made an exasperated noise. "Well, don't outrage your feelings. I'll find out anyway."

Letty was going around the apartment, touching things, putting her hand on surfaces. "Maybe not so much bent as muddled," she said finally. Then, as her hands went on, she said, "But she had been in quite serious trouble."

"What kind?" O'Neill asked.

"I don't know. I don't know. There was a death."

"Well, she was murdered."

"That's not the one I mean."

"Her mother was murdered," Claire said.

"Yes, but that isn't what I'm talking about."

"She had an abortion," O'Neill said.

Letty, whose hands were out above a book on the table, stopped. "Yes, that was sad. It made her sad. And it made her angry."

Claire handed her the book on Christian Eros that she had been holding. "Without looking at the title, does this tell you anything?"

"I never look at the title on a book I'm feeling," Letty said indignantly. She was holding the book and staring straight ahead. Suddenly she put the book down. "This is not a happy book," she said firmly.

O'Neill grinned. "My parish priest would agree with you." He hesitated. "What's the book about?"

"Sad sex. Sad, because she felt wrong reading it."

"What does it tell you about the man who lent it to her?"

Letty's hand turned and reached for the book again, but her eyes continued to stare straight ahead. "Another unhappy person. It was an unhappy day they came together."

"Are you telling me that the man who gave her that book killed her?"

"No, I don't think so." Abruptly, Letty sat down.

"Are you all right?" Claire asked.

"Yes," Letty said. She looked almost pale.

"By the way," O'Neill picked up the horoscope and handed it to Letty. "When did you do this for her?"

Letty looked at the chart. "About two months ago."

"Then you met her?"

"No. I did it by mail. I do quite a few that way. Somebody told her about me. I got a letter and a check in the mail. In the letter she told me her date and hour and place of birth, which was all I needed to know."

"And then you sent her her chart?"

"Not right away. I didn't want to do it. I wrote and gave her the name of at least two astrologers who I knew are quite competent, and returned her check with the letter."

"Why didn't you want to do it?" Claire and O'Neill asked at the same time.

"Because . . . because a truly dreadful feeling came over me when I thought about her."

"Meaning?"

"You know, one sees these things in the form of pictures sometimes, and the ones I saw about her made me not want to do her chart."

"What kind of pictures did you see?"

"Killing. A knife plunging down again and again."

O'Neill sucked in his breath. "And who was holding the knife?"

"I don't know. I couldn't see. Just a hand, holding it." Letty sounded on the brink of tears.

"But you did the chart anyway," Claire said gently.

"Yes. She sent the check to me with another letter. She said she wanted me to do it, and was there something wrong with her or her money? She sounded quite desperate. Finally, I did the chart. But I stayed away from any predictions and dealt only with her personality and characteristics and so on. And I emphasized strongly all the things she should avoid. I thought there might be a chance I could . . . could, well, head her away from whatever was threatening her. But obviously I couldn't."

Letty was sounding so distressed that Claire felt an urge to comfort her. "You did your best."

"Yes, I know. And we can't question God. What seems terrible to us may be the right thing in His Eyes."

"I thought psychics didn't believe in God," O'Neill said.

"Of course they do," Letty said indignantly. "You know better than that."

"How can any good come from a girl being savagely murdered?" Claire said angrily.

"For now we see through a glass, darkly; but then face to face."

Recognizing the quotation Claire smiled. "I take your point, but things like that have a daunting effect sometimes on my faith."

"That's because we see things lineally. In the eye of God, time is a place in which everything happens at once." She hesitated. "I feel . . . I feel I have to tell you something. I'm afraid. I'm afraid there will be another death."

XI

THERE WAS A STILLNESS IN THE ROOM. CLAIRE FELT A SHADOW draw closer to her. It was so real it was almost visible.

"Don't worry," O'Neill said abruptly. Then he said to Letty, "Do you know who the victim will be?"

She shook her head. "No. I'm terribly sorry. I wish I did."

Claire said, "Is there anything else—anything at all—about Ida, or about anything to do with this, that you can tell us?"

"I wish I had something of hers—not just a book—something personal to hold. It helps."

"There's a whole bunch of stuff in the bedroom," O'Neill said. "Why don't we go in there."

Probably because she had not known Ida well, Claire felt more uncomfortable in the bedroom than the living room, as though she were violating Ida's privacy. The room was smaller than the living room, and the bed, jutting out from the wall beside the door, took up a lot of space. Curiously, Claire noticed there were no closets. "I suppose this was built before the days of closets," she said.

"Oh yes," Letty agreed. "That's why there's an old-fashioned wardrobe over there. See?"

Painted white, like the molding around the top of the room, the wardrobe was in an indented area between the fireplace and the wall and looked almost built in. O'Neill strode over and opened the doors. On one side was a long space with a bar at the top. Hanging from it were some dark skirts and jackets and brightly colored dresses. On the other side were drawers.

"All right, Letty," O'Neill said. "Look at whatever you want."

But Letty didn't move. She stood there with her eyes closed. After a moment or so O'Neill said, his exasperation showing, "What are you doing, Letty? Are you seeing something?"

"I'm praying," she replied. "And it wouldn't hurt you to do the same. You ought always to do that before you go touching and handling some poor person's things. They retain part of that person and should be treated with respect and prayer."

O'Neill mumbled something.

Letty opened her eyes and went over to the bed. Then she opened the drawer in the night table beside it. Putting her hand in, she drew out a thin silver chain with a medallion. Again, she didn't look at it, but held it, staring ahead. After a while she put it back.

"I can't do any more," she said.

"Couldn't you get anything from it?" O'Neill asked.

"Yes. But it was muddled."

"What do you mean, muddled?"

Letty didn't say anything. But her face looked distressed as it had in the living room.

"What—"

"Don't bully," Claire said. "Letty's doing her best, and while I know nothing of the psychic—as a matter of fact I'm a little afraid of it—I do know that you can't hurry it or bully it or expect it to provide messages like the Dow Jones or the Associated Press."

"You understand more than you will admit," Letty said to her. "You probably use it quite a lot in your job."

Claire found herself suddenly wondering if she'd ever told Letty Dalrymple her own function in the Church. "I suppose your neighbor whom I worked with told you what I did."

"I don't think so, although I could be wrong. But I would know anyway. You help people."

Claire felt herself blushing.

"What do you mean, muddled?" O'Neill persisted, stubborn as a bird dog.

Letty hesitated, then she said unhappily, "I feel death when I hold it. But Ida is already dead."

"You said you were afraid that somebody else would die," Claire said.

"Yes."

Claire went over to the drawer and looked at it. There, lying by itself on the blue shelf paper inside the drawer, was the silver chain and medallion. Curious, Claire picked it up and looked at the design on the small silver disk: a winged knight in armor, his sword piercing the dragon at his feet. "St. Michael the Archangel," she said.

"Yes," Letty said. "Put it back, Mrs. Aldington. Please."

O'Neill made an impatient noise. "She's not going to steal it."

"It's not that."

Claire dropped the chain back inside the drawer. She felt her heart hammering inside her.

"There's something unfinished, undone," Letty said.

"I'll say," O'Neill grunted.

"Well, couldn't it just be her life?" Claire asked.

"Yes, of course, but there's something else—"

"May I ask what you're doing in my sister's bedroom?" a voice said behind them.

All three turned. The Reverend Hector Blake, his narrow face rigid with anger, was standing just behind them in the small hall. Then he strode in. Claire was still beside the open drawer of the night table. He took one look and turned on her.

"How dare you! How *dare* you come into my sister's room and rummage among her things like this! I should think that even for you that would be beyond the pale!"

Claire felt the blood surge back into her face. "I was asked to come here by Lieutenant O'Neill. I am not rummaging among her things. And I don't know what you mean by 'even for me.' I'd like very much for you to explain that."

"Take it easy, Reverend," O'Neill said. "Since we are having a hard time getting a lead on who killed your sister, I asked Mrs. Aldington to come here and see if anything in the apartment might give her a clue. After all, she's in the same profession. And by the way, how did you get in?"

"I have keys, of course."

"And you were pretty quiet. I usually hear people coming into doors."

"I heard voices and was deliberately quiet so I could find out who it was before they tried to get away."

"Considering that there's no other way out but the stairs, I don't know why you were bothering to sneak up. There's nowhere we could get past you."

"Since I haven't been here before, I couldn't be expected to know that. And who is this lady?"

Claire had an immediate sinking feeling that he would not be pleased when he found out who Letty was.

"My name is Letitia Dalrymple. I'm a psychic."

"A psychic! That's all that's needed. I never heard of such rubbish! As a priest I find the whole idea offensive in the extreme, and must ask you, Lieutenant, to remove yourself and these two women, neither of whom is fit to talk or give advice about Ida. If that's all the New York Police Department has to lean on, then it's worse than I have suspected it was. Why don't you go all out and kill some animal and read the entrails?"

"What a horrible thing to say!" Letty protested. "You may be unhappy, but you have no right to accuse people the way you do, and as for suggesting killing an animal—"

"And I would very much like to know what it is that both you and Mrs. Blake wanted to see me about," Claire put in. "All you have done is threaten over the phone and make wild accusations about something I'm supposed to have done to Ida. I want to know what it is, here and now, when I have witnesses."

"Very well. You deliberately set out to get Brett Cunningham away from Ida."

"First of all, it's not true. I've told you. Brett has told you. Why do you cling to it? And why did your mother threaten me and Brett with some kind of media exposure—exposure of what?"

A closed look came down over his face. "I'm not at liberty to discuss this."

"Why not? And if you're not at liberty to discuss whatever it is you wanted to talk to me about, then why did you call me up and why did your mother insist she was coming to see me?"

"This is my sister's apartment. I insist you all leave immediately. I shall be moving some things in here soon, and I want to have it to myself."

"Technically, the apartment's still in police possession," O'Neill said. "But since you're next of kin, we don't mind your using it."

"Thank you." Hector bit out the words.

"And you haven't answered Mrs. Aldington's question."

"I don't have to answer any questions, Lieutenant. Now could you please leave me alone."

CLAIRE, LETTY, AND O'NEILL STOOD ON THE PAVEMENT OUTSIDE the house. It was now dark. Lights shown behind the long windows of the graceful houses. For a moment Claire had the illusion that the houses and the street were caught in a time bubble, unchanged for a hundred and forty years. It was so strong, she stood absolutely still, as though frozen. Then a car started up and O'Neill spoke and broke the spell. "I think the guy's nuts."

"He's very afraid of something," Letty said. "And he is also angry."

"You could certainly describe him that way," Claire admitted drily. "I have a feeling that all of this about me and Ida is a curtain in front of something else. What do you think, Letty?"

"I think I want to go home. I don't mean to be unhelpful, but the cupboard's bare. There's no more I can feel or tell you right now."

"You've been wonderful," Claire said.

O'Neill cleared his throat. "Yeah. Thanks a lot. You always come through."

"I don't know what I came through with."

"Food for thought," Claire said. She added grimly, "And a warning."

Letty waved and walked away.

"Where are you going?" O'Neill asked Claire.

"To the vet's. I have to pick up—Good heavens!" She whirled around. "Letty," she called.

Letty, who was ten yards beyond them on her way to Ninth Avenue, turned.

Claire walked towards her with O'Neill following. "Did you ever know a woman named Althea? I'm sorry, I don't know her last name, but she has a cat called Dalrymple."

"Of course. Althea Tierney. She lived in the Village near me and had heard about my work. When her brand-new kitten disappeared, she called me, and when I was able to help her find it, she named it after me. How is she?"

"She's now a bag lady. She sits at the corner of Sixty-third and Lexington, with all her goods around her, and Dalrymple wears a harness and sits with her.

"Oh dear, oh dear. I told her she ought not—but she was very stubborn. I'm so sorry. How is Dalrymple? He must be fifteen or sixteen by now."

"He is. He got sick and she asked me to take him to the vet, which I did. Now he has to come home with me to recuperate before he can go out on the streets again."

Letty sighed. "When she discovered I was English she used to call me or come and see me quite a lot. She was doing a book on Arthur and what might have happened if he had won that last battle. She had an absolute thing about him."

"She still does. She hallucinates most of the time, and she thinks she's sitting on the cliffs of Dover holding off the Norse invaders, waiting for Arthur's return."

"She was beginning to get ill when I knew her."

"What did she do then?"

"She taught mediaeval history in one of the colleges here. One of the good ones."

"Does she have a family?"

"Yes. But I don't know where they are. Would you like me to take Dalrymple? I have a cattery—about eleven of my own, but I could keep him in a separate room and look after him."

Claire felt an immediate sense of relief, which she thrust behind her. "I said I'd take him for a while, and I think I should. Besides, I work right opposite the corner where she sits. So I can give her news about Dalrymple easily."

"If you want a lift to that vet, you'd better come now," O'Neill said. "I have to get moving."

"All right. Thanks anyway, Letty. Let's keep in touch."

DALRYMPLE LOOKED THINNER BUT MUCH BETTER WHEN CLAIRE picked him up at the vet's and paid the bill.

"Give him these twice a day for a week," Dr. Rosenthal said. He tickled Dalrymple behind his ear. A loud purr throbbed out. "I wish Althea would go to the hospital and get herself stabilized and take her medicine. It would be a lot better for Dalrymple. She's been lucky so far, and she does keep an eye on him. But I worry about big dogs coming along. Dalrymple's not young, and the fact that he's on a leash, which keeps him from getting lost, might also keep him from escaping if he's attacked. Call me in a couple of days and let me know how he's getting on."

CLAIRE INSTALLED DALRYMPLE IN HER OWN ROOM WITH HIS OWN water and food and his litter box in her bathroom. After dinner, when Dalrymple had had a chance to get used to his new surroundings, she let Martha bring Patsy in. When the kitten pranced up to the big black and white cat, he gave a ritual hiss but did not seem seriously offended. While Claire was brushing her teeth before going to bed, she noticed him grooming Patsy and being groomed in return.

She'd been in bed for about half an hour when the phone rang. Brett, she thought, or hoped, and snatched the receiver off the phone beside her bed.

"Don't get too comfortable," the genderless electronic voice said.

Claire felt an onset of fury. "How dare you call me at this hour—whoever you are! My children are asleep." The moment she said that she regretted it. Even to mention her children to this evil maniac struck her as putting them in danger. She was immediately confirmed in her feeling.

"Ah yes, your children. So vulnerable, children! You must be very careful with them."

Claire could feel herself shaking, whether from rage or fear she couldn't be sure.

"You think you're getting away with this, but you aren't!"

"No? If you could do something about it, you would have done it before now." And, inexplicably, the voice giggled.

Claire drew in her breath. There was something about that giggle that reminded her of something or someone. But all she said was, "You're drunk—or stoned!"

There was the sound of another voice in the background, but not clear enough to identify in any way. Then, "You'll be very, very sorry." And the person hung up.

Claire did not sleep the rest of the night. After an hour or two, she gave up the struggle and sat up and read for a while. Then, at dawn, she lay down again and dozed briefly before her alarm went off at six-thirty.

At breakfast, which was around the kitchen table, Claire said to Martha and Jamie, "Did either of you hear the telephone ring last night around eleven-thirty?"

"Yes," Martha said. "I thought it might be Brett."

"It wasn't, unfortunately. I've been getting . . . well, crank calls. Threatening crank calls. I mentioned them once before. This time, he, she, whoever it is, mentioned you. I don't want you to be frightened. But I do want you to be careful. Please, please go around with a bunch of others whenever you can. I know you do, anyway. And unless you go on a class outing, don't go into the park. Promise me!"

"I promise," Martha said. Her eyes looked large and a little alarmed.

"Jamie?" Claire looked at her son.

"I'm not going to go skulking around like I was scared of somebody." He had a mulish look on his face that Claire associated with his Much Macho act.

"I'm not asking you to go skulking. I'm asking you not to go alone anywhere. I don't think that's a lot to ask, just for a while."

"Well, what am I supposed to do when I have to go someplace and there's nobody around? Ask somebody to go with me? The guys'd die laughing. I can't do that, Mom."

"I'm not asking you to do something that embarrasses you. I'm just suggesting that you kind of attach yourself to other kids when you're going to the park for a game or some other place."

"I will if I can, but I'm not making any promises."

Claire did something then that she rarely did: she lost her temper. "Yes you will, Jamie. I'm worried half out of my mind. I'm being threatened, and I'm not going to have you sit there and decide in some lordly way whether or not you can bring yourself to help me. This is an order. You will not go about by yourself alone. Is that understood?"

Jamie stood up, swung his arm in a Nazi salute and said, *"Heil* Hitler!"

"Come off it, moron!" Martha said, "Can't you be of some help?"

Claire got up. "Obviously not." She went into her room and checked on Dalrymple, who seemed lively and glad to see her. Then she called O'Neill's office. He was not in, a Sergeant Wisnovsky told her. "Anything I can do?" he added.

Claire hesitated, then decided not to begin from the beginning with a policeman she didn't know. "Please ask him to call me," she said. Then she put on her coat and left the house.

She arrived at St. Anselm's as morning prayer was beginning and achieved some degree of calm listening to the familiar words of the Venite. "O come, let us sing unto the Lord; let us heartily rejoice in the strength of our salvation . . ." It had been some time, Claire thought gloomily, since she had felt like heartily rejoicing in anything. Perhaps that had been her problem. What she needed was less worry and more rejoicing. But at the moment, and given a sleepless night, it would have to be an act of faith . . .

GERRY WAS HER FIRST CLIENT. THE GIRL HADN'T BEEN IN HER office for more than ten minutes when Claire realized she had gone back to drugs.

"When did you start using again, Gerry?" she asked.

"I'm not . . . I don't . . ." But the denial stuck. Tears came out of her eyes and trickled down her cheeks.

"Why? What happened?"

"Somebody I knew before came back to town . . . He was using, and he wanted me to . . . so I did."

"Who?"

"His name is Jesse." She sounded zombielike and miserable.

"Jesse," Claire repeated. Where had she heard that name recently? "Are you in love with him?"

Now definitely crying, Gerry nodded.

Claire said slowly, "I don't have to tell you, do I, that
that way promises nothing but disaster?"

"I know. But when he comes around and offers me a joint
or a pill or a snort of coke I . . . don't seem able to say
no. At least I say no, but he just laughs and then gives it to
me. And I don't refuse."

"If he's an addict himself, it's no use on earth to appeal to
him. I take it he is."

"Yes. He threw it for a while, but then something—I
don't know what—made him go back. He just says it was
boring being straight."

"Would you like to go back to the rehab?"

"Yes. I would. But not just yet. I can't give him up now. I
just can't."

Claire sat there silent for a minute or two, listening to the
occasional stifled sobs that broke from Gerry. Lecturing
Gerry, scolding her (even if Claire had wanted to do that,
which she didn't) would, she knew from experience, do no
good. Not herself an alcoholic, Claire had been to AA open
meetings and learned there and from friends and clients who
were members that only the person concerned could do
anything about it, and only when he or she wanted to. "You
didn't cause it, you can't stop it and you can't cure it," she
had heard one alcoholism counselor say to a family member
of an alcoholic.

"I can't treat you when you are using drugs, Gerry, you
know that. But as soon as you want to stop, let me know."

Gerry, still weeping, departed.

Claire checked with Darlene to see if Lieutenant O'Neill
had called, but he hadn't.

Later that morning, Claire was on her way out of the
parish house to report to Althea about Dalrymple when she
bumped into Douglas Barnet and Sarah Buchanan.

"We're going to lunch," Douglas said, looking far more
cheerful than his usual austere self. "Want to join us?"

"I'd love to, but I have some errands to do. Let me have
a rain check." She smiled and watched them get into a taxi.
Sarah, she thought, a pretty woman anyway, was looking

even prettier than usual. Remembering seeing the two of them at lunch when she and Peggy Anderson and Pen Morgan were at the Academic Club, she wondered if she was witnessing the beginning of romance. For obvious reasons, it made her think of Brett. Where was he, and why didn't he let her know where she could reach him? Determined not to be a stereotypical jealous woman, she pushed the unanswered questions from her mind and crossed the street to Althea's corner.

"You'll be glad to hear that Dalrymple's well and is eating," she said.

"I am glad." She hesitated. "And thank you. How long before I can have him?"

"I have to take him back to Dr. Rosenthal's in a week. If he's all right then, I can bring him to you right away."

Althea was looking more strained and sibyl-like than usual. "I miss him," she said. "The enemy is gathering."

"I saw Letitia Dalrymple," Claire said. "She said she knew you several years ago and that she found Dalrymple for you when you had lost him. And that you had named him after her."

"I never look back," Althea said. "It's dangerous. And you ought to be careful, too. You have enemies."

Claire had no desire whatsoever to enter into any of Althea's fantasies or hallucinations. "I'm always careful," she said. But that assertion rang other changes in her mind. "Are you talking about Norse enemies? The ones you're watching for?"

"Men," Althea said. "They follow you. I watch them and they follow you."

Claire had promised herself time for some much-needed shopping during the lunch hour. But she found that she was uninterested in either a new sweater for herself or a new skirt for Martha. She would, instead, she decided, get a sandwich and some coffee at the nearest deli and take it back to her office.

Back at her desk she opened the brown bag and stared at her sandwich. Then, instead of taking a bite, she dialed

Lieutenant O'Neill's number, though without much hope of finding him. If he had received her message he would have called her.

To her surprise he answered the phone. "You're in!" she said.

"I was just going to call you. What's up?"

"I got another call last night, this time threatening the children."

"What did he say?"

Claire told him, repeating word for word the message that had burned itself into her mind.

"He didn't actually threaten."

"Wasn't that a threat?"

"No, not legally, though he was obviously intent on making you think so."

"What do you mean—legally?"

"I mean we're abysmally short-handed. I can try to get police protection for your two children, but I'm pretty sure they won't give it to me. Just make sure the kids don't go out alone."

"That's a lot easier said than done."

"I know. I'm sorry. And I want you, too, to be careful. No more solitary rambles in Central Park!"

"I can assure you I'm not about to. By the way, a . . . a friend of mine told me a few minutes ago that she saw men following me."

"What friend?"

"Does it matter?"

"You don't want to say?"

Claire sighed. "Althea—the bag lady. The one I was talking to Letty about yesterday. I suppose that will make you think it's not reliable, that she made the whole thing up."

"Not necessarily. But I can't help wondering if those men she sees following you aren't apart of the Norse invasion she's trying to stave off. But that doesn't mean I don't still want you to be careful."

"No, I will be. I promise."

After she'd hung up, Claire looked at the phone for a moment, then dialed Brett's direct line. The same ubiquitous young man answered. Claire almost hung up, but she made herself say as graciously as she could, "Would you please ask Mr. Cunningham to call me when he is free."

"I'm afraid it'll be a while," the young man said with irritating good humor.

"Why?" Claire asked baldly, though she didn't expect anything but an evasive answer.

"He's out of the country," the young man said. "Sorry!"

Claire then dialed Jamie's school. "Could you ask James Aldington to call me when he can," she requested of the school secretary.

"Anything wrong, Mrs. Aldington?"

"Oh no. I just want to speak to him."

"I'll give him the message."

IT WAS AROUND FOUR IN THE AFTERNOON WHEN THERE WAS A knock on her door.

Claire was with a client and was irritated that whoever it was had not been stopped by Darlene. Any member of the staff knew better than to interrupt her. Excusing herself, she got up and opened the door. "Please—" She started to say, when she saw it was Pen.

"Am I interrupting something?" Pen said. "I'm fearfully sorry."

"I'm in the middle of a therapy session. May I talk to you in about an hour? Will you be home?"

"Oh yes. It's nothing urgent. I just happened to be in the area and thought I'd drop in and see Douglas, but he doesn't appear to be in and the girl downstairs didn't seem to think he'd come back from lunch. So I decided to bother you instead. So sorry."

"Douglas was going out to lunch with Sarah Buchanan when I last saw him. You could call her if you want. She's at the church headquarters at Forty-third Street."

"Oh, I don't think I'll bother her. Thank you so much."

"Sorry about that," Claire said to her surprised and

annoyed client. "We can take an extra five minutes to make
up for it."

But the session was fated not to be a full one. Ten minutes
after she'd got rid of Pen, Claire's phone rang.

"I can't think what's got into people," she said, staring at
her phone. "All calls go through Darlene and she's been
told to hold them on pain of excommunication. Except, of
course, in an emergency . . ." Claire stared at the phone
for a second, then snatched up the receiver.

"Yes?" she said.

A voice she recognized immediately as belonging to the
headmaster of Jamie's school came through. "Mrs. Aldington?"

Fear snaked through her. "What is it, Mr. Simmons?"

"I'm afraid we can't find James. He seems to have
vanished."

XII

"HE'S MISSING?" CLAIRE SAID. "YOU CAN'T FIND HIM ANY-where?"

"I'm afraid not. The secretary gave your note to one of the students in James's class. But the boy didn't get around to telling her that James wasn't in his class until a short while ago. Then she came to me. I tried your apartment. Your cleaning lady was there, but she was quite firm that James wasn't. I've questioned some of the boys. Two of them say they saw James at the lunch break when he was buying something from a stationery store near here. He told them to go on, which they did since they were late. But he didn't come back."

Her first feeling was fear. Her second, bitter self-reproach. Because she had lost her temper at him, because she had humiliated him in front of his sister, Jamie would take special pleasure in polishing his Much Macho image by doing exactly what she had asked him not to.

"Oh my God!" she said. "And the stationery store at the lunch break was the last anyone saw of him?"

"Yes."

"That must have been four hours ago. I don't mean to blame somebody else—but I wish the secretary had tried to deliver my message herself. We would have known right away."

"I know. And I told her that. And she is devastated. I'm terribly sorry. Please let me know as soon as you have any news. In the meantime, is there anything I can do?"

"I can't think of anything, unless you ask some of the other boys. But can you give me your home number just in case?"

"Of course."

Claire didn't even remember her client until she hung up. "I'm sorry, Linda," she said to the young woman sitting across from her. "This seems to be a fourteen-carat emergency. I'm going to have to phone the police now. I'll make it up to you next week."

Linda, a pleasant young woman, got up. "I'm sorry about this. I hope everything comes out all right. Don't worry about the time." And she was gone while Claire was phoning Lieutenant O'Neill.

He wasn't in, but the sergeant who answered the phone seemed to know who she was and something about her case.

"How long's he been missing?" he asked. "Only since lunch? No need to panic yet. He's probably out at some candy store with other kids, or playing hooky."

Claire knew he was trying to be reassuring, but she felt her anxiety and anger rising. "I hope you're right. But my children have been threatened. I want police action right away."

"I'll get in touch with Lieutenant O'Neill immediately, but you know kids!"

"Yes. I do. My own kids. They know my circumstances. They wouldn't disappear for fun. Now *do* something!"

"Yes ma'am."

Claire hung up and found her hand was shaking and her

heart was pounding. Her next thought was Brett. But he was out of the country. A great longing for his calm good sense came over her, followed by resentment that he was away when she needed him, and further, that he didn't trust her enough to let her know where he was.

She dialed her apartment. The phone rang six times before she hung up. Obviously Connie, the cleaning lady, was gone, and Martha had not come home yet. Claire put the receiver back briefly then dialed Martha's school. When the school secretary answered, Claire asked to speak to Martha. After a few minutes, the secretary came back and said that Martha was in the middle of dress rehearsal for the school play that was going to have its first performance the following night, and the drama coach said she couldn't possibly come to the phone now. Could she—the secretary—please take a message?

Claire thought for a moment. The fact that Martha's play was about to go on had slipped her mind and she felt vaguely remorseful. "Just tell her please, please, to come home with the others tonight the way we discussed. She'll know what I mean." Claire thanked her and hung up.

For a few minutes she sat there, trying to will the phone to ring. More than anything else in the world she wanted to hear from Jamie, to hear that he was all right and had simply taken off to give her a scare and assert his manhood. If he was truly all right, she would thank God—and wring his neck. Failing that, she wanted to hear from Brett or O'Neill.

But the phone didn't ring. The next thing to do, she knew, was to call the homes of Jamie's friends. Pulling her address book out of her pocket, she started systematically telephoning. As she was told by one boy or mother or housekeeper or maid after another that Jamie was not there and was not expected, she realized that Jamie was extremely popular. His list of friends seemed endless. When the friend himself answered, Claire queried him about when and where he had last seen her son. None had seen him since the morning, except for one of the boys who had seen him in the stationery store.

"Did he say anything to you about any plan of his?" Claire asked.

"No. He didn't. I just thought he'd be back at school in a couple of minutes."

Claire repressed an impulse to ask the twelve-year-old boy if Jamie had seemed to have anything on his mind or to be troubled by anything. If nothing were wrong, and Claire was trying to convince herself that nothing was, then she would have to deal with her own very angry twelve-year-old for having asked one of his friends such a sappy question.

Finally O'Neill called. It was past five by that time, and Claire felt weak with anxiety. Quickly she told him.

"Okay," O'Neill said. "I know how you must be feeling. I've tried to have somebody keep an eye on both of your children, but we can't spare extra men all the time. Look, I know it's probably no use to say this to you, but calm down. On a purely statistical basis, the chances that anything bad has happened to him are small. He's a sensible boy, intelligent, a city kid with street smarts, not somebody from a small town. He knows what the score is and he's been warned. So remember all that. I'm going to have to go now and see what steps I can set in motion at this end."

Claire was sitting, wondering what next step she should take, when Larry appeared in the doorway.

"The scuttlebutt says that Jamie has gotten lost. Is that so?"

"Yes," Claire said. "That is so. And don't tell me how sensible and intelligent and wise he is and how foolish it is of me to worry."

"I won't. I take it that's what everybody else is saying."

"Yes."

"How about praying?"

"If every mother of a sick or lost or stolen child had her prayer answered—"

"It might not affect whether or not you get him back. I don't think prayer's about manipulating events. I think it will improve your own faith, and since I also believe in telepathy, it might put praying into Jamie's mind, and there's no telling what that might inspire him to do."

"Umm," Claire conceded.

"Want a ride?"

"Yes," Claire said. "Do you have your car here, or are you planning to take a taxi?"

"I have my car."

They were silent going up Park Avenue. Then Claire said, "You can drop me on the corner of Eighty-second Street. It's eastbound and you can't make a left turn."

"All right."

When he stopped the car, he said simply. "I'll call you later to see how things are. Don't forget what I said."

To her relief Martha was in the apartment. Claire looked at her, "Do you know about Jamie?"

"Yes. Jamie's headmaster called to see if you had heard anything and he told me. Mom, anybody who took on Jamie—"

"Martha, everybody's been trying to tell me how grown-up and sensible and smart he is. He's all that, but he's also a little boy."

"Yes. I know."

"How did the dress rehearsal go?"

"Fine. And I did come home with Ellen and Susie."

"Thank God."

The phone rang. Claire said, "If it's one of your friends, would you please get off the phone immediately. You don't have to say why. But I want to leave the phone open. Tell them I'm expecting a long-distance call or something."

Claire heard Martha murmur into the phone and then replace the receiver. At eight Lieutenant O'Neill called to see if she had heard anything.

"No," Claire said. "Do you know anything?"

"No. But we're working on it."

"Do you have any ideas?"

He interrupted. "I'm sorry. I don't. Try not to worry. I have to go now."

* * *

THE HOURS SEEMED ENDLESS. TO PUT SOME KIND OF STOP TO her own horrified thinking, Claire turned on a television show of which she remembered nothing later. Watching the people on the screen was like watching puppets in mime. The words bounced off some wall around her. Inside that wall, she was recalling what she never knew she had retained—the details of every kidnapping of every child in the past year or so, especially the childen who had been stolen in New York. It was as though her unconscious had memorized each agonized word from every parent.

Martha sat beside her saying nothing, but occasionally reaching out and holding her hand. At some point Douglas Barnet called.

"Pen and I are tremendously sorry. Our prayers will be with you. And you must know that if there is anything at all we can do . . ." He finished up, "God bless."

God bless whom, Claire thought wearily. The kidnappers? As though he were sitting there beside her she could hear Larry say in his calm, reasonable voice, "Well you never know what effect it might have on them, do you?"

At ten Claire said to Martha, "Go to bed. There's no need for both of us to be sleepless."

"I can't sleep either, and I'd rather be here with you. Unless you want to be alone."

"No," Claire said, and reached out her hand. "I'd much rather be with you, too."

After a while something made Claire say, "Are you wondering if it were you, would I be going through the same hell?"

Martha hesitated. "It sounds horribly self-centered, but it did cross my mind."

"It's not self-centered, or if it is, it's human. The answer is yes, I would."

AT ELEVEN-THIRTY CLAIRE WAS WATCHING THE CABLE NEWS WHEN the phone rang. She leaped towards the hall.

"Yes," she said.

"It's Brett," his voice said. And then, "Your voice sounds different. Is something the matter?"

"Oh God, Brett, I've needed you so much. Where have you been? Jamie's missing."

She heard him draw in his breath. "When. Tell me everything."

Claire poured it out to him. At the end, he said only, "I'll be around in a few minutes."

When he rang the bell, Martha let him in. He walked straight into the living room and took Claire in his arms. "It's all right," he said, patting her back as she cried. "I don't know how, but I am quite sure it's going to be all right."

Illogical as it seemed, Claire felt a growing conviction that he was right. After a while they sat down on the sofa. Martha, yawning mightily, had disappeared. "I can't seem to keep awake any longer."

Claire said, "No, darling, go to bed. Remember you have the play tomorrow."

"Are you going to tell me where you were and what you've been doing?" Claire asked Brett when Martha had gone.

"Not quite yet, but very soon," he said. "Now start at the beginning and tell me again about Jamie. Don't leave anything out."

So she talked. She talked about everything she could think of concerning Jamie and their quarrel. After she'd finished, he said thoughtfully, "Why do people kidnap children?"

A feeling of nausea rose in her. "For sexual purposes," she said. "It's been haunting me ever since I talked to the headmaster."

"So much so, I imagine, that you haven't thought of any other possible reason."

"Such as?"

"Money. Ransom."

"But I don't have any money. I mean, we're comfortably fixed, but we don't have real money in the sense of wealth."

"It depends from whose standpoint you're talking, doesn't it? To somebody who makes three-fifty an hour, what you have in the bank, or what he thinks you have in the bank judging by the place you live in and the schools your children go to, what you have is real wealth. And *I* have money. To anybody who knows you and your life at all, I, and whatever I have, must figure in."

"That probably shouldn't make me feel one degree better, but it does."

"Of course. If there is a bartering chip that would enable you to get your son back, you wouldn't be a normal mother if you wouldn't walk over anything and anyone to get it."

AT TWO O'CLOCK CLAIRE, LOOKING AT BRETT'S FACE, SAW, AS though for the first time that evening, how strained he looked, how deeply the lines were etched. He's thinner, she thought.

"Brett—" she started.

At that point there was a sound that was both familiar and unexpected: a key turning the lock of the front door.

Claire was unaware of running towards the hall, simply that she was there and that facing her, looking both frightened and sheepish, was Jamie.

"Ma?" Jamie said.

She was hugging him and he was hugging her back. "I'm sorry, Ma, you must have been scared stiff. I didn't know—"

Brett appeared behind them and asked, "James—what happened?" Then, in a voice Claire had never heard before, "I trust you didn't just take off, because if you did, I, personally, am going to give you a hiding you richly deserve."

"I did not! At least, I didn't mean to."

"What does that mean?"

"Well you see this woman came up to me in the stationery store . . ."

"What woman?" Brett and Claire asked at once.

"Just a minute," Brett said. "Did you come home by yourself or did somebody bring you?"

"I came home by myself. After she took off the gag and untied my hands."

"What gag? Who?" Claire was trying to control her voice, but it had a tendency to rise. Above all at this point, she did not want to sound hysterical. "Jamie, I'm sorry to behave like a mother, but come here and let me hug you again."

"That's all right," Jamie said. "I don't mind your behaving like a mother. I mean, I'd really like to have had you around in the past few hours." At which point he gave her a hug and seemed, suddenly, to be much more her twelve-year-old son than the budding adolescent Much Macho.

"I told you once before, value it," Brett said.

"Let's go into the living room," Claire suggested. "I think we could all sit down."

"Mom, I was so scared back there that I lost my appetite. But I didn't get dinner and now I'm hungry."

"Come into the kitchen, both of you," Claire said. "I'll fix you something to eat and you tell us what happened."

While Claire was putting together a sandwich of school-boy proportions, Brett and Jamie sat down. "Now," Brett said, "Begin at the beginning. You were in the stationery store."

"Yeah, I was getting some drawing paper when this female, who was looking at paper beside me, started talking and asked me what art class I was taking. I told her and she said well maybe it would be better to get another kind of paper and then asked to look at my pencil. She was being real helpful . . . Mom, I know you said not to go around alone, but a stationery store for God's sake, all the school uses it."

"So she talked you out into the street, right?"

"Yeah. She said she knew a better art supply store five blocks away, and if I had time she could take me there and it would make my drawing easier. Well, I haven't told you, but I've been interested in art lately. I've found I can draw and I like it. So I thought I'd go with her. She said she'd drive me back to the school, and Ma, she's a girl. I just didn't think—"

"And when you got in the car, somebody knocked you out one way or another, right?" Brett asked grimly.

"Yeah. I couldn't believe it was happening. For a minute or a second it was like it wasn't real, but then it was. What they did was put something over my mouth from behind, and then something over my nose. It smelled funny. And then the next thing I knew I woke up on a bed somewhere and my hands were tied and I had a gag on. I was scared. I mean, you see something like that in the movies and it's exciting. And anyway, you know it's going to come out all right. But when it's real, it's awful."

Claire put a large sandwich down in front of Jamie. She turned to Brett. "Wouldn't you like something?"

"Just some coffee. What happened then, Jamie?"

"Nothing for a while. I tried to struggle, but it wasn't any use. And then I tried to move my jaw around, but it made things worse. I could hardly breathe. So I got even more scared and just lay there for a while, trying to think of what to do. It seemed like forever. I tried everything I'd heard of, like breathing slow. Maybe I breathed too slow. Anyway, I went to sleep, I don't know for how long.

"Then after a while I woke up and I realized people were talking in the next room. I could hear their voices, but I couldn't really hear what they were saying. It was kind of faint, like they were in the other side of the room away from the door leading into mine. Anyway, I decided to listen, so I rolled off the bed—I could do that—and then lay still because I made an awful thump when I fell. But I guess they didn't hear me. Nobody came in. Then after a while I started rolling as quietly as I could over to the door so I could hear them better. You know you'd think it'd be easy to roll over, but it wasn't."

"Not when your hands are tied," Brett said.

"No. And what's more, it hurt where they'd tied my

wrists, but it wasn't too bad. I got over to the door and put my ear on the floor next to the crack."

"Did you hear anything?" Claire asked, putting some coffee down for Brett and some decaffeinated down for herself.

"Yeah, I heard them. One of them said, 'The next thing is to let him know we've got the kid. One move to the feds and the kid goes, and so does his kid.'"

"What on earth—?" Claire said. She glanced at Brett. "Do you know what he's talking about?"

"Yes. I do."

"You mean this is something you've been mixed up in?"

"You could say that."

"Well considering it's my child they've taken, I think the least you could do is tell me about it."

"I didn't tell you because I was afraid for you if any of the people I've been dealing with thought you might have information about them. That's why I stayed as clear of you as I could. But obviously, not clear enough."

"What have you been doing, and who have you been doing it with?"

He took a deep breath. "I'm not sure of all the ramifications yet, but Adam was not only mixed up in drugs, he was also a dealer. I didn't learn this until I went out there to see him. Being bright, as well as addicted, he turned out to be a successful dealer—until, of course, he stopped being able to function. If he'd only bothered to put those brains of his to some constructive purpose! But it's no use railing about that now. He did what he did.

"As you probably know, because it's been in the papers, there's a brisk trade between some of the South American countries and the drug dealers in the States. The FBI called me and asked if I could go down to some of the countries on a supposed business trip and find out there what I could through some of my business and investment contacts. I didn't have much hope, because I was reasonably sure that the people I dealt with had no more to do with drugs than I did. But I was wrong. Adam, in his repentant mood, gave me a couple of names. I went south and discovered that some of those names led to the most respected and respectable citizens. I got in touch with their internal police, and had the satisfaction of knowing that they were named and arrested.

"But I knew that I hadn't begun to get names here in the States. One attempt was made on Adam's life in the rehab he's in. A phony aide was caught trying to give him a lethal shot, so there's been a guard put on him.

"In the meantime, Ida called me and said she wanted to talk to me. That's the lunch that you resented so much."

"I'm sorry," Claire said contritely.

"It's all right. I was rather flattered." He reached out and took her hand. "She said that a boy she—and to some extent, Adam—had grown up with had gone the drug route and was now clean and was interested in hearing how Adam was. I trusted her, of course. It never occurred to me not to. So I told her the facts I had and also told her about my projected trip to South America. One way and another I spilled plenty of beans," he said grimly. "One does not suspect people in one's own family."

"You mean she was involved with the drug dealers?" Claire said, shocked. "That's hard to believe. She was an ordained priest."

"I don't think she was involved in the way that you mean it. I believe she was perfectly sincere in her interest in this childhood friend, and that she was an innocent actor in the whole thing. I think the drug dealer here wanted information about Adam because he was afraid Adam had told me about their international dealings, which, of course, he had. And I think he hoped Ida would get all the information from me for him. Which she did. They knew I had once worked with military intelligence, and they were afraid of what I would do if I knew how much Adam was involved with the drug dealers in Latin America. And, of course, they were right. I went to the FBI immediately, and then went abroad for them."

"I didn't know you were with military intelligence,"

Jamie said. "Gosh, that's neat. Were you also with the CIA?"

"For a while, or at least I worked with them."

"How does their kidnapping Jamie come into this?" Claire asked.

"For blackmail on you and therefore on me. What I'd like to know, Jamie, is how you finally got away?"

"Well," Jamie took a giant bite of his sandwich and munched for a few moments before he said with a relatively full mouth, "It'd be great if I could say that I outwitted them. But I didn't. After a while I could hear their footsteps going out of another door to the room they were in. I didn't want them to find me there, by the door, and think maybe I heard something, so I rolled back to the bed. It took me quite a while to get up first on my feet and then lie back down, and I was so tired from that I guess I went to sleep. I don't know how long I slept, but when I woke up it was dark. I lay there for another long while and wished I'd done what you said, Ma—stuck with other kids. But I dunno. Maybe I would have talked to that woman anyway. I was really feeling rotten at that point and pretty depressed and my head ached. Maybe I dozed again.

"Suddenly the door opened and somebody came in. It was dark in the room and in the hall outside, too, because no light came in the door. But a woman whispered to me, 'I'm gonna let you go. If you tell anybody, they'll kill us both.' So she untied my hands and then pulled off my gag. I told her thanks, but she put her hand over my mouth. She said then, 'When I leave, go downstairs and out the door and then to the end of the block. Here is some money, it's all I could find. Go home as fast as you can.' I asked her where I was. She said she wouldn't tell me except that it was Brooklyn, and that getting home was my problem. Then she left.

"I went downstairs as quietly as I could and out the front door and then walked to the nearest avenue. I didn't know where I was. She'd given me two dollars, but it wasn't enough to take a cab, even if I could find one. I walked and walked and walked and finally came to a diner that was open. I went in and asked how to get back to the city. The guy looked at me pretty hard and I didn't want to say anything else in case he was some kind of crook, too. He told me where the closest subway was. I got there and then asked the guy in the token booth how to get to Eighty-sixth and Lexington in Manhattan. He told me what trains to take, but it took a while. I had to wait around a lot. The trains didn't come that often, I guess because it was late. Anyway, here I am."

"Oh Jamie, I think you did wonderfully. And you kept your head! And thank God for that woman! Did you see her at all? Was she the same woman who had lured you into the car?"

"I couldn't tell, Ma. It was dark. And she was whispering."

"Well, you were wonderful!"

"I didn't do too much, except wander around Brooklyn for what felt like hours."

"Jamie," Brett said. "While you were listening, did you hear any names at all? Did anybody address anybody by name?"

"No, I don't think—yeah, once. A woman spoke, the same one who talked to me in the art store. When she finished, one of the guys said something to her and said her name."

"What was it?" Brett asked.

"Gerry."

XIII

"GERRY!" CLAIRE SAID, AMAZEMENT IN HER VOICE.

"Do you know her?" Brett asked.

"I know a Gerry. She's one of my clients. Gerry Moser. She used to be on drugs, was off for a while, and got a lot better, but then regressed and finally admitted she was on drugs again because her boyfriend had more or less lured her back to them. But surely . . ." Her voice trailed off.

"Surely what?"

Claire looked at Brett. "It's hard for me to imagine that Gerry is involved in anything as . . . as truly awful, as criminal, as this."

"Yes. We're inclined to think of criminals as other kinds of people—not ones we know. But if she were back on drugs, and thoroughly hooked, then there's not much she wouldn't do to get them." He glanced at Claire's face. "Sorry," he said. "Did she ever say what her boyfriend's name was?"

"Yes. The last time I saw her she did."

"What was it?"

"I can't remember and my notes are at the office. I'm sure it'll come back to me. But it's not there right now."

"I think the police had better be informed about Jamie's return and about this development."

"Good heavens! I had forgotten all about them." She went over to the wall phone and dialed a number. Then, "Is Lieutenant O'Neill there? Thanks." A few seconds later she said, "Lieutenant? This is Claire Aldington. Jamie's home. At about two o'clock. Yes, I know I should have phoned you sooner. In all the excitement I forgot. He says that a woman approached him when he was in a stationery store near his school." Quickly Claire told the lieutenant the rest. "He says the woman he heard in the next room was named Gerry. And Gerry Moser is one of my clients who, I know, is back on drugs. She said that her boyfriend induced her to go back. No, I can't—Yes I can. She referred to him as Jesse . . ." Claire paused as she saw Brett raise his head. "Just a minute, Lieutenant. Hang on." She lowered the receiver. "Does the name mean something to you?" she asked Brett.

"Yes. It certainly does. Jesse Pope was the boy Ida grew up with, the one who got into drugs and she was trying to salvage. He also knew Adam."

"My God! Now I remember! Of course. I saw him at St. Paul's when I went down there. He was the one who looked like the aging hippie. And I saw his picture in Ida's photograph album down in her apartment—only I couldn't place it at the time."

Claire and Brett stared at one another, until Claire became aware of squawking from the reciever in her hand. Hastily she raised it and repeated to O'Neill the conversation between her and Brett.

"That's quite a tie-in," O'Neill said. "We'll discuss it when I get there."

"You're coming now? But it's the middle of the night. Don't you ever sleep? All right, I've been up a lot lately, too. But I want Jamie to get some rest. He's been through a lot. Very well. We'll wait here, but please don't plan for a long visit. We all have to get to bed."

She hung up and turned around. "I don't know when Lieutenant O'Neill sleeps. He's coming over here now, and when I pointed out that we needed sleep, too, he said he wanted to talk to Jamie while his mind was still fresh."

"It's probably a good idea," Brett said. "I'll stay until he goes." He looked vaguely abstracted.

"Lieutenant O'Neill coming to see me?" Jamie said. "That's awesome. Wait till I tell the kids."

"Don't let it go to your head," Claire couldn't help saying.

"I wonder, which one of those people was the one to call you on the phone—that genderless voice that you told me about?" Brett said.

Claire stared at him. "I'd forgotten about that, unbelievable as it seems. And it's no use asking Jamie whether one of the people he overheard could be the voice on the phone. He never heard that voice."

"And you have never recognized it?

"No. There was a minute—just a flash—when I thought I did, but it didn't last long enough and I can't put it together with any specific voice I'm aware of hearing."

"Martha heard it once," Jamie said. "He called when you were out and said a lot of stuff about if we wanted to see you again we should tell you not to tell anything you knew."

"She never told me," Claire said.

"No, we decided you had enough to worry about."

"Well you should have. You're not old enough to be making decisions like that."

"Martha thought that as well as me, so you might as well get mad at her, too, even though you never are. It's always me."

"That's not true, and you know it," Claire said. "I wonder if I ought to wake Martha up, since O'Neill is coming. I hate to do it."

"Maybe so," Brett said.

Claire went to Martha's door and knocked. There was no answer. Claire turned on the light and then went over to the bed and put her hand on Martha's head. "Martha!" she said.

"Umm."

"I'm sorry to wake you up again at this hour, but Lieutenant O'Neill is coming and I heard you talked on the phone to the man who's been threatening me."

"Yeah."

"And Jamie's home," Claire said. "Not much the worse for wear."

"I know. I woke up in the general commotion, and I intended to come out and give him a hug, but I went back to sleep. I'm glad he's back and okay. Sure I'll talk to the lieutenant."

"When did you take that call?"

"Sometime last week. He called in the afternoon before you got home and then started saying that if I didn't make you understand you couldn't tell anything to anybody, but especially the police, then they could get you or one of us."

"Why in God's name didn't you tell me?"

"Because I thought you had enough on you now, and I didn't think it could do any good. He was a creep!"

"You keep saying 'he.' Are you sure it was a man?"

"No, not really. I just sort of assumed it."

"Had you ever heard it before?"

"No."

Martha swung her legs out of bed and reached for her robe just as the front door bell rang.

Claire went out into the hall and opened the door. Lieutenant O'Neill plus one other man was standing there.

"Sorry about the hour and all that," O'Neill said, coming in. "But I'd like to talk to Jamie before he's had time to embroider what happened and then not know what's true from what's untrue."

"Come into the living room," Claire said. "The kitchen's really not big enough to hold all of us."

When they were all in the living room, O'Neill turned to Jamie and said, "First of all, congratulations on getting away, however you did it. Now, I want you to tell me everything that happened. Don't leave anything out, even if it seems unimportant."

So Jamie told his story again. When he got through O'Neill said, "I think you showed a lot of guts and calm."

"Thanks," Jamie muttered.

O'Neill turned to Claire. "You say that this Gerry could be Gerry Moser, your client?"

"Yes."

"Do you know where she lives?"

"Not offhand. I have her address in my office."

"Would you remember if it's Manhattan?"

Claire paused. "I'm not sure. But I have a feeling she might live in Brooklyn."

"Where's your phone?"

"In the hall or the kitchen."

O'Neill strode into the hall and lifted the receiver. Claire heard him instructing someone to find Gerry's address and phone number. Then he came back.

"Now Jamie," he said, "I want you to describe as near as you can where the house was that you were in."

"But I can't. I just walked and walked and turned corners, but I—"

"Didn't you see or notice any street signs? Not one?"

Jamie sat there staring at the policeman. "I don't think— yes, I do remember one. Kelly Street."

"Kelly Street. Let me see if I'm right that it's in Williamsburg?" He pulled a booklet out of his pocket and flipped through some pages. "Yes. Williamsburg. Do you remember any other streets? Any numbered streets?"

Jamie shook his head. "No. And I only saw Kelly Street after I'd been walking a long time, I mean, it wasn't near where the house was."

"Umm. You were lucky not to have been mugged in that area. Did anybody follow you?"

"No. But I walked as fast as I could and kept close to the buildings. It was scary."

The phone rang. O'Neill got up and picked up the receiver. "O'Neill," he said. "Okay. Thanks." He came back. "Well, Gerry Moser lives farther out than Williamsburg but in that general area. He glanced at Claire. "Didn't you tell me she had a good PR-type job? What would she be doing in a place like that?"

"For one thing, she had been on drugs before, and if she had a place in Manhattan probably had to let it go, and had hung on to her apartment in Brooklyn while she was trying to kick the habit. Now that she's back on something, her chances of ever moving are dim."

Claire stared down at her hands, regret for Gerry's now abandoned hope fighting with her anger at what was obviously the girl's involvement in Jamie's kidnapping.

"Do you think that getting Gerry back on drugs was part of the master plan to kidnap Jamie?" she asked O'Neill.

"Probably. In some way or other, this Jesse found out that Gerry came to you for therapy. This made you much more accessible."

"From Ida?" Claire asked. Then, "No, Ida wouldn't know anything about my clients. And the fact that Gerry was my client doesn't really have much to do with the kidnapping itself. I don't see her importance to them."

"Do you have pictures of your children on your desk?"

"Not on my desk," Claire said. "But on the mantelpiece in my office."

"So Gerry could have got a pretty good idea of what Jamie looked like. Did she ever question you about the pictures? Ever mention them?"

"Yes, once. She asked who they were and how old they were and—now that I come to think of it—how recently the pictures were taken. This was a few weeks ago. I answered her questions, although at the time I thought they were some kind of diversionary tactic to get us off the subject of some of her problems."

"So if you told her the picture of Jamie was fairly recent,

then it would have been an accurate likeness for them to go on. Did you ever, as far as you remember, tell her what schools Jamie and Martha went to?''

Claire stared at him for a moment. "Yes. Not when we were talking about the pictures, but some other time, when she was discussing her problems at school, she asked me about the schools that Martha and Jamie went to. Again, I thought she was just throwing in a red herring to keep me off painful subjects. But I did answer her.''

"So Gerry also knew where Jamie went to school." He turned to Jamie. "You said that a woman came up to you in a stationery store. Do you have any idea whether or not that was the same woman that let you out of the house?''

Jamie thought for a moment. "I don't know. I sort of took it for granted that it was. But I couldn't swear. I mean when she told me she was going to let me out she was whispering, and I couldn't tell. Anyway, I wasn't thinking about it.''

"No one can fault you for that. But I would bet that your instinct was right: It was the same woman.''

"But if she got me there," Jamie said, "why would she let me go?''

"Yes, that question has been on my mind, too," Brett said. "And the only answer, or at least the most obvious answer, is that they may have told her originally that they meant you no harm, and then later, in that conversation in the room next to yours, she learned different. Which makes me grateful to her.''

"Yes," Claire said. "Me, too. I wish I could talk to her.''

"For what purpose?" O'Neill asked.

"To see if I could help her get out of this mess. She wouldn't be in it if it weren't for that boyfriend of hers.''

"Maybe. She has some responsibility, too." O'Neill said. "Maybe he held out the drug but she didn't have to take it. Anyway, I wouldn't let you call her. It could be dangerous for you and Jamie.''

"What are you going to do now?" Claire asked.

"This minute, I'm going to ask your daughter Martha about her recollection of that threatening call." He turned towards Martha who was sitting in a straight chair beside the desk. "Can you remember exactly what he said?"

"I think so. Mostly. He said, 'Is your mother there?' When I said no, he said, 'Please give her a message for me.' I said, 'All right, only let me get some paper.' And he laughed. Almost giggled. Then he said, 'You won't need any paper for my message. Just tell her that if she doesn't stop meddling in things that are none of her business and she tells anything to anyone, especially anyone in the police or press, then she or Jamie or you will be killed.'"

"I still don't know what it is I am not supposed to tell anybody," Claire said.

Brett turned to her. "He, whoever he is, and his friends are going on the assumption that I have a lot of information about drugs and how they get into the country and who has them, and that I have naturally told you."

"But then I don't understand why you haven't been threatened."

"I have. Several times. I just didn't tell you."

"Your mother and brother seem to be unsure as to whether the caller is a man or a woman," O'Neill said. "Can you imagine the voice now, and can you imagine it coming out of either a man or a woman?"

Martha closed her eyes for a moment. "Yes. I can. It could be either. But you know, there was something else funny about the voice. It had sort of . . . well, a tinny echo."

"Electronically disguised," O'Neill and Brett spoke at once. They looked at each other and smiled. Then O'Neill said, "Well, that seems a dead end for now. We'll keep working on it, and I think I'll ask you to let me monitor your calls coming in here. We can put a man in the basement."

"What good will that do?" Martha said, looking vaguely alarmed. "I mean, I get a lot of calls."

"Don't worry, we're not interested in any gooey stuff going on between you and your boyfriends," O'Neill said.

Martha blushed furiously. "Yes, but what's the point?"

"If whoever answers the phone can keep the person,

male or female, talking long enough, we might be able to trace the call.''

"Oh.''

"That's what they do in the movies,'' Jamie said.

O'Neill turned to Claire. "You still can't track that flash or whatever made you think you might recognize something in the voice?''

She shook her head. "Sorry, no. The moment it trickles to the surface I'll let you know.''

"Tell me,'' Brett said to O'Neill, "Now with this link from Jesse to Ida, and then to Gerry, what do you think it has to do with Ida's death?''

"I don't know,'' O'Neill said. "But there seems to have been a free traffic of information, if nothing else, among the three of them. I ran a check on this Jesse, and he's been into drugs and dealing for quite a while.''

Claire said, "Then you think Ida's and her mother's deaths have to do somehow with drugs alone?''

He didn't answer for a moment, then he said, "I have a feeling there's something else. The Episcopal clergy are not that numerous. Yet in a short period of time, a clergywoman is murdered, her mother is also murdered, and the son of another clergywoman is kidnapped. I don't see what the additional connection is, but reason would indicate that there would have to be one.''

"I'm afraid I agree with you,'' Claire said.

O'Neill got up. "All right. Thanks for letting me come over right away. Mrs. Aldington''—he turned to Claire— "if by any chance you remember what made you think, however briefly, that you recognized the caller, call—at any time.''

"All right.''

"I guess I'll go on out with them,'' Brett said. "You all need to get some sleep.'' He gave Claire a firm kiss, ruffled Jamie's hair, smiled at Martha and left after the two policemen.

"I like him,'' Jamie said.

"So do I," Martha agreed.

Claire sighed. "So do I."

Claire herself was up early the next morning, being
unable to sleep, but she called the two schools and
explained that Martha and Jamie would be late. Then she
delivered them herself in a taxi. "Do I have to ask you
both," she said, before the cab dropped Martha off first,
"not to go around alone, now, after all that's happened?"

"No," Jamie said. "I'll stick to the bunch."

"Me too," Martha agreed.

THE NEXT DAY WAS A SATURDAY. AFTER SOME THOUGHT, CLAIRE
called a theater broker and made a reservation for the three
of them for a matinee showing of a popular musical that
none of them had seen.

After the matinee, she took them out to dinner. All three
of them enjoyed themselves and Claire felt safe with the
three of them together at all times.

On Sunday, Claire was scheduled to celebrate the Eucharist at eleven. Neither of the children was an enthusiastic
churchgoer, and with the ominous example of various
clients who traced a dogmatic atheism to having been forced
to go to church when they were young, Claire had not
insisted they go. This Sunday, she did. "I want you both
there in a pew near the front where I can see you at all
times."

This was perfectly agreeable to Martha, who was more of
a churchgoer than Jamie. Jamie, who had been unnaturally
good and compliant for two days, reverted to type and
muttered under his breath about bullying.

"You're not being bullied. After all that happened,
thanks to your determination not to be pushed around two
days ago, I think a little willingness to go along would not
be a bad thing."

Jamie mumbled a bit, but went. When Claire looked out,
as she recited the ancient liturgy (albeit in what she
considered a flat-footed modern translation), she saw her

two offspring sitting side by side in the third pew, Jamie looking unnaturally clean and tidy in a tie and jacket and with his hair combed. The sight brought her a sense of fulfillment and peace.

That afternoon all three went to the Bronx Zoo and came home around six, tired and ravenous.

While Claire fixed dinner she turned on the radio in the kitchen to an all-news station. Half listening as she browned some lamb chops, she suddenly jerked to attention and stood, unaware that she had stopped all action until she could smell the burning meat. Over the radio a man was saying, "The body of a young woman was found in Brooklyn this afternoon, beside one of the more deserted streets in Williamsburg. The woman has been identified as Geraldine Moser."

Smelling the meat, Claire snatched the pan off the fire and added some water to prevent the lamb chops from being ruined. But she did it automatically, without conscious thought, and while she was straining to hear if there was any other news about Gerry's killing over the radio. But they were onto sports now, and she knew from long experience that a major earthquake in the metropolitan area would not budge the sportscaster from his schedule.

But while she was still maneuvering the chops around the pan, Martha and Jamie suddenly shouted from the living room, "Did you hear that, Ma? Gerry Moser's been killed!" Then they burst down the hall and into the kitchen. "Did you hear—" Jamie started again.

"Yes, I heard. Martha, could you come and try browning these over a low flame while I call O'Neill? I almost burned them, so be careful."

Somewhat to her surprise, since it was a Sunday evening, O'Neill came to the phone. "We just heard about Gerry Moser being killed," she said. "I suppose you're aware of that."

"Yeah. Maybe they didn't like her letting Jamie go."

"Do you know yet who did it?"

"No. Any more than we know who's behind Jamie's being taken. But we're working on it."

Shortly after that, Brett called. "I suppose you've heard the news."

"Yes. And I'm exceedingly sorry."

"I'm also calling to make a radical suggestion. I'd like to be able to protect you better, and I can do it if I can live there with you, or you and the children could come in here. What I am suggesting," he said, ignoring her attempt to interrupt him, "is that we get married right away. Like tomorrow. Or at least as soon as we can get a valid license. We can do the ceremonial part later."

Claire was aware of being torn in opposite directions. Part of her wanted to shout "Yes" and be at the proper bureau at nine the following morning. The other and more dominant part was dismayed at the flouting of the religious ceremony and all the ritual that went with and before it.

"Brett. I can't. You know I can't. It isn't that I wouldn't like to."

"No, I don't know why you can't. Tell me."

"Because I think it would be inappropriate under the circumstances."

"That's an awfully old-fashioned viewpoint for anybody as up and coming and so 'full of wise saws and modern instances' as you are."

"As You Like It," Claire said automatically. "I'm sorry if I sound stuffy. But ceremony has its place, and it particularly has its place with somebody who's a priest. I'll be happy to make it any time after this month, or better, still, the next two months. It isn't that I'm not eager . . ."

"But not that eager," Brett said.

"No, don't make it a rejection," Claire said. "Getting married is more than a date for a drink. The thought of the domestic arrangements involved either in your moving here or our moving there is more than I can cope with in the midst of all this."

"I find your prioritries a little odd, but I won't press you. Good night, my dear."

* * *

WHEN CLAIRE GOT THROUGH WITH HER MORNING CLIENTS, SHE received from Darlene a list of messages that had come in for her. One of them was from Sarah Buchanan.

Claire was happy to see that. She had felt that their lunch had ended on a less than happy note, with Sarah, along with so many others, disliking her friendship with Lieutenant O'Neill and feeling, therefore, a little suspicious about answering her questions.

Claire dialed Sarah's office and was glad to find her in, this close to lunch.

"Hi," she said cheerfully. "How are you?"

"Fine," Sarah answered briefly. "There's something I want to talk to you about and I thought we might have lunch. But in the meantime, I went ahead and made another date."

"Sorry I couldn't answer earlier. But I don't like to interrupt my clients' therapy sessions for anything less than a total catastrophe."

"No, I see. We'll have to make it later in the week, although . . . well, it can't be helped."

"I take it it's something important," Claire said.

"Yes. But I really don't want to discuss it on the phone."

"How about a drink tomorrow evening? I could meet you over near you somewhere."

There was a pause. "All right. What about The Balcony or whatever it's called in the old Commodore. I've forgotten its new name."

"All right. What time?"

"Five-thirty?"

"I'll see you there, then."

"And Claire—" Claire, on the point of hanging up, was drawn back by the sound in Sarah's voice. She almost sounded afraid.

"Yes?"

"Crazy as it may sound, please don't tell anyone about our date. Anyone at all. Okay?"

"Okay. I promise."

* * *

CLAIRE HUNG UP AND STARED AT THE PHONE. AS SHE SAT THERE, she was gripped by an overwhelming urge to get up and go over to Sarah Buchanan's office and talk to her now. But she had clients and a week's worth of unanswered mail, and when she glanced at her watch she saw it was already too late. Sarah would have left for lunch.

The afternoon wore on slowly. Between clients, Claire was nagged by her feeling that she ought to make an effort to see Sarah that day. But she was due at Martha's school for the play that evening, and Dalrymple, who had been doing remarkably well, was due for his final visit to Dr. Rosenthal's before being returned to Althea.

Thinking about that, Claire came suddenly to the realization that she hadn't seen Althea at her usual post for several days. Picking up the telephone, Claire dialed Larry's inside number.

When he answered she said, "Larry, have you seen Althea in the past day or so? I was thinking about her now because I'm going to the vet's this evening to see whether Dalrymple's ready to be returned to her. Then I realized I hadn't seen her since, well, the middle of last week. I can't understand how I could have missed her, except that I don't always leave by the Lexington Avenue entrance to the parish house. Have you seen her or talked to her?"

"No," Larry said slowly. "I can't remember exactly when I did last see her, because I, too, have been trotting in and out of some of our other doors. Let me go check now."

"I'll go with you," Claire said. "I'll meet you in the hall downstairs."

But when they got to Althea's corner, there was no sign of her.

"She isn't one of the homeless who sleep in the hall downstairs, is she?" Claire asked. "I've never seen her when I've been on duty."

"No. I've told her often that she's welcome to come, but I can't absolutely guarantee that she can bring Dalrymple.

I'd be happy to smuggle him in, but I don't think that all our vigil committee—to say nothing of the other homeless—would feel the same. I had to tell her that, and she said she'd made other arrangements anyway. I have a vague feeling she once told me that she sleeps in some cat-loving super's basement in the Village. What time's your appointment with the vet?''

"Six. I'd better start moving there now."

"I'll give you a ring to see if you found anything out."

"The trouble is that I'm supposed to go to Martha's school play, which is opening tonight. But I do have an answering tape. Leave a message and tell me how late you can be called back.

"YOU HAVEN'T HEARD FROM ALTHEA?" CLAIRE ASKED THE VET.

Between them, on the examining table, Dalrymple sat in sleek comfort. As the doctor stroked him a purr rumbled from his interior.

"No. But I didn't think anything about it because I knew she was quite comfortable about Dalrymple's health and well-being in your house."

"He's certainly welcome to stay as long as is necessary. Even Motley has arrived at a sort of *modus vivendi* with him, though I can't say they're the greatest of friends. I wish I knew what to do next. I suppose I could call the Coalition for the Homeless. But there are so many of them—the homeless, I mean—that it seems like asking about the needle in the haystack."

"I have a feeling that anybody who has anything to do with the homeless will remember Althea."

"You're probably right." Claire opened up the carrier she had bought for Dalrymple. "Come on, hop in." When she had fastened down the top she said, "I'll keep you informed. I'm glad he's in good condition. It'll be something positive to report to Althea when we do find her."

MARTHA WAS AS GOOD IN HER ROLE AS *JULIET* AS CLAIRE could have hoped, and the audience gave her an ecstatic ovation. Even Jamie, whether out of a sudden conversion to the bard's masterpiece or loyalty to his half sister, applauded vigorously.

"You know, Ma," he said while they waited for Martha to change and join them, "she's good. She could practically be on television."

"Tell her that," Claire said. "She'd be thrilled."

"I don't think she thinks too much of my opinion."

"Risk it. What can you lose?"

"I can look like a moron if she just floats by like I was a fireplug."

"She won't. Now be friendly."

"You were great," he said when she emerged.

"Really?" Martha said. "Did you really think so?"

"Yeah. I did. I mean you're almost as good as some of the people on television."

Claire drew in her breath and waited for tears, anger, or a cold rebuff. But to her relief, Martha giggled. "Thanks." She turned to receive Claire's praises and those of the rest of her school friends and faculty. These went on for what seemed to Jamie a long time.

"She's like a movie star," he grumbled *sotto voce* to Claire.

"This is her moment, Jamie, let her enjoy it. You'll have yours."

"Yeah? Doing what?"

"Whatever it is you most want to do."

WHEN THEY GOT HOME THERE WERE TWO MESSAGES ON THE tape, one from Larry Swade asking Claire to call, the other from Lieutenant O'Neill, also requesting her to call.

While Martha and Jamie went off to fix themselves a midnight snack, Claire dialed Larry's home, not without some trepidation. It was past eleven, and when he told her to call back, he might not have meant to leave it so open-ended. But she wanted to find out about Althea.

He answered on the first ring.

"Hope this isn't too late," Claire said.

"No. I wanted you to call back, and I've unplugged the phone in the bedroom, so it shouldn't wake up Wendy. First the good news. I've located Althea. Now the bad. She's in Bellevue."

"In psychiatric?"

"Unfortunately no, in the sense that I'd like her to consent to stay in a good psychiatric facility long enough to get herself stabilized and be resolute about remaining that way. She was brought in by ambulance when a public-spirited citizen found her. She'd been badly beaten, and from the little I could find out, would probably have been killed if the people who did this hadn't got scared and run off when the good Samaritan or Samaritans showed up. She's okay. She'll survive. But she'll also be there for a while. She's conscious most of the time and has been asking about Dalrymple, only of course the people in the hospital didn't know who he was. Maybe you could call them and tell her that her cat's okay. Or go down there and see her."

"Of course I will. What a horrible thing. For heaven's sake, were they mugging her? She doesn't have anything."

"I didn't get a lot of information, but I have a feeling that the authorities don't think so. They think that, for whatever reason, they wanted to kill her."

"But why?"

"Maybe because she knew or had seen something."

"That's awful, Larry. I'll go there tomorrow morning. Thanks for telling me."

"I take it Dalrymple's fully recovered."

"He's blooming. And Martha was a great success."

"You may have another Katharine Hepburn on your hands."

"What a wonderful thought. I'll tell her you said so."

After she hung up, she dialed O'Neill's number, wondering if what he had to say might have anything to do with Althea.

He answered immediately. "O'Neill."

"This is Claire Aldington. Would this have anything to do with Althea?"

"Your bag lady friend?"

"Yes. She got beat up."

"I don't know anything about that." He took a breath. "Your colleague Sarah Buchanan, the lady priest . . ."

"Yes?"

"She was found murdered in her apartment about two hours ago. She was cut up and mutilated the same way as Blake."

XIV

"*SARAH . . .*" *CLAIRE WHISPERED. THEN SHE CRIED*, "*I* should have insisted on seeing her."

"What did you want to see her about?" O'Neill asked.

"She wanted to see me. When I picked up my messages after a morning of therapy there was one from her. She wanted to see me for lunch. She said there was something she wanted to talk to me about. But when I didn't get back to her soon enough she had gone ahead and made another date. We agreed to meet for a drink tomorrow. Just before I hung up she asked me not to mention to anyone that she wanted to talk to me. I should have just gone over to see her."

"Don't beat yourself! She didn't say it was urgent, did she? If she had, you'd have gone over. And when she didn't hear from you right away, she went ahead and made another appointment. That doesn't sound like somebody who needed to see you immediately."

"I can't help feeling that if I had seen her and talked to her she might still be alive."

"You're not God," O'Neill said testily.

"No, I'm not." Claire paused. "But what an awful thing. Do you have any leads at all as to who did it?"

"None. It's not a doorman building. Nobody saw anyone come in. She was discovered by her cleaning lady."

"How long had she been dead?"

"Maybe eight hours."

"But it looks like the same maniac?"

"From the type of cuts and slashes I'd say so."

Claire paused. "Some killer seems to have gone on a rampage: Ida, Mrs. Blake, Gerry, and now Sarah. And Jamie's kidnapping, which would probably have ended in his death if Gerry—if it was Gerry—hadn't released him." She was silent for a moment. Then, "You said that Ida was drugged and then killed and her body was taken to the place in the park where she was found."

"True. So?"

"So is this killing different in that respect?"

"Yes. She was killed in her apartment."

"I wonder what that tells us?"

"It tell us," O'Neill said slowly, "that whoever it was knew that he couldn't get away with killing Blake easily in what amounts to a converted private house. So he had to kill her somewhere else."

"And he made sure that we wouldn't know where that somewhere else was by carrying Ida's body to Central Park. Wouldn't that be even more risky? There are people there, in cars if not on foot, at all hours of the night."

"He almost certainly took the body in by car. And then, if it were late enough, he could wait until there were no cars coming and take the body out and dump it."

"Do you know yet if Sarah had been drugged first?"

"Not yet, officially, but somehow I think she probably was."

"So we come back to who and why."

"Yeah."

"Are you any nearer to the answers of those questions?"

"I'd like to say yes, but the answer is no, not really."

"Do you know who killed Gerry?"

"No, any more than we know who kidnapped Jamie. It all hangs together. Any ideas?"

"No . . ."

"You don't sound too sure. Are you holding out on me?"

"No. Not intentionally. But I have a feeling that there is something I know or have forgotten. If I could just get hold of it, dredge it up . . ."

"Then we'd know everything."

"Maybe not everything, but . . . well, something. Is there anything you know, Lieutenant, any clue or fact that you've uncovered, that could help me?"

"Well, one of the reasons we're sure the person who killed Blake also killed Buchanan is that he's left-handed."

"How do you know that?"

"By the way the knife went in."

"Anything else?"

"This was not indicated by Blake's death, of course, but I'd say that Ms. Buchanan knew him, because there's no sign of struggle. One reason we think that she was drugged first is that two glasses, freshly washed and clean of any prints, are in the kitchen on the counter beside the sink. That would indicate a so-called friendly drink that turned out not to be so friendly. You never did find out who Blake's current boyfriend was, did you? I'd now like to know who Buchanan's was. Could you work on that for me?"

"Yes, of course."

"And when whatever it is at the back of your mind floats to the surface, you'll let me know, right?"

"Right."

THE NEWS WAS FULL OF SARAH'S DEATH. THE RADIO BLARED IT out as Claire dressed, and the headline "Second Woman Priest Murdered" stared at her from the newspaper as she picked it up from outside the door.

"You're always telling us to be careful," Martha said. "What about you?"

"I'm being very careful."

"I think you ought to be extra careful," Jamie said. "After all, you're a woman priest."

"How are you going to the church today?" Martha asked.

"By public bus, the way I usually do. I really don't think anybody can do anything to me there."

Yet she couldn't help feeling that the shadow she had sensed before had come yet nearer.

"MR. BARNET WANTS TO SEE YOU," DARLENE SAID AS SHE entered the parish house.

She went straight back to his office, and saw him standing there with Pen.

"My dear," the latter said, coming across to her, "please, please be careful."

"Yes." Douglas came across and stood beside his sister. "Claire, I hope that you are really taking every precaution possible. The police must surely find out who did this before too long, and until then I'd like to have your assurance that you will be doubly careful. Try not to see people you don't know. We value you highly, you know." Unexpectedly, he reached out and grasped Claire's arm. It was an oddly moving gesture from an undemonstrative man.

"Thank you," Claire said. "I appreciate your concern. And since I have a high regard for my own safety, I can promise you that I'll be caution itself."

"I was wondering," Douglas said, "if you'd like to go away somewhere. I'm sure you need a vacation, and I think now would be a wonderful time to take it."

"Douglas, am I hearing you right?" Claire said. "It's not yet Easter, and you know nobody's free for anything until after that. I realize my own work is not as cyclical as others', yet I do feel I ought to be on hand in case I'm needed to fill in. And I can't just abandon my clients like that. But thank you again, anyway."

She paused, then said, "Douglas, I wanted to talk to you, anyway. Lieutenant O'Neill has asked me, as somebody within the Church, to see if I can find out a couple of things, as he asked me for Ida. I know you had lunch with Sarah a while back. Did she speak to you of a boyfriend at all?"

He shook his head. "As a matter of fact, the good lieutenant has already been on the phone about that. She didn't. Our talk was almost entirely of the Church or Church-related matters. She could be very amusing sometimes and I enjoyed getting her—well, somewhat irreverent views of various goings-on."

Maybe he was the boyfriend, Claire found herself thinking. His face, always rather craggy, now looked drawn, and there were shadows under his eyes. She wished, for a moment, that Pen weren't there. It was more than likely that Douglas might be a little more candid away from the presence of his sister. "Well," she said, glancing at the clock on the wall to her right. "I'd better get upstairs. My first client is due in five minutes. Let me know about the funeral arrangements if you hear before I do," she said to Douglas.

"Let's have a lunch," Pen said, walking with her to the door. "I've come across one or two problems in my committees, and without Peggy Anderson here, one wonders the best tack to take. I'm sure you could give me excellent advice."

"Of course," Claire said, rather shocked at her own lack of enthusiasm. And then she remembered Pen's patronizing, even derisive attitude towards her after their previous lunch, an attitude that had seemed prompted by Claire's cooperation with the police.

"I know you didn't fully approve of my helping Lieutenant O'Neill," she said, always one to speak what she thought, rather than let it sit around and pick up complications. "But as you can see, the matter is crucial; there have been several deaths, and I do feel that anything that anyone can do should be done."

"Yes. I'm sorry I gave you that impression. It was silly of me. Did you know Sarah well?"

"Not terribly. Better than I knew Ida, but that wasn't a lot. I knew she was upset—"

At that point Douglas, who was on the phone, called out, "Pen, can you come here a moment. I'm trying to set up something about that hospital committee and we need you."

"Go on," Claire said. "I really do have to run now." And she walked rapidly down the hall and up the stairs.

As she walked into her office her own phone rang.

"Are you all right?" Giles Fairmont's voice said. "What's going on is really unbelievable."

"Yes," Claire said. "And horrible." She paused, but she felt that the time to tread on eggs around Giles had passed. "Forgive my bluntness, Giles, but did you know Sarah at all, know in the sense of going out with her?"

"Still the lieutenant's helper?" he said, but the gibe wasn't as sharp as it could have been.

"Indeed yes, more than ever. I think everyone should give him all the help in the world at this point. Who knows, I may be next."

"Yes, well, I see your point. All right. No, I did not know Sarah particularly well, even though she helped out here most Sundays. Unlike Ida, she was not in the least flirtatious."

"Ida? Flirtatious?"

"Very. It didn't go really well with her militant feminism, but she could switch from one to the other without pausing for breath. Jesse, who knew her as a child—"

"Yes, Jesse," Claire said, interrupting. "I've just learned that Jesse not only knew Ida, but he also knew Gerry."

"Gerry who?"

"Gerry Moser."

"Who's Gerry Moser?"

"Don't you read the papers or watch televison news?"

"No. I have better things to do with my time. Most of the

papers print establishment lies, and I don't own a television set. Have I missed something important?"

"Gerry Moser—she was murdered—was a client of mine. She was also Jesse's girlfriend. She had once been on drugs and had lately returned—pushed, she led me to believe, by her boyfriend."

"Jesse's not on drugs. He kicked them a couple of years ago."

"Would you stake your life on that?"

"Yes, I would. He doesn't lie to me."

"I'm afraid you might lose that life. I think he does. My son, Jamie, was kidnapped a couple of days ago. It's all right," she said as he started to interrupt, "he's back now—thanks to Gerry, I'm almost certain. Where does Jesse live?"

"I suppose you're asking in your familiar role as cop's helper."

"Giles—my son was kidnapped. They were going to kill him."

There was a silence. "I suppose, if, as I think, Jesse is innocent, then he has nothing to fear, although he's been chased by the police plenty in his life. He lives in Brooklyn, near the Williamsburg area."

Claire let out her breath, looked up and saw her client standing in the doorway. "Thank you. I'll call you back. I have a client waiting now."

As soon as she had hung up, she said to the client, "There's a chair outside. Would you wait there for a moment. I'll be with you as soon as I make one phone call."

When O'Neill answered the phone, Claire said, "I have some information for you. My friend the Reverend Giles Fairmont knows Jesse Pope and reluctantly told me he lives in Williamburg."

"Okay. By the way, about this Hector Blake. It turns out he isn't a priest at all."

"He isn't? But he acted as a priest at Ida's funeral and

read part of the liturgy. Everyone I know thinks he's a priest."

"We just got the news from Scotland Yard. We knew he'd just arrived over here, and for the heck of it since he was Ida's brother we gave his name to the English police, not because we had any particular suspicions about him. He's been in a lot of trouble over there."

"I think I'd better tell the rector about this. Have you talked to him—Hector Blake—since you found out?"

"No, we've been trying to find him."

"He's not in his sister's apartment? He said he was going to move there."

"He didn't, apparently. He just stripped it bare and sold a lot of her stuff. According to our informant in London, he was banking on her marrying your guy, Brett Cunningham. He figured he could touch Brett for a sizable loan and get himself out of the jam he's in now over there. Talk to you later."

Claire just sat there. Then she dialed the rector's inside number. "Yes?" he said testily when he picked up the receiver.

"I've just been told by the police that Hector Blake is not a priest, has been in trouble with the law in England, and is now nowhere to be found."

"I knew that about his not being a priest. There was something bogus about him that made me call a friend in the Church in England. He would have been listed in at least three directories I can think of if he'd been ordained, and he wasn't in any one of them. I didn't know he'd been in trouble with the police, but it doesn't surprise me."

"I wish you'd told me, Doug. He's been extremely unpleasant to me, accusing me of getting him into some kind of trouble, threatening me. It would have been nice to know he was a nut of some kind rather than thinking he was a priest."

"I'm sorry," Douglas said briefly. "I've had one or two things on my mind."

Claire was sorely tempted to say, So have I. But she held

her tongue and hung up. "Come in, Leslie," she said to her client. "I'm sorry to have kept you waiting."

At lunchtime Claire hailed a taxi and went down to Bellevue Hospital. She had learned Althea's ward and bed number from Larry, but discovered, when she got there, that Althea had already been transferred to the psychiatric department. The rules there about visitors were strict, but with her clerical collar on, Claire did not have too much trouble getting in to see her.

"I'm very sorry about your getting beat up," she said when she finally located Althea. The latter still had a black eye and one side of her face was swollen. Also, she had an Ace bandage around one wrist. With those and the depressing hospital gown and paper slippers she was forced to wear, Althea looked a far cry from the grande dame of Lexington and Sixty-third Street.

"Yes," Althea said listlessly. "But I've been beaten up before."

"Why were they doing it? Did they think you had money?"

"No, I think they thought that I had been watching them and would tell you."

Claire almost jumped. "You did tell me men were watching me. Was that why you were attacked?"

"Yes."

"I'm sorry. I'm really sorry that you got beaten up on my account."

"It's all right. How's Dalrymple?"

The beating had changed and subdued Althea, but not, Claire was relieved to see, in her feelings towards Dalrymple.

"He's fine. As a matter of fact, Dr. Rosenthal said he could go back to you any time now. I think he misses you, because whenever I come home, he's standing at the door of my bedroom, waiting to get out."

Althea didn't say anything for a moment. Then, "The

doctors here want me to stay for a while and get stabilized on medicine."

"We'll keep Dalrymple, if that's what you're worried about."

"Yes. I had a mother, and I have a daughter, living with my aunt. But I love Dalrymple more than any of them. Can you understand that?"

"Yes. As it happens, I've been lucky in that there are people in my life that I have loved a lot. But I can understand how you feel."

Suddenly tears started falling down Althea's cheeks. "If I stay here and get stabilized, where will I live when I come out? They'd have to find a shelter for me, and then I couldn't have Dalrymple."

Claire opened her mouth to enumerate all the advantages that would come from Althea's being medicated and stabilized on anti-psychotic drugs. But no words came out. She would indeed have to go to a city shelter somewhere, and the chances were overwhelming that she would not be allowed to have her cat.

"What about your family? Isn't there any—er—money there, that could help you find a private apartment?"

"I ran through all the money that was mine. My daughter won't speak to me because I'm crazy and embarrass her. My aunt won't have anything to do with me for the same reason. If I got stabilized and if I stayed that way for a while, they might think about helping me out. But it would take years, and it would be too late for Dalrymple." She started to cry.

"Maybe if you give me their address I could write and explain how important Dalrymple is to you."

Althea shook her head. "Mr. Swade tried. They won't listen."

"Then what are you going to do?"

"I'll have a hearing soon. I'll pretend to be okay, and if the doctors try to hold me, I'll threaten to sue them. There is the patient's law, you know. I don't have to stay here—not if I'm not dangerous to myself or anybody else."

"And you'll go back to Lexington and Sixty-third?"

"Yes. Dalrymple and I." She looked slyly at Claire. "Would you honestly advise me to do anything else?"

Claire opened her mouth, and then after a moment closed it again. After a while she got up and said, "Is there anything I can do for you?"

"You're doing a wonderful thing for me already. You're looking after Dalrymple." The woman reached out and grasped Claire's hand in her own. "God bless you!"

WHEN CLAIRE GOT BACK TO THE PARISH HOUSE SHE WENT BACK to Larry's office and reported her conversation with Althea. "And you know, you'll think I'm crazy, but I couldn't tell her not to go ahead with her plan. She might be stabilized, but she'd be depressed and miserable."

"And the Norse invaders would finally land, don't forget that."

They started at each other and then laughed.

SHE HAD JUST FINISHED A SESSION AROUND FOUR O'CLOCK WHEN her phone rang.

"Thought you'd be interested to know that we set up a watch in Williamsburg and finally saw Jesse going into one of the tenements there. So we raided it and found him and quite a lot of coke and some heroin. We also arrested the former Reverend Hector Blake. He was walking there as bold as brass when we nabbed him."

"Did you have a right to do that?"

"He had on his round collar, so we jumped him on the grounds of impersonating a clergyman. In the meantime, after I first spoke to Scotland Yard, they had run across his tracks in a big drug deal and were very eager for us to lay hands on him. Apparently he came over here fully determined to get his sister back into favor with Brett Cunningham so he could get his hands on some of Cunningham's money. That, according to him, had been Mrs. Blake's aim all along—to recoup the family fortune by having Ida marry Brett Cunningham. His phone campaign against you was to frighten you off Brett, or Brett off you, especially if he could make Brett believe that you were nuts.''

"Did he kill his mother, for heaven's sake?''

"No. Jesse did that. Common sense was not Mrs. Blake's leading virtue. I guess having known him as a child, she couldn't take him seriously as a criminal. She threatened to tell you about his involvement with drugs and with Ida, as well as Hector's impersonation. I think he panicked at this point and thought this might lead you therefore the police to him. So he dressed up like a bellhop, got into her hotel room and killed her. He's confessed to that. He also confessed to killing his girlfriend, Gerry Moser.''

"Why did he do that?''

"A drug-induced fury after she let Jamie go.''

"What about the other two murders—Ida and Sarah?''

"He swears he had nothing to do with those, and he's managed to get confirmation that he was out of town the night that Ida was killed. Also, he really doesn't have a motive. So we still have those to account for.'' He sighed. "The investigation on those two is not progressing. I can't help coming to think that they have nothing to do with Mrs. Blake's murder. She was killed with a blow to the head for what she knew and for what she could pass on. There's something ritualistic about the other deaths.''

"Yes,'' Claire shivered a little. She paused and then said, "I know that Brett has been doing some work about the international drug trade for some branch of Intelligence. Do you know anything about that?''

"Yes. We do. We're very indebted to him. He has the kind of connections that we couldn't hope to get. I think in a sort of way he's doing it for his son.''

"Well, I wish he'd call me.''

"If I see him, I'll tell him. You two have a fight?''

"Not exactly. He wanted to marry me immediately so he could move in and protect me. But I held out for a church wedding. I'm sort of sorry now I did, although my reasons at the time seemed perfectly rational. I suppose by today's standards they also seem ludicrously old-fashioned.''

"Well," O'Neill said, "you are a priest. Albeit female."

"Yes. And I have two children in my charge. I've always believed in the precept: Don't tell, do."

"My parish priest would be proud of you—at least that part of you."

"Maybe he wouldn't be so proud if he knew I now regret it."

"Do you regret not telling him to move in?"

"I guess I regret not thinking of some way around it."

"You could have got married."

"That's where this conversation started. By the way," she said abruptly. "Do you know where he is?"

"Yes, but that's confidential."

"Thanks a lot."

"It's your own fault. If you had agreed to marry him right away, you'd know, too." He hesitated. "May I make a personal request?"

"Of course."

"Will you please be careful. Ida Blake and Sarah Buchanan were both women priests. So are you. They were both young, attractive women. So are you."

"Thanks," Claire said. "I will."

"For God's sake," O'Neill said irritably. "Couldn't you at least have invited Brett to sleep on your sofa?" He hung up.

CLAIRE HAD TWO MORE CLIENTS, WHICH MEANT SHE WOULDN'T get home till nearly seven. But she had a casserole in the refrigerator and knew she could call Martha and have her stick it in the oven when she was ready to start for home.

She had seen one client and was waiting for the second one when something Letty Dalrymple had said jumped up in her mind. Quickly dialing the psychic's number, she was about to hang up on the fourth ring when a breathless Letty said, "Hello?"

"It's Claire Aldington. I'm sorry if I'm interrupting something."

"It's all right. In fact I'm glad. I was trying to clip Petal's claws, and she was being most uncooperative. I've been thinking about you all day. I feel that you must be careful."

"I intend to be. Letty, I just remembered something. When I was looking at that chain and medallion in Ida's apartment you said something like, I feel death when I hold it. What did you mean?"

There was a silence that seemed to stretch on and on. Finally Letty spoke. "I think I meant that she had been given it by the person who killed her. It wasn't as clear then. It is now, somehow. Maybe I knew unconsciously that I knew, and was willing you to call me."

After the last client had gone, Claire called O'Neill. "That chain and medallion of Ida's that Letty was holding when we were standing in the bedroom—well, something made me call Letty just now and ask her what she meant when she said it made her feel death when she held it."

"And what did she say?"

"She said she meant that the murderer had given Ida that chain. Lieutenant, do you know if there was any chain and medallion like that among Sarah's things?"

"Just a minute. Hold the phone."

After a few minutes he was back. "Describe the medallion to me," he said.

"It had a winged armored figure holding a sword. St. Michael the Archangel."

"Yes. I'm holding another one. It was in the envelope containing Buchanan's things."

XV

It took all Claire's discipline to keep her mind on her client and her client's affairs, but she managed it. Then she called O'Neill back. "Do you know anything more about the chain?"

"Yes, and no. It doesn't have any of the usual silver marks and, according to one expert we called in, was probably privately made by somebody as a hobby. So we know that, but it doesn't get us anywhere."

"I see."

"Yeah, well, I've had about six hours' sleep in the last three nights. I'm going home and hit the sack and I suggest that you do too. And be careful. One more thing. Don't tell anybody about the chain. It may get to the point where we tell the press to see if anybody can help. But right now, we want to keep it quiet."

"I won't tell anybody."

When Claire got home, she was stunned to find Brett

sitting there with Martha and Jamie, reading his *Wall Street Journal* while they were watching television.

"Hi," she said, walking in. "How nice to see you."

"I'm glad you feel that way. Nice to be here."

She then saw a big roll next to the bookcases. "What's that?"

"My sleeping bag."

She looked at him and grinned.

"He was going to sleep in the living room in his sleeping bag," Jamie said, "but I told him the sofa pulled out and he could sleep there. I'm right, aren't I, Ma?"

"Of course." She went over and kissed Brett. "I'm very glad you're here." Then she kissed the others.

Jamie mumbled something as he turned back to look at the television screen.

"What was that, Jamie?"

"I just don't see why you don't get married."

"We're going to," Claire said. "Soon."

"How soon?" Brett inquired. "I thought you didn't like soon."

"I don't like City Hall. I'd like a church ceremony, however informal. So, why don't we see how soon we can set that up?"

"Great!" Martha said. "Then Brett can get rid of the sleeping bag."

"WERE YOU SERIOUS ABOUT THAT?" BRETT SAID LATER ON, when Jamie and Martha had gone to bed. Motley was in with Jamie and Patsy with Martha. Dalrymple was sitting on Claire's lap.

"Yes, I was."

"Do I have to sleep in here?"

"Only because of the children. But because of that you do."

"You're right."

"But there's no law against some heavy necking."

"How old-fashioned that sounds," Brett said, coming over to the sofa.

* * *

SARAH'S FUNERAL WAS HELD IN NEW HAMPSHIRE, WHERE SARAH had been born and grew up. The papers and television news kept the matter fresh by having almost daily some item about what one anchor man called "the clerical murders."

There was, however, a memorial service for Sarah held at St. Anselm's, which Sarah's friends in New York and many of the clergy attended.

Claire, who had been asked to read one of the lessons, was up in the chancel. Brett and Pen Morgan were in one of the front pews. After the service, Claire, who had been stopped by several people as she had come from the vesting room, finally caught up with Brett outside, where he was talking to Lieutenant O'Neill.

"I'll be back in about three days," Brett was saying to the lieutenant. "I can come downtown then."

"Are you being arrested for something?" Claire inquired, slipping her arm through his.

"Not that I know of. The lieutenant wants me to make some kind of a deposition or statement about my role in the drug bust. There's going to be a press conference about it tomorrow morning and you'll read all about it in the paper."

"So it was more than just Gerry's and Mrs. Blake's murders."

"Yes. It had a lot more ramifications," O'Neill said.

"Anything new on the other murders?" Claire asked. Deliberately she kept her voice calm. But as she spoke she could feel her own tension. Was it her imagination, or were people giving her sidelong looks as they left the church. Would she be next?

"Not too much, I'm sorry to say." He pulled on his gloves. "We have more or less decided to give the press that bit about the silver chain and medallion. Somebody who knows something about it might come forward."

"What chain and medallion?" Brett asked.

O'Neill told him. "I always feel a little defensive about doing something because a psychic suggests it, but I must say Letty has been on target several times, and she did say the murderer gave the chain to Ida, and then we find one among Buchanan's things. That's too much to ignore."

"You're right. It is," Brett said. He frowned.

"Is it the thought of Letty—the psychic—that makes you frown?" Claire asked.

"No. It's because that chain and medallion strike a bell somewhere."

"Where?" O'Neill and Claire asked together.

"The trouble is, that's all it does, strike a bell. I can't get any further with it than that."

"Well when you do, let me know," O'Neill said. "It could be useful."

A young woman, obviously from the press, came sidling up. "Ms. Aldington, since you are also a woman Episcopal priest, would you care to tell us how you're feeling now?"

"Now that you've seen your daughter's body laid out in the hallway," Brett said.

"What's this?" the reporter said, her eyes widening, her pencil scribbling.

"Now see what you've done?" Claire said. And then to the reporter, "He was only joking."

"About what?" the reporter snapped.

"About the tendency of the press to stick a mike in front of a woman whose six children have just been burned to death to ask her how she feels."

"You don't believe in the First Amendment and the freedom of the press?"

"Of course," Brett said smoothly. "And I wish that the media felt the responsibility of the press with the same passion."

"May I quote—" the reporter started.

"Come on," Claire said impatiently to the reporter, "we have just come from the memorial service of a woman who was a friend. Don't choose this moment to pick a fight. There must be other stories elsewhere."

Fortunately, the reporter's colleagues called to her and, with an angry look at Brett, she left.

"You shouldn't have baited her," Claire said to him.

"I know. But it was irresistible."

"Maybe she'll find it irresistible to put something about you in the paper."

He grinned down at her. "I don't care. I'm not running for office."

"I take it you're going away again," she said.

"Yes. This time on a sober business trip, but I'll be back in three days."

Douglas and Pen walked up. "It was a good service," Douglas said. He glanced at his watch. "Still only eleven-thirty. I'd better get back to the parish house. Are you coming, Claire?"

GILES CALLED AN HOUR OR TWO LATER. "*I OWE YOU AN* apology," he said in his crisp, direct way. "I was wrong about Jesse and I realize now if I hadn't been as bewitched by my own biases, he might have been put somewhere safe before he killed two people—certainly before he killed Gerry Moser."

"That's handsome of you, Giles. Thanks." Claire's sense of mischief bobbed to the surface. "Does this mean you can now be counted with the Tory establishment?"

"No, it does not. It just means that the next time I get going I'll try to remember I can be wrong."

"*I HAVE NEWS FOR YOU,*" LARRY SWADE SAID AT THE END OF THE afternoon as he hove in view in her doorway.

"Good news, I trust. I could do with it."

"Well, it's all in how you look at it. I'm sure Dalrymple will be happy. Althea will be returning to her former residence on Lexington and Sixty-third Street. There was a hearing this afternoon and according to the doctors she behaved like a model citizen throughout the entire affair. She was represented by a civil liberties-type lawyer, who maintained that the hospital had no right to force her to stay. The judge finally decided in her favor. So she will be returning to us tomorrow morning."

Claire stared at him. "I suppose I should be terribly

upset, but I'm not. She'd be miserable in some SRO, medicated but without Dalrymple."

"I agree. What I feel strongly is that there should be some provision for people who do not want to be hospitalized but who can't cope on their own."

"Would they let her have Dalrymple?"

"Since all medical opinion at this point agrees that elderly people are far better off with their pets, there ought to be some way for her to keep him."

"She's not elderly."

"Don't quibble."

"I still wonder where she spends the nights."

"So do I. At least we now know that Britain will be safe from the Norse invaders."

Claire grinned. "Don't you have anything to do?"

"Lots. What about you?"

"Also. But I never felt less like doing it."

Larry put his head on one side. "Come out and have a drink. You looked peaked."

"I feel peaked."

"I can't say I blame you. You'll be quite safe with me and then you can relax. I will then see you home."

But when they got to the main hall downstairs, they bumped into Douglas and Pen.

"Where are you two off to?" he inquired.

"Larry was taking me out for a reviving drink," Claire said. "He thinks I look peaked."

"Come to think of it, you do," Douglas said.

"Surely Brett's the man to cheer you up," Pen said.

Larry made a portly bow. "I stand in his shoes, since he told me he was leaving on business tonight."

"I think all four of us should come back to our apartment. We could all do with some reviving cheer," Douglas said. "Come along now."

"Well, I don't want to put Pen out," Claire murmured. She found she didn't in the least want to go to Douglas and Pen's apartment.

"I won't take no for an answer," Douglas said.

Claire would have liked to make some acceptable excuse if it hadn't been for two things: Douglas was her boss, and he really did look as though he needed some cheering. Always an austere man—except, Claire found herself thinking, that day when he and Sarah were going to lunch— he now looked almost driven.

"All right," she said. "Just for a short time."

THE RECTORY, A FINE COOPERATIVE APARTMENT OWNED BY ST. Anselm's, was only two blocks away. Claire had been in it before, but she was always surprised by the size of the rooms and the height of the ceilings. Unlike her own apartment, this one had been built in the days when walls were thick, rooms were spacious and families, especially rectory families, were large. As she walked with the others into the front hall, she wondered again how Douglas and Pen, rattling around an apartment that could quite easily hold eight people, enjoyed living here.

"It's a bit large for us," Pen said cheerfully, putting her black raincoat in a hall closet. "But it's wonderfully comfortable."

Dressed, as usual, in her gray suit, black rabat, and round collar, Claire was, strictly speaking, attired for any occasion. Pen was more fussily dressed than Claire had seen her before. Underneath the raincoat was a silk suit with a high ruffled blouse. It was handsome and it was expensive, but Claire couldn't help thinking that Pen would have looked better in something more tailored.

"Come in here," Douglas said, leading the way past the open door of what looked like a study and into a large living room overlooking Park Avenue. On a table by the wall was a tray with drinks. "What'll you have, Claire?" Douglas asked, going over to the table. "We have gin, scotch, bourbon, vodka."

"I think a weak scotch and soda," Claire said. She really didn't want an alcoholic drink, but felt that to ask for a soft one would somehow not go down well with Douglas and

Pen. They might take it as not fully accepting their hospitality.

However Larry, who apparently did not have such qualms, asked for a soda.

"Really?" Pen said. "Are you sure?"

"Yes, quite sure. It's really uncouth of me, I know," Larry said. "But I don't much care for alcohol."

"Whatever you like," Douglas said. He gave Larry a soda with some lime in it, and then poured what looked like whiskey on the rocks for himself and his sister. He was about to sit down when the phone rang.

"Oh bother!" Pen said. "Do you want me to get it, Douglas?"

"No. I'll take it in the study." And he went out of the living room.

The conversation among the three left in the living room was labored. Douglas was gone a long time, for which, Claire thought in a spasm of cynicism, she didn't blame him. But then why are we here, she found herself wondering? Pen seemed distracted, so Claire and Larry soldiered on to fill the awkward pauses with chit-chat about the parish, the committees and various problems that had arisen during the week.

Douglas finally reappeared, looking grim. "Sorry about all that," he said. "But I'm afraid I'm going to have to leave you all. A rather difficult situation has come up and needs immediate attention. Larry, I shall take you with me because I may need your help."

"Anything I can do," Larry murmured. "Probably Claire could help, too," he said.

"No, no," Douglas said, "the two of us will be enough. You stay, my dear," he said, turning towards Claire. "I know Pen will be glad of your company."

"I really must get home," Claire said, rising and putting down her almost untouched drink.

"No, do stay," Pen said. "I feel really depressed after this afternoon. It would be an act of kindness. I'll put you in a taxi to go home quite soon. I promise."

Claire's desire to leave was overwhelming. But without having announced a definite appointment beforehand, she felt she would seem ungracious. "Well," she said, "I do have to get home. But I'll stay a short while longer."

"That's kind of you," Pen said.

Larry looked at Claire, his round face plainly worried. As though he were public print, Claire could read what he wanted to say but couldn't without mortally offending his boss and his boss's sister.

Claire grinned. "Run along, Larry dear. When you get home, give Wendy my love and tell her she owes me a lunch."

"Will do."

Claire heard the two men talking to each other in the hall. Such was the thickness of the old walls that even though the living room door was open, she couldn't hear what they were saying.

"These old apartment buildings were built for the ages," she said to Pen. "You should see ours. It was put up in the late fifties and I can hear people changing their minds in the next building, not to mention water flushing, beds creaking and so on. It can be quite embarrassing."

"We had a cottage like that in England. Jerry-built from the word go. There was no such thing as imparting a secret there . . ."

As Claire heard the high, bright voice chattering on, she found herself glancing at her watch. How soon could she decently get away? To make the time go faster, she said, "How are you making out on the committees that Peggy told you about?"

"Very well, though I can see some of the good ladies really need a firm hand . . ."

Doggedly, trying to fill the slow moments with chatter about the church and the parish, Claire plodded on. What's the matter with me, she thought? Rarely did she have trouble manufacturing conversation with people.

"Here, let me fix you another drink," Pen said.

Claire tried to hold her hand over her glass. "I really don't want any more."

"Of course you do. Now, this is much better." And before Claire could do anything, Pen had whisked away her glass and substituted another darker one in its place. "You'll feel better if you take a sip of that. Now go on. I'll just put something in mine."

Obediently, and to get rid of Pen, who was standing over her, Claire took a swallow.

Afterwards, she couldn't remember which came first, a curious sensation, as though everything had receded to a distance, or her realization that as Pen had got up and down from her chair, the ruffled neck of her blouse had unbuttoned and come apart. There, in the hollow of her neck, was a silver chain and medallion.

Claire stared at it for a moment. "Where did you get that charm?" she asked, and, as she struggled to get the words out, had her first inkling of what was about to happen to her. She tried to get to her feet.

"This?" Pen said, and pulled it out from her blouse. "Oh someone I know in England makes these. I bought quite a few, just to give her a boost, you understand, and to give them to friends."

Claire took in the words. But she couldn't make herself get out of her chair. Her legs seemed paralyzed. All she could do was to say despairingly, "You! It was you!"

"I have to protect my brother, you know," Pen said in a perfectly normal voice. "He was meant to be a celibate, and I was meant to look after him. I've known that for years, and therefore I have to remove the women who seem to want to attach themselves to him. First it was Ida, then he developed this silly crush on Sarah, and now you. I recognize the signs."

Claire's brain was still working, though slowly. But she knew she was caught. There was no way out, because she couldn't move.

At that point, the telephone rang.

"We'll just let it ring, shall we?" Pen said. "Or perhaps

I'd better answer it." She got up and went through a connecting door to the study. "Stay quite still, won't you?" she said over her shoulder. And she laughed. Then she picked up the receiver. "Oh, hello Larry. No, she left quite a while ago. No, I don't think she was going home. She said something about an errand."

Claire gathered herself. She couldn't move, but her voice wasn't completely gone. With all her strength she shouted. But the noise that came out was barely audible.

"There now," Pen said, putting down the receiver and coming back into the room and over to her. "I should also tell you that I consider that a woman—any woman—who tries to take over the sacramental duties of a man like my brother is committing some kind of blasphemy and should be punished. As you will be punished. . . ."

The level, insane voice went on, the eyes watching her. This, Claire thought, was what Ida and what Sarah had heard. This was the terror they must have felt.

At that moment, Claire knew she was going to die. Her final conscious thought was a prayer for her children. Just as unconsciousness closed over her she heard a noise, a noise that sounded almost like a shot.

SHE WOKE UP AND STARED AT THE WHITE CEILING, WONDERING why it looked unfamiliar.

"How are you feeling?" Brett was sitting beside her bed and smiling at her. She moistened her lips. "What happened?"

"That mad woman, Pen, slipped you a Mickey Finn, in preparation, of course, for dispatching you altogether, the way she did Ida and Sarah. Fortunately, we were able to stop her."

Claire turned her head and smiled a little. "How?"

"Suddenly I remembered where I had seen the chain and medallion you and O'Neill were talking about. It was when Pen took off her outer coat during the memorial service. The button at the top of her blouse slid open. She was turned towards me, folding her coat beside her, and I saw it clearly.

It was quite distinctive. But I suppose, as with a lot of things we see, I didn't really register it. There was no reason to. Which is why I couldn't remember it right away. But suddenly at the end of the day, I did. I called O'Neill and told him, then I called you at the parish house. Somebody there said you and Swade had gone back to the rectory with Douglas and his sister. I was about to call Doug and tell him I was coming over immediately when O'Neill called me, looking for you. I told him where you were.

"He told me to meet him in the lobby of the rectory. When I got there, he had called Douglas and persuaded him to leave the apartment with Larry, because he was now sure that Pen had killed Ida and Sarah and thought there was a good chance she might use this opportunity to dispense with you, and he wanted, if possible, to catch her red-handed. I almost felt sorry for Douglas."

Claire swallowed and said weakly, "I'm surprised he agreed."

"I think he was feeling overwhelmed with guilt over not telling O'Neill right after Ida's death that Pen had a history of mental illness. But he wanted so much for her to be well, and he had convinced himself that she was and could not possibly have had anything to do with Ida's dying. And then, of course, when Sarah died, he blamed himself.

"I wasn't at all happy loitering down there in the hall with God knows what happening to you upstairs, so to appease me, O'Neill had Larry call from the phone in the lobby and ask for you. He figured that if he was wrong, if you were perfectly safe, then Pen would call you to the phone. So when Pen pretended you had left and added for good measure that you had gone on an errand so that any late arrival at home would be accounted for, we knew it was time. So we went up."

"What was that shot?"

"It was O'Neill shooting out the old-fashioned bolt in the front door. Apparently at some point Pen had gone out and slid it home so that even if Douglas had wanted to get in, he couldn't. We found you passed out in a chair, and Pen with a kitchen knife in her hand."

"Where is she now?"

"In the psychiatric section of this hospital. I think that Douglas finally gave his assent to catch her that way on condition that she would not be taken directly to the precinct but be ensconced in the hospital. Of course she's there under police guard."

Claire stirred. "There were a few minutes when I was convinced I was going to die. I hope I remember that for the rest of my life, so that I'll never stop appreciating life itself." She paused. "Are Jamie and Martha okay? Do they know what happened?'

"More or less. They send you their love. Once I am convinced you're okay, I'll go and spend the night there. You'll be home tomorrow yourself."

She reached out a hand. "Thank you."

"Do you remember anything at all after you passed out and were brought here?"

"Bits are coming back. Unpleasant bits involving a lot of throwing up and being walked up and down. I take it they were trying to counteract my Mickey Finn."

"Yes. Luckily you only took a swallow. Larry said he was sure you were suspicious of something. Were you?"

"Not of Pen herself until I saw her chain and medallion. But that was after the others had left and I thought it was too late. But before that I was terribly uncomfortable. I suppose Letty would have a psychic explanation—that I knew about Pen on some level, but not consciously. All I was aware of was that I loathed being there and felt guilty about it."

"In future," Brett said, "listen to those feelings." He hesitated.

"I suppose Pen went to Sarah's apartment planning to kill her."

"Yes. They had a dinner date or something. Then Pen quite happily admitted she insisted on going back with Sarah and bought a bottle of wine on the way, which she also insisted they drink. It was not hard to drop the knockout pill into the wine and, when Sarah was unconscious, stab her.''

Claire shivered.

Brett put his hand on her arm. "All right, darling?"

"Yes. But I know now how she must have felt. I knew what was going to happen—or at least what I was sure was going to happen—and also knew I was too paralyzed to do anything about it. It was the most horrible feeling I've ever had. Where did she kill Ida?"

"In the rectory apartment. As you know it's a huge place. She told O'Neill that she waited until Douglas was out of town and invited Ida to dinner and then doped her drink. But she actually stabbed her in one of the rooms they keep closed off. O'Neill said they went there after her confession and there are traces of blood all over it, though she had tried to clean it up. And she had kept the door locked so the cleaning woman wouldn't go in. After Ida was dead, Pen carried her downstairs by the fire staircase and out the garage door in the basement. Then she put her in their car and drove her to Central Park. As you know, Ida was small and light and Pen is as tall as most men and is strong. She'd have had no trouble with that."

"And all because she felt that Ida and Sarah and I had designs on Douglas? She really is insane."

"Yes. Douglas finally admitted that Pen had always talked of herself as his soul mate and companion and when he married, had bitterly resented his wife and had as little to do with her as she could."

"How did she die?" Claire asked.

"O'Neill asked that, too. Apparently in a car accident in which Pen could not have been involved."

"But you'd think, wouldn't you, that Douglas would have seen Pen's attitude as odd, at the very least. Or am I being wise after the fact?"

"You have to remember that Pen is a lot younger than Doug, that in his mind she was always the adoring little sister. He was back here when she had her first mental breakdown and was hospitalized. He thought it was simply strain over her father's death. I'm not even sure he knew about the next one; he was busy himself over here, was newly married and not really paying attention. After Ida died, he says now, Pen's history of mental illness crossed his mind, but he simply thrust it away. He is, as you know, the kind of man who is inclined to ignore unpleasantness until he can't ignore it any more. This has certainly been a lesson to him."

"So Doug was Ida's secret boyfriend that nobody wanted to tell me about."

"No, it was her cousin Jesse Pope. As you know, his interest in her had more to do with her marrying me and whatever money I might have than anything else. But there was a touch of the crusader in Ida. I think she felt that Jesse was a brand to be snatched from the fire."

"And Hector, her con man brother, was in cahoots with Jesse?"

"Yes. And he did his considerable best to blacken your name to his mother. Which is why she talked to you the way she did. But I have a feeling that when she announced she was coming to your apartment, the night she was killed, she might have been intending to warn you, because she had had a stormy session with Hector and had come to have a fairly shrewd idea of what he and Jesse were up to."

Claire lay there, thinking about it all. Then, "I've been meaning to ask you, how is Adam?"

"Better than I had hoped, I'm glad to say. I talked to him on the phone today. I'm almost afraid to say it, but I think he's growing up."

"What will happen to him about his drug-dealing past?"

"I don't know. The best I can do is get him a good lawyer and stand by." Brett paused. "What encouraged me most was that, for the first time, he seems willing to accept his own responsibility for what happened."

After a moment, Brett reached over and took her hand. "Do you feel up to talking about marriage?"

"Yes," Claire said, surprised at her own vehemence.

"That's good. I have made an appointment with Larry to perform a small, private ceremony a week from today. That'll give us time to get the license and do all the other bureaucratic shuffle. How say you?"

"I say yes!" She reached up and pulled his head down for a long kiss. A little later she added, *"Con gusto, con amore!"*

CONSPIRACY
INTRIGUE
MURDER

From **Fawcett Books**

27 million Americans can't read a bedtime story to a child.

It's because 27 million adults in this country simply can't read.

Functional illiteracy has reached one out of five Americans. It robs them of even the simplest of human pleasures, like reading a fairy tale to a child.

You can change all this by joining the fight against illiteracy.

Call the Coalition for Literacy at toll-free **1-800-228-8813** and volunteer.

Volunteer Against Illiteracy. The only degree you need is a degree of caring.

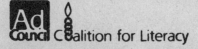

Ad Council Coalition for Literacy

LV-3